THE FOUNDLING BRIDE

Helen Dickson

MILLS & BOON

Published in Great Britain 2017
by Mills & Boon, an imprint of HarperCollins*Publishers*
1 London Bridge Street, London, SE1 9GF

© 2017 Helen Dickson

ISBN: 978-0-263-92592-0

Our policy is to use papers that are natural, renewable and
recyclable products and made from wood grown in sustainable
forests. The logging and manufacturing processes conform to the
legal environmental regulations of the country of origin.

Printed and bound in Spain
by CPI, Barcelona

Lowena watched his gaze drop to her mouth in a state of anticipation that was reaching dizzying heights.

Marcus took two steps to close the distance that separated them, his gaze still focused on her lips. She caught her breath. She could feel his warmth, the vital power of him. The size and heat of him had the power to shock her. Sensations of unexpected pleasure flickered through her. She was powerless to prevent what she hoped with all her heart would happen next.

Taking her arms, he drew her to his chest. Their faces were close together, his breath warm on her lips. Her trembling hands reached up to hold him. Under her clutching fingertips the muscles of his shoulders beneath his coat coiled and quivered reflexively. Placing his finger below her chin, he tilted her face to his, lowering his head and covering her mouth with his own.

Author Note

Cornwall, steeped in its history of smuggling and shipwrecks and ancient legends, has provided inspiration for numerous authors—and I am no exception. It never fails to capture my imagination.

Some years ago I wrote *Highwayman Husband*—the setting was Cornwall and I really enjoyed writing it. I've spent many memorable holidays in that lovely county, and I was drawn to writing another book set there.

After ten years of soldiering, it is on a smugglers' night that Marcus Carberry returns to Tregarrick, his home on the south coast of Cornwall. Here he becomes reacquainted with his hostile older brother and the innocence of Lowena Trevanion. Having experienced an unhappy affair in the past, he is in no rush to step up to the altar—but Lowena is a challenge he has not bargained on…

Helen Dickson was born and still lives in South Yorkshire, with her retired farm manager husband. Having moved out of the busy farmhouse where she raised their two sons, she now has more time to indulge in her favourite pastimes. She enjoys being outdoors, travelling, reading and music. An incurable romantic, she writes for pleasure. It was a love of history that drove her to writing historical fiction.

Visit the Author Profile page
at millsandboon.co.uk for more titles.

Prologue

1761

Beresford House was a large, rambling old place. It stood away from a small Devon village, perched on a rocky promontory overlooking the sea. It was the home of the old and distinguished Beresford family, and until twelve months ago it had housed three members of the family, until Sir Frederick Beresford had died of a fever, leaving his wife and only child Meredith alone.

Twenty-year-old Nessa Borlase stood in the cold, dim light of the house, which smelled of death, and looked with great sadness at her young mistress. She was in her white nightdress, and at the side of the bed was her four-day-old daughter in her crib. The fever that had taken this girl's father had spared her, only for death to take her in childbirth. Her labour had been an interminable agony. When she had finally thrust the babe out into the world she had lived just three days before breathing her last.

When her labour had started, her mistress's mother, Lady Margaret, had retired to her room, leaving Nessa to minister to Meredith, her pregnant daughter. When Nessa had gone to her and begged her to send for the physician she had coldly refused.

Suddenly the door was thrust open and Lady Margaret stood there. As her gaze passed over her dead daughter there was no change in her self-righteous, steely-eyed expression. It was as cold an expression as Nessa had ever seen on a woman who had just lost her only child.

'So, she's dead, then.' Her voice was as cold as her eyes.

Nessa swallowed audibly and nodded. 'Yes—just now. I—I was just coming to tell you.'

Lady Margaret nodded, her eyes settling on her granddaughter in the crib. Her eyes were wide open, but the child was too young to comprehend what was happening, that her mother had just died. However, seeming to sense the malevolence in the woman—her grandmother—she began to whimper softly.

Something cold and heavy descended over her heart as Nessa went to the motherless babe and swept her up into her arms and held her close. 'The babe is hungry. I must feed her.'

'I don't want her here. Take her away—anywhere, I don't care, as long as she is out of my sight.'

Bewildered, Nessa stared at her. She couldn't believe what she was hearing. 'Take her away? Forgive me, my lady—I don't understand. Where…?'

'To Castle Creek. Where else would she go if not to that libertine of a father of hers? And do not insult my intelligence and pretend you don't know who I mean. Don't play the innocent.'

She was so certain of herself, so dreadfully intimidating as she stood beside the bed.

'You played *your* part in the wretched affair when they were carrying on behind my back.'

Nessa was feeling colder by the minute, and Lady Margaret's words hammered on her nerves. 'But Sir Robert is still in Mexico. There will be no one at Castle Creek.'

'There are servants. Let *them* deal with her. It's not my concern. It's either that or the orphanage.'

Nessa remained silent, but inside her anger stirred. Suddenly this embittered woman put her in mind of a witch—and she even seemed to hiss. It was the only way to describe the low-pitched, hate-filled words. If Nessa had hoped for compassion in her for her dead daughter, she knew better now. There wasn't an ounce of compassion in this woman.

In her grief at losing Meredith, her beloved mistress, Nessa wanted to shout her anger, to remind her that if she hadn't been so against her daughter seeing Robert Wesley there would have been no need for them to carry on behind her back. She took a deep breath to calm her jangling nerves, telling herself not to sound desperate, not to plead for the babe in her arms, but to be reasonable.

Lady Margaret's hatred was deeply rooted in the past. Robert Wesley's father, whose family had been greatly involved with the mining of silver and lead in that part of Devon for decades, had been her first love, and she had never forgiven him for throwing her over in favour of Robert's mother. Nothing would have persuaded her to allow her daughter to form a liaison with his son.

As young as she had been, Meredith had been possessed of a passion for Robert Wesley she hadn't been able to control. Lady Margaret had seen it—lust, she had called it. Lust, not love. And in her opinion lust was wicked—a sin that destroyed.

In the beginning Meredith had concealed her condition from her mother and the other servants, but it could not be concealed for ever. When she had told her mother she was to bear Robert's child, her mother had railed and stormed unendingly, her face twisted with fury, accusing her of behaving no better than a peasant girl and calling her a whore.

Had it been anyone else who had fathered the child she would not have objected so strongly and merely forced a marriage, but she had not allowed her daughter to marry Robert Wesley. It had been too appalling for her to contemplate—and Nessa's young mistress had been too young and too weak to disobey. Lady Margaret had not even allowed her to write and tell him of her predicament, and had kept her confined to the house, allowing her to see no one but her maid.

But the servants had talked among themselves in hushed whispers, and when Miss Meredith had taken to her bed they'd made up their own minds about what ailed the young mistress.

Lady Margaret had had no intention of letting her daughter keep the child. But, whatever her objections to the child's father, neither did she wish to become involved in any scandal. People would talk, and she *did* mind about that. Not that she cared for their opinion, but to draw attention to one's self in any way she considered ill-bred.

She had decided that when her daughter had

been delivered of the unwanted burden, if it survived she would see it dispatched to an orphanage in another county. She had not expected her daughter to die, and now it no longer mattered what happened to the child.

'And me, my lady?' Nessa's voice was low, her expression controlled.

'You?' Lady Margaret spoke as if addressing someone completely stupid. 'What *about* you?'

'Am I being dismissed?' Nessa asked.

'Yes, you are,' she replied, her face a mask, her mouth inflexible. 'Your services are no longer required in this house.'

Nessa looked at the pale figure of her young mistress, feeling a deep sadness. 'But—I can't leave,' Nessa objected. 'Miss Meredith—'

'Is dead. She no longer has any need of you. You heard what I said. Oblige me by taking the child far away from this house. I don't want you here.' Her eyes dropped to the child. 'Either of you,' she added.

Nessa was stunned by the viciousness of Lady Margaret's words. 'But—my lady—you can't do that,' she ventured bravely. 'The child is your granddaughter…'

'And Robert Wesley is her father,' she snapped back.

Decency and honesty came first in Nessa's

mind, and she could not understand how a woman could discard her own grandchild. 'But—but what you are doing, my lady, is—is cruel.'

Lady Margaret's eyes sliced over her. 'You—a servant—dare preach to *me* about cruelty. Life is like that. Now get your things and go.'

'But—my money—and a character…

Lady Margaret walked to the door, then turned to look back at the servant. 'A character? I don't think so. Get the child ready. I'll give you whatever money is owed to you before you leave. I have nothing more to say.'

She gave her a last withering look and left.

With the child held in one arm, and carrying a bundle containing her few worldly possessions in the other, Nessa left Beresford House. Not that she was sorry to leave. In fact she was relieved to be gone. Tall, and carrying herself upright, Nessa was near to weeping—but anger prevented it.

The big problem was what she should do. She wondered what life had in store for her. It was important that she found work, otherwise she would be unable to ensure that regular money went to her mother and father. They lived across the Tamar in Cornwall, and they both suffered from ill health. Without her money they would be turned out of their cottage. But who would employ her? She had not been given a reference, and without a character she would not find it easy to find employment in service.

With these thoughts heavy on her mind she followed a route which took her along the two miles of pathways to Castle Creek, mentally damning Lady Margaret with every step she took. The woman should be ashamed—getting rid of her granddaughter as she would a stray dog.

It was a hot day, and the child was heavy in Nessa's arms. She was wondering at the reception she would receive when Castle Creek came into view. Commanding a view over the English Channel, it was a solid, square-built house, with crenelated walls and innumerable windows. It was bigger and more imposing than any house Nessa had ever seen. She found it quite awesome.

Reaching the lodge, she knocked on the door. Getting no response, she peered through the window. It appeared no one was at home. She carried on up the long drive to the house and reached the heavy wooden doors. The shutters were closed, and when she pulled the rope that rang the bell inside the house sounded hollow and empty.

An old man in working clothes and a floppy felt hat who was tending the gardens told her that the old master had passed on two months back. His son, Sir Robert, had been in Mexico on silver mining business. He had been notified immediately, but before arrangements had been made for him to return home he'd been fatally wounded. The house had been closed and the other servants dismissed until further notice.

When the man had shuffled off to go about his work, Nessa stared after him. Clutching the babe in her arms—an orphan, she realised—she looked around. The beautiful house had a look of desolation about it, a feeling of emptiness, as though all the life it had known since the day it was built had been whisked away for ever.

What was she to do? What was to become of them? She had to find work, and the child would only hinder her. But for now there was nothing for it but to take the child with her to Cornwall.

The journey was hard. Without the usual method of feeding a young baby, she had to buy milk to spoon-feed her.

She had a spinster aunt who lived in Saltash, but being a harsh, self-righteous woman she would not take kindly to her turning up with an infant. Perhaps by some miracle something would turn up.

One thing she was sure of—Lady Margaret might not want her grandchild, and she, Nessa, had no part of her, but she would *not* take Miss Meredith's defenceless daughter to any orphanage.

* * *

Two days after the lumbering farmer's cart carrying Nessa Borlase and her young charge crossed into Cornwall, leaving her at a crossroads to go her own way, with her spirits crushed and no hope of finding a place for herself and the baby, a young boy rode over the undulating terrain.

Gripping the spirited roan with his strong legs, Marcus Carberry bent low over its glossy neck as he rode—at great danger, it seemed, not only to him but to the animal, as he galloped with complete abandon across the great expanse of undulating parkland. At any other time he'd enjoy courting danger—the thrill of it. But today he rode his horse hard in an attempt to rid himself of his brother's harsh words.

Edward, his half-brother—the elder by six years—had arrived home from school. To his disappointment, Marcus had known immediately that Edward's resentment towards him was unchanged.

'Come, Edward,' their father had said. 'Aren't you going to say hello to your brother? You haven't seen him for almost twelve months.'

Edward had regarded Marcus with cold, malevolent eyes as he'd pulled off his leather gloves, and from his expression Marcus had known that

Edward could quite happily have gone another twelve months and more without seeing his younger brother.

'It's good to see you, Edward,' Marcus had said, in an attempt to reach out to his brother, despite his aura of barely concealed ferocity. 'You are looking well.'

'So are you,' Edward had replied, before turning his back on him.

Marcus had stared at his straight back, angered by his attitude. His dislike of his brother at that moment had been so intense that he'd been afraid of losing his temper—and with it any advantage he might have.

Marcus's mother, Lady Alice, was Lord Carberry's second wife. Edward had been born to his first wife, who had died as a consequence of a carriage accident. At five years old, Edward had not welcomed his father's second marriage. Even at so young an age he had resented the intrusion of a stranger into his well-ordered world—and he had resented it all the more when Marcus had come along, followed three years later by his sister Juliet.

In the distance the blue sea met the sky, and to the left of him a large lake on which many species of beautiful birds glided serenely and silently over the smooth surface was half a mile away. The boy gave it no more than a cursory glance as he rode towards the woods in the distance.

Once there, he slowed his horse and followed a narrow path into the trees. It was cool within the confines of the wood. The beech and the oak trees were heavy with leaf, dappling the path. In patches where the sun came through he felt the heat of those stray sunbeams as he rode through.

At ten years old he was a handsome boy. His eyebrows swooped fiercely upwards and his heavily fringed eyes were a startling silver-grey in a face as dark as a gypsy's. His mouth had a hint of hardness, even in one so young, but at his age it was mobile, and he smiled easily and often. His hair was thick, and as smooth and black as a raven's wing.

Hearing a rustling ahead, he paused and waited, smiling and looking with awe at the beautiful creature that suddenly appeared—a deer, slender and graceful, with long legs and stick-like antlers growing out of its proud head. Startled, it stopped and stared at him, before bounding away. The darkness that had shrouded him with his brother's return melted away.

Laughing easily, the boy dismounted and led his horse along the path, delighting in the rabbits that ventured from the undergrowth and loving the peace of the wood which was shrouded in timeless tranquillity. The May sunshine had turned the beauty of the woodland and the quiet glades of ash and sycamore and venerable oak to every shade of green and brown.

He was so entranced with his surroundings that he could not believe his ears when he emerged into a circular glade and heard what he thought to be a young animal crying. The ground was thickly carpeted with delicate white wood anemones and bluebells, their scent quite intoxicating. Looking about him for the source of the noise, he found his eyes drawn to what looked like a bundle of rags beneath a canopy of leaves. He was sure he saw it move, and suddenly what looked to be a tiny hand reached up and thrashed the air.

Tentatively he moved towards it, unable to believe his eyes when he found himself looking down at a baby. It was wrapped in a pink woollen shawl which the infant, clearly objecting to being so confined, had worked loose with its wriggling about.

Marcus glanced around, unable to believe the baby was unaccompanied—surely someone would appear at any moment to claim it. Hunkering down, he studied the tiny scrap of humanity with interest.

'Well, what have we here?' he murmured.

The infant was female, by the look of it, and couldn't be any more than a few days old—although he was none too sure, not having much knowledge of babies and never having given them much thought.

He felt a prickle of curiosity. She was a lovely-looking child to be sure, he decided, simply lovely. His heart softened towards the infant. She was distressed. Great fat tears brimmed from her incredible eyes and her face was red and screwed up with anger and exasperation.

'Hush, now—stop yelling,' he murmured softly, touching her cheek gently with the backs of his fingers.

He thought he must have a magic touch when she stopped crying almost immediately. Her eyes were as bright as two great blue jewels beneath their burden of moisture as they became fixed on his. When he held out his finger and placed it within her palm she gripped it and clung to it with a strength and fierceness incredible in one so young.

Maybe it was an instinct of self-preservation that made her grip so hard, as if she sensed she had been abandoned and stood the greatest chance of survival with this strange boy who had found her. Taking his finger to her mouth, she sucked on it hard, bringing a smile to Marcus's mouth.

'So you are hungry, are you, little one? Well, what is to be done with you? I can't leave you here, now, can I?'

Retrieving his finger, he was about to get to his feet when, feeling a strong sensation of being watched, he glanced around him. He hoped someone would emerge from the trees and claim the child. When no one did, and beginning to realise that would not happen, he gently picked the child up and carried her to his horse. Mounting with some difficulty, and settling into the saddle, he cradled her in from of him.

He would take her to Izzy. She would know what to do.

Izzy Trevanion was the only child of a parson and his wife, and from Somerset. She had been educated by her father, and when she was of age had found employment as a governess to three young girls on an estate bordering Tregarrick, which had been the home of the Carberrys for generations. On her marriage to Colin Trevanion, the head steward at Tregarrick, she had left her employment to look after Colin and raise their family. They lived in a cottage on the Carberry estate.

Riding up the path towards the cottage, Marcus found the aroma of a tasty stew cooking in Izzy's oven assailing him. It was plain fare Izzy prepared for her family, unlike the fancy dishes at Tregarrick. But Izzy's stew was probably mutton with fresh vegetables, to be followed by a tasty suet pudding—well-cooked, nourishing, and mouthwateringly tasty.

Having heard the horse, Izzy came out to see her visitor. Marcus knew she had a soft spot for him. He remembered the times when he had found his way to her cottage, when she had lifted him up and folded him to her ample bosom and told him stories which had held him agog. Now, wiping her hands on her apron, she smiled a welcome— but the smile faded when he swung himself out of the saddle with one hand and holding a child with the other.

Izzy watched the youngest of Lord and Lady Carberry's two sons approach, waiting with an air of expectancy, her hands on her hips. She gasped, her eyes fixed on the infant. 'My goodness, what have we here?'

'A baby, Izzy. I found her in the woods.'

A slight breeze ruffled the child's curls and the sun shone warmly on her pink cheeks. Izzy stared at her in amazement. 'Found her? But—you don't just *find* a baby. Who was she with?'

He shrugged. 'I wouldn't know. She was quite alone.'

Carrying the child ahead of Izzy into the house,

he was greeted by Hester, the oldest of Izzy's three daughters. She was kneading dough on a floured board. At eight years old, with a shock of brown curls and bright green eyes, Hester was a pretty girl, and already adept at running the cottage and controlling her younger sister Kenza, who was whisking eggs in a bowl. Annie, the latest addition to the household, was asleep in a basket beside the fire.

As one, the two girls at the table came to a halt to gape in wonder at the baby. It was a homely scene.

Marcus loved Izzy's cottage. There was always a welcoming warmth and a place by the fire. There was also a stove, and all manner of kitchen things hanging on the walls. The sunlight shone on copper pans, and the dresser against one wall was crammed with blue and white crockery. A vase of wild flowers sat in the window, and a large black cat stretched out on the rug in front of the stove.

'Poor little mite,' Izzy said. 'Someone will be looking for her.'

'How do we know that?' Marcus said. 'She didn't lose herself. Someone put her there on purpose—abandoned her. She must be unwanted by those who did it. Imagine what would have happened to her if I had not come along. It's too dreadful to contemplate. It's a crime, Izzy—an act of wickedness. That's what it is. Who could do that to an innocent babe too young to fend for itself?'

Izzy shrugged, taking the infant from him. 'Some poor girl who found herself in trouble and couldn't cope, I'd say. She wouldn't be the first to find herself in that unhappy state—no money and the stigma of bearing a child out of wedlock,' she uttered sympathetically, and instantly offered up a prayer for the mother of this child and her misfortunes.

'Perhaps you're right. But someone's been looking after her, and she looks well fed. Until we find out who she is she must have a name. We can't call her "the girl", can we? What shall we call her, Izzy?'

'Eh, Master Marcus, I've no idea. She must have a name already.

'But we don't know what it is.'

'Then what do you suggest, Master Marcus? You can choose until we know more about her.'

Marcus looked at the child, whose steady gaze hadn't moved from his face since he'd found her. They were the loveliest eyes he had ever seen. He studied her for a moment and suddenly felt his heart stir with warmth towards this tiny scrap of humanity. As she continued to stare at him, with her wide and trusting eyes, he found himself quite enchanted by her, with her mop of deep red hair. Just looking at her sent a wave of tenderness through him.

The strange feelings hit him with an impact that stunned him, creeping into his heart and arousing a love quite different from the love he bore his adored mother and Juliet, and at the same time made him want to be her protector should she ever need one.

'Lowena,' he said suddenly. 'Until we know different we'll call her Lowena—for joy.'

Izzy stared at him. 'Lowena? That's a nice name, I must say.'

'I think so too,' Hester remarked, leaving the bread to come and take a look at the child. 'Lowena is a pretty name.'

'Thank you, Hester,' Marcus said, smiling warmly at her, which brought a soft flush to her cheeks. 'I see nothing wrong with it. And you're right. It's a pretty name for a pretty girl. I found her among the anemones and bluebells, so I suppose we could call her Bluebell, but I think Lowena is better. Lowena it is.'

'And what are you going to do with her—with Lowena?' Izzy asked. 'Will you take her to the house? I don't suppose Lord Carberry will be too happy about you turning up with a foundling waif.'

Marcus frowned when he thought of his father,

knowing how he would react if he were to turn up with an abandoned child, spoiling the well-ordered running of his home.

'You're right, Izzy, Father wouldn't like it one bit. Besides,' he said, a shadow passing over his eyes, 'Edward's home and he wouldn't like it either. I'll have to tell Mother, though. She would want to know, and maybe she might learn something of Lowena's family on her visits to the village. I'll make some enquiries of my own. Perhaps I will find out who she belongs to.'

'She's a plump little thing. You are right. She's not been neglected,' Izzy remarked, reaching out and fingering the pretty smock the child was wearing. 'Her clothes are quality, so she obviously belongs to someone well-to-do. And see,' she said, fingering the elaborately embroidered initial on the blanket she was wrapped in. 'The letter B. Well, that could be significant, and a start as to discovering her identity. But in the meantime what are you to do with her?'

Folding her arms across her large bosom, Izzy looked at him hard, knowing perfectly well what the young master was about to ask her.

Marcus removed his attention from the child and, placing a cajoling arm about Izzy's waist, smiled infectiously, disarmingly, as though to ask forgiveness for what he would say next—for there really was nothing else he could do. And because Izzy was so fond of him he knew she would not refuse.

'You'll look after her for me, won't you, Izzy? You have a brood of your own—one more won't make any difference.'

'Will it not?' she said, glancing at Hester and Kenza, their chattering voices filling the kitchen once more. 'With three mouths and my husband to feed how will I manage?'

'Babies don't eat much, Izzy, and I'm sure Mother will help.'

Izzy hesitated, looking at him hard again. Master Marcus had discovered how to manipulate those who cared for him from an early age. Whereas his brother, Master Edward, was rebellious, given to fits of temper and nastiness when he could not get his own way. He was proud and haughty where Master Marcus was generous and tender-hearted and full of irresistible charm, and all those around him—from the cook down to the scullery maid—could not help but respond to him—especially Izzy and her girls, who adored the very ground upon which he walked.

Izzy sighed, unable to refuse his request. 'With that clever brain of yours, that pleading look in your eyes, Master Marcus, and the way you have of getting the better of others—especially me, even with my strong powers of reasoning—you know I can't refuse you anything. But when people ask where she came from what am I to say?'

'The truth, of course,' Marcus replied, satisfied that he'd got his way and gently chucking Lowena under her softly dimpled chin.

'I'll look after her for the time being, Master Marcus,' Izzy said, cradling the child in her arms and thinking what a lovely little thing she was. 'You know I'll take good care of her. But I want you to promise me that if anything should happen in the future—what I mean is if we fail to find her family and should anything happen to me—*you* will take care of her, see that comes to no harm.'

Noting the gravity of Izzy's words, Marcus nodded, and his answer was spoken quietly, equally as grave. 'I will, Izzy. I promise.'

'That's all I ask. Now, then, let's get her settled and I'll see about feeding her. I don't suppose Annie will mind sharing...'

Before Marcus left the cottage Izzy was already unbuttoning her dress and settling down beside the hearth to feed the new and what she believed to be the temporary addition to her family.

As the years passed Lowena flourished within the warmth of Izzy's family. She was a happy child, adored by all who met her.

Izzy never made any secret of the fact that she was a foundling. Enquiries had been made, but no one could throw any light on where she had come from, and as time went by it ceased to matter…

Chapter One

1780

The crowd melted away, making a pathway before Captain Marcus Carberry as he walked from Fowey Harbour with long, purposeful strides. Some turned to look again at the well-built figure of the tanned military man in his late twenties. His face was disciplined, strong, striking—and exceptionally handsome. He was conspicuous in his tight fitting-red jacket with its cross-belt of white which emphasised his powerful chest, and tapering white trousers above knee-length black boots emphasised long legs and muscular thighs.

Having left the ship outside Fowey's deep harbour, on its way to Portsmouth, and rowed to shore, he was eager to get home. Looking around the familiar bustling streets he felt his heart swell. For him, the war in America was over. Having served the ten years he had signed up for with the army, he had been on the point of extending his post, but the death of his father had brought him back to Tregarrick.

Cornwall was in his heart, and he had always known he would come back. Everything he had ever cared about was here. Breathing deep of the salt sea air, he thought even the cloying stench of fish that hung over the harbour smelled sweet after five years of war.

And then there was the family mine—Wheal Rozen, named after his grandmother. From the moment his father had taken him there as a boy he'd set about learning all there was to know about mining and everything connected with it, from anyone who was prepared to talk to him. The memory of the times he had spent at Wheal Rozen as a boy and then as a youth, listening to the noise and action of the great pump engine demonstrating its power, made his body tingle.

Now, on his father's demise, Marcus's elder half-brother Edward had inherited the estate—which was the way of things—but his father had left Marcus one hundred per cent ownership of the mine, so all the decision-making would be up to him, and the freedom to explore for further mineral deposits was his priority.

As soon as he had eaten at a hostelry he hired

a horse and headed out of Fowey. The horse would be returned in due course. It was already dark. He knew it was dangerous to travel at night but, believing his uniform would protect him against anyone who might be tempted to way-lay him, and eager to get home, he set out for Tregarrick.

Thoughts of his brother brought a hardening to Marcus's jaw and an ache to his heart, and as he covered the miles he was unable to stave off his anxiety as to how his homecoming would be received by Edward.

Marcus knew better than to expect him to welcome him home with warm words. Spoiled and fawned over by an adoring mother, Edward was one of the most unprincipled men he knew. He and Marcus had led separate lives, meeting only when one or the other had come home from school, and later when Marcus came home from the military academy. After a lifetime of resent-ment Edward was unlikely to have had a change of heart towards Marcus. But if he had, Marcus would welcome that and hold out his hand.

As brothers they should be able to forgive each other anything—shouldn't they?

Almost at the end of his journey, and seeing a flash of light out at sea, he dismounted and walked to the cliff's edge. His eyes were drawn down to the beach, where dark figures moved and horses waited. From his vantage point Marcus knew he was witnessing the centuries-old Cornish tradition of smuggling.

It was something he had grown up with, and he knew that to those involved in the trade it was a way of life. For the families with many mouths to feed times were hard, and smuggling was their way of trying to make ends meet—the ring-leaders often became rich on the strength of it. But those who got involved in this illegal trade did so at a high cost, for the penalty for smuggling would be found at the end of a rope...

Tonight the wind was blowing and the sea was choppy. Conditions were perfect for the run. The night was dark, with only a half-moon showing now and then between heavy clouds. Lowena didn't like being on the cliffs after dark, but Edward had left her with no choice.

Edward Carberry! The mere thought of him had the power to fill her with fear and hatred. It was hard to believe that a man of such high standing in the community, and indeed the whole of Cornwall, would involve himself in the illegal and highly dangerous practice of smuggling. But since taking up employment as a servant at Tregarrick, Lowena had come to realise that her employer was clever and as slippery as an eel—and notorious for his ruthlessness.

It was as though smuggling gave him a much needed outlet for adventure, and the danger provided heightened his emotions. He also seemed to take great delight in cocking a snook at the Government in faraway London, for the exorbitant taxes imposed on the people of Cornwall to fund its wars and other schemes that did not concern the county.

As soon as she had started work at Tregarrick, after Izzy's death, Lowena had caught his eye. When she'd resisted his advances, he had taken a perverted delight in drawing her into his ring of smugglers. She had courageously stood up to him, and told him she wanted no part of it, but he had left her in no doubt that if she did not comply she would have to seek employment elsewhere.

With no family to support her and nowhere else to go, Lowena had had no choice but to do as she was told.

Had his brother Marcus been at home then things would have been different. In all the years she had known him Lord Carberry's younger half-brother had shown her nothing but kindness and consideration. He had often come to see Izzy when he was home from school, to sample some of the wonderful appetising food that she'd put on her table.

How he'd loved to talk! And how Lowena had loved to listen, with her eyes wide and nothing to contribute but her admiration of this handsome youth. Tenderness still shook her every time she thought of him. *He* would not have allowed Lord Carberry to use her in this manner.

Her heart warmed as she thought of him now. Izzy had told her that Mr Marcus had all the characteristics his half-brother had always envied and resented. Lowena remembered that his features were quiet and intent, that they were also strong and noble—in all he was taller and significantly more handsome and manly than Edward Carberry. Edward's features were fine—his eyes a watery blue, his hair ash-blond.

It wasn't the first time Lowena had been dragged from her bed when there was a run. She knew the routine. She was positioned at the highest point along this part of the coastline, and it was her responsibility to light the beacon of furze should trouble appear. Someone else was guarding the narrow track that ran down to the cove—the one that led to the high moor, which was dominated by a bleak, hostile landscape and where no one lingered longer than was necessary.

The wind snapped at her hair and she shuddered as she looked down into the cove, unmoving, watchful, staring into the darkness, hoping and praying that all would go to plan so she didn't have to light the furze.

A cloud moved off the moon, shedding light on the small horseshoe cove. This was where, on a terrible stormy night, a ship had once found itself at the mercy of the wind, the sea and the rocks—where it had floundered and broken up. Wreckers had soon been drawn to the stricken vessel, before the customs men had appeared on the scene. They had looted the vessel, killing without mercy anyone who had survived.

It was said that on certain nights the souls of the dead could be heard on the wind, as if they refused to move on and continued to haunt the environs of the cove.

Ever since that night people had said the cove was cursed, and no one came here—which was to the smugglers' advantage. It was a haven for smugglers—if they knew how to pilot a boat among the reefs.

Two strings of horses were already on the beach. They were hardy workhorses, along with specially adapted saddles which could carry the heavy casks of liquor and chests of tea.

The men in the boats were professional seamen, the shore party less so, being made up mainly of agricultural labourers and miners. A successful run could earn them as much as two weeks working on the land, and it was with Lord Carberry's approval that they brought with them carts and horses wherever they could be found, to assist in the landing.

Edward's estate manager, William Watkins, was keeping his eye on proceedings and giving orders to the men on the beach.

Looking out to sea, Lowena saw a light. It flashed three times. This was the signal indicating to those on shore that the ship they were expecting was there for the rendezvous, hidden in the darkness out at sea. The men in the boats began rowing towards the light in the treacherous waters, careful to avoid the submerged rocks and soon being swallowed up in the darkness.

The suspense was unbearable to Lowena as she paced back and forth along the cliff edge. It was a cold night and her heart was racing, her eyes blinded by gusts of wind.

After about an hour or more the boat returned. The men jumped out carrying their oars and placed them on the sand. They worked swiftly, unloading the cargo with silent speed and loading it into carts or securing it onto the horses and leading them up the narrow valley which opened into the cove.

Some of the smuggled goods would be taken up-country to Devon or beyond, and some would be stored locally, to be sold in the community. Lord Carberry had established contacts to shift the goods.

As the horses began to move off with their heavy, lucrative load, Lowena gave a sigh of relief and yawned. At last she could return to the house and her bed.

Suddenly something made her turn her head and look along the cliff. Straining her eyes in the darkness, she felt cold fear grip her. Her heart almost stopped when she saw the silhouette of a man, watching the activities below. His feet were slightly apart, his back straight, his hands clasped behind him. Instinctively she shrank into the shadows. How long had he been there? What had he seen? It was too late now to light the beacon.

Holding her breath, Lowena slowly edged towards some tall shrubs, hoping he hadn't seen her. When she looked again the man had gone. Her gaze scanned the blackness all around her, but there was no sight of him. Not wanting to wait a moment longer, she turned and headed for home. Moving swiftly along the path, she felt her foot stumble against a stone and only just managed to keep herself from falling.

Straightening herself, she came face to face with a tall figure in the uniform of a soldier. A dragoon—he had to be a dragoon. At the sudden appearance of this ghostly apparition, looming large and menacing, she trembled with fear. A bolt of terror shot through her and she stood rooted to the spot, unable to move or to speak. When he stepped closer to her she pulled herself together, and with no thought other than to escape turned to run. But the man caught her arm in a vice-like grip.

'Don't be a fool,' he growled. 'Stay where you are.'

Stunned and stricken dumb, Lowena heard that low, deep voice and thought she was in some kind of nightmare. She spun back, her eyes wide, staring up at him through the tangled mass of her hair. Her heart was beating hard and seemed to roar in her ears. The man towered over her, and in the darkness she could just make out his face.

She felt herself drawn to him, as if by some overwhelming magnetic force, and for an instant something stirred inside her. She experienced a feeling of strange, slinking unease—the unease of shadowy familiarity—and she shivered with a sense of deep foreboding.

The blood drained from her face. Recognition hit her and she gasped, thunderstruck.

It was Mr Marcus, back from the Americas. At least it looked like him.

With her hair strewn across her face and in the dim light she prayed he hadn't recognised her—not now, not when she must look a frightful sight and was breaking the law. Struggling fiercely to release herself from his grip, closing her ears to the low curses he uttered, she succeeded in freeing herself and fled.

On reaching the back of the house at Tregarrick she let herself in, breathing a huge sigh of relief that he hadn't recognised her or followed her. In her room, high in the eaves, she lay in bed staring at the ceiling, her body taut, her head in a whirl. She tried not to think of Mr Marcus, wondering if perhaps it hadn't been him who had taken hold of her, if she had been mistaken and it had been one of the dragoons from the barracks at Bodmin who had accosted her.

After a while she heard a dog bark in the stables and the whinny of horses. Voices sounded outside and she knew the men had returned from their night's work in the cove. She froze, her desire to flee this house overwhelmingly strong.

Covering her face she began to sob, and great tears oozed from her eyes. 'Oh, Izzy,' she moaned, with a wretchedness that came straight from her heart. 'Why did you have to die? Why did you have to leave me?'

There was no help for her.

Two hours later, when the two half-brothers finally faced each other across the drawing room at Tregarrick, the air about them had turned cold, lapping around them like a winter sea. It held the two of them in its deathly chill.

Edward took judicious note of the taut set of his brother's jaw, and the small lines of ruthlessness around his mouth, and could see he was a youth no longer. Marcus presented a towering, masculine, imposing figure. An aura of authority and power seemed to surround him. It was etched in every line of his lean, taut frame, and he possessed a haughty reserve that was *not* inviting.

Edward mentally despised the implacable authority and strength in Marcus's manner and bearing, which no doubt stemmed from his military training and the ensuing years fighting the war in America.

'Ah,' Edward said, his eyes cold. 'You survived the war, I see… So the soldier condescends to return home? Good of you, Marcus. Better late than never, I suppose.'

Marcus's lips curled in derision. 'I am the sort who clings to life, Edward, as you should know.

I was sorry to hear about Isabel,' he said, his tone flat as he referred to Edward's wife.

Edward's face hardened and became closed, but not before Marcus had seen a hidden pain cloud his eyes.

'Mother told me it was a riding accident that killed her.'

'These things happen,' was all Edward said, clearly irritated that his brother should remind him of that time in his life when he had been at his most vulnerable. 'I am surprised to find you here at this late hour. You must forgive my absence. I have been occupied with other matters tonight.'

'I saw.'

Edward smiled thinly, pouring himself a drink. Dropping into a leather chair by the fire, he stretched out his long booted legs. 'As long as you were the only one who saw then I am not concerned.'

Before Marcus had left for America he had known that Edward had become the leader of a well-organised smuggling ring operating hereabouts. It would seem nothing had changed.

'I had thought you would have put the trade behind you with your new position. Even the cleverest smuggler will make a mistake eventually—and then he will be either arrested or dead.'

Edward's brows lifted imperturbably. 'I and

more than half the population in Cornwall do not see smuggling as a crime. Those involved in various ways either buy, sell, or drink—respectable ministers of the church, doctors, lawyers, and… oh, yes…even magistrates and excise men. They all look the other way for a drop of fine French brandy or a bolt of silk or lace for their ladies.'

'You are good at impressing people, aren't you, Edward? People who don't know that beneath your fine clothes and affectations you are in possession of a ruthlessness and cruelty which will stop at nothing to possess or destroy what you cannot possess. But there are those who are law-abiding and will not turn a blind eye to your activities for ever. You would do well to remember that you are not beyond reach of the law.'

Marcus had spoken quietly—too quietly for Edward's comfort—and there was a judgemental expression in the cold, pale eyes assessing him.

'The law can go to hell,' Edward bit back, with apparently righteous indignation. 'The various schemes I devise with those across the Channel for our mutual profit will continue until I call a halt. I shall continue to land contraband in that cursed cove until I can no longer elude the Revenue men and the dragoons.'

'Nevertheless it is still a crime, and should you get caught your title will not save you.'

'So you imagine I might be arrested?' Edward said, tilting his head to one side and peering at his brother through narrowed eyes. 'Perhaps you may propose to do something yourself.'

Marcus shrugged. 'What can I do that the excise men can't? I can't forbid you to cross the land to the cove, since you own it. But you will not escape without retribution—and if you were not my brother it would be all the sweeter if it were by my own hand. I *know* you, Edward. The methods you use for disposing of those who get in your way are not mine. I am first and foremost the King's servant. Eventually you will be caught, and you will have to stand trial and suffer the ultimate penalty for your crime—and when you do you will ask yourself if it was worth it.'

Edward laughed lightly, unconcerned by his brother's argument. 'The men who work for me are as audacious and cunning as I am. We are not such amateurs that we would leave contraband lying around for the excise men to find.'

'And those in the community who are not directly involved? Huge rewards are offered for the successful conviction of smugglers. Does it not concern you that someone might speak out?'

'Anyone tempted by the rewards will know that their lives would be short if they were to do that. The Cornish coast is long, Marcus, with many hidden coves riddled with caves. Smuggling goes on from Land's End to the Tamar and beyond. The excise men and the dragoons cannot be everywhere at once. But I suppose if I should be arrested that would please you, would it not? To become Lord of the Manor?'

Marcus didn't answer. He knew Edward was trying to bait him, but he refused to be drawn.

'The funeral is over, Marcus,' Edward said, having had enough discussion of smuggling and wanting a change of subject. 'Our father has been interred in the church next to my mother.'

Marcus knew exactly what he was alluding to. He wanted to remind him that his own mother took second place as their father's second wife. 'I know. That's as it should be. I came as soon as I received Mother's letter.'

Edward glanced at his brother. 'Is it your intention to return to the war, or are you home for good?'

'I'm sorry to disappoint you, Edward, but I am here to stay. My time with the army is at an end. I'm weary of war—which is not going well for the English.'

'I am aware of that. The world has not passed me by here at Tregarrick,' Edward replied drily.

'I am surprised to find you still at home, Edward. In her letter informing me of our father's demise Mother mentioned something about you going to London. I imagine that now you have the estate to manage you will not spend so much of your time in the city as you have in the past.'

'Why not? I employ Watkins to oversee the work here. He worked well for my father—'

'*Our* father,' Marcus corrected coldly.

Edward smiled thinly, arrogant in his demeanour. 'Whatever you say.'

'Have you considered getting yourself an heir, Edward, and marrying again? It's two years since Isabel died.'

'I will—when I am good and ready. It has crossed my mind to go up to London for a time, and I might have a look around for a woman who suits my needs while I'm there. I'm in need of some pleasurable diversion. However,' he said, swirling the brandy round the bowl of his glass and settling back into the chair, his lips curved in a self-satisfied smile, 'at this present time I have to say that a certain young woman at Tregarrick is proving to be the most charming diversion since she has come to work at the house.'

'Really? Do I know her?'

'You should. You were the one to bring her here after all!'

The dawning of understanding filled Marcus's eyes. He stared at Edward. 'Lowena?' His face hardened. 'Are you telling me that you and Lowena…?'

Edward laughed mirthlessly. He could almost *feel* the effort his brother was exerting to keep his rage under control. 'Absolutely. She has the face of an angel—a beautiful, fallen angel in every sense. She certainly has fire in her veins. You know the type… I'm tempted to remain in Cornwall a while longer. She helps in other ways, too,' he said quietly, meaningfully, watching his brother carefully for his reaction. 'She is particularly alert on the nights when there is a run and we need someone to man the beacon—or *woman*, in her case.'

There was nothing subtle about his mockery. It was direct. Marcus looked at him, lounging in his chair, arrogant, smug, self-satisfied, with a triumphant light in his eyes. He shook his head, as if to clear it of the monstrous thought his intellect was already beginning to form, but it clung on with the tenacity of a limpet on a rock. The mere thought that Edward had made Lowena a pawn in his illegal ventures almost sent him over the edge.

'Are you telling me that you have involved Lowena in smuggling?'

Edward looked at him. 'Why not? She is in my employ, so she has to do as she is told. She does have her uses—in many ways.'

Marcus went cold as what Edward had implied settled round his heart like an iron band. An awful, impossible thought came sliding slowly into his mind. It was too wicked for words—and yet suddenly he knew. He had a deep-rooted conviction that it had been Lowena he had encountered earlier—the girl who had been standing as lookout on the coastal path. He hadn't been able to see her identity because of the dark.

It was bad enough that Edward had implied that he was in a sexual liaison with Lowena—which Marcus refused to believe—but to be told that she took part in his nefarious practices was hard to take in and to accept. Edward had never been one to look beyond his own gratification. The mere thought of his brother tarnishing that sweet girl with his corruption sent a pain through his heart.

What Marcus remembered about Lowena was pure and good—all Edward would see was some sweet flesh to feed on. He had not changed. But then he had not expected him to. Edward lived his life close to the wind, in a dubious, discreditable way, caring little for the gracious things.

Contemptuous of his unworthy brother, Marcus filled his voice with scorn. 'I will not have Lowena's character impugned by innuendo, Edward.'

'Innuendo?' Edward laughed mirthlessly. 'My dear Marcus, who said anything about *innuendo*? Miss Trevanion has grown up to be the most accommodating beauty. Wait until you see her. You will not be disappointed.'

Edward was boasting with an unpleasant brand of sarcasm and resentment that Marcus had heard before. His anger simmered quietly within him, but when he spoke his voice was full of menace. 'Lowena is nineteen years old—'

'A very *delectable* nineteen-year-old. You've been absent too long, brother. Your sweet little Lowena has grown up.'

'I'd sooner see her burn in hell than for you to get your hands on her.'

Edward smiled, not in the least intimidated by his younger brother's angry words. 'That's rather harsh, Marcus, but I believe you. However, it's a bit late in the day for that.'

Marcus looked at his brother hard. Edward's face was a mask of sexual greed as he anticipated the corruption of someone beautiful and innocent. There was avarice in his pale blue eyes— avarice and pitilessness, along with self-interest. There was also contempt for those he considered his inferior, and an indifference to those he destroyed in his search to relieve the boredom which drove him like a sickness—a sickness that had possessed him ever since he was a boy.

'Your words show you in a bad light, Edward. If you attempt to touch her again you will have me to answer to. She is not a prize to be conquered. I demand that you remember that.'

Edward's eyes narrowed dangerously. 'You tempt me to put you to the test just for the sheer hell of it.'

'Lowena is a young woman of great intelligence and tenacity. She is vulnerable and, having played a large part in bringing her to Tregarrick, I consider myself to have an obligation to protect her.'

He'd promised Izzy all those years ago that he would look after Lowena, should she find herself alone, and he would abide by that promise.

'She is a *servant*,' Edward sneered callously.

'She is also a human being and should be treated with respect.'

'What goes on in the lives of those in my employ is no concern of mine.'

Edward's eyes were as cold as steel as they met his half-brother's, and the muscles in his cheeks tensed with ire. At that moment he saw that Marcus was every inch a man, and any questions he might have had over what might result from Marcus's time in the Americas and his arrival in Cornwall were answered.

Edward glared at him as their eyes parried for supremacy in a silent battle of unspoken challenge. It was Edward who looked away first.

When he spoke the mockery was gone and his voice was purposeful. 'I answer to no man, Marcus, least of all to you.'

'I would not expect you to.'

'Nevertheless I speak the truth. Lowena is very diverting—which you would know all about had you not gone away to widen your horizons.'

'I was a soldier, Edward, fighting a war. Listening to you, anyone would think I had gone abroad on the Grand Tour. Unlike you, I had no estate to inherit and secure my future. I had to make my own way.'

'Until Father willed the mine to you,' Edward uttered sharply, the tone of his voice telling Marcus how much he resented that fact. 'You must have known he would.'

'On the contrary. But he knew you had no interest in it.'

'Whereas you have?'

'Of course. You always knew that. So did Father.'

'Nevertheless, he should have made us equal partners,' Edward retorted, his expression hardening. He suddenly felt at a disadvantage—a unique experience for him.

'Has it not crossed your mind that his reluctance to do so might have had something to do with your tendency to gamble, Edward? With your impetuous behaviour and lack of judgement? With such shortcomings as those he might have thought you needed keeping on a tight rein.'

'He trusted me with the estate,' Edward pointed out, regaining his confidence.

'Because he saw that as your right. The mine is a separate entity, started by his grandfather. I think Father knew what he was doing when he willed Wheal Rozen to me. From the report I received in America from the mine manager, I gather Wheal Rozen is highly profitable, so there will be no need to bring in outside capital for further exploration. So you see, Edward, you are not rid of me after all. But you can rest assured I shall endeavour to keep out of your way as much as it is possible to do so.'

'Under the circumstances, that shouldn't be too difficult,' Edward said, getting out of his chair.

'Since we inhabit the same house, it is inevitable that we shall bump into each other now and them.'

About to take his leave, Edward half turned and looked at him hard, a smug smile curving his lips.

'The house? And what house might that be, brother? Tregarrick? *This* house?' He laughed—a laugh that was brittle and without humour. 'Of *course*! You don't know! But then—how could you?'

Something dark and ominous began to unfurl within Marcus. 'Know? Know what?'

'Your mother has moved out to the cottage. Knowing how fond you are of your mother, and knowing you would wish to reside with her, I had your things removed from Tregarrick.'

'Moved out? Did she go of her own free will or did you order her to leave?'

Edward shrugged. 'Does it matter? She went, anyway.'

The knowledge that Edward had relegated his mother to the cottage angered Marcus beyond words, but he would not take him to task over it until he had spoken to his mother.

'I will speak to her tomorrow, but before I leave for the cottage there is something I have to take care of.'

'And that is…?' Edward asked as his brother strode to the door.

As Marcus had expected, a servant was hovering in the hall should Edward need anything.

'Bring Miss Trevanion to me.'

She stared, nonplussed. 'Miss Trevanion? But—but she is in bed, sir.'

'Then wake her—and tell her to pack her things.'

His tone of authority had the girl scuttling away.

Marcus went back inside the room and gave his half-brother a dark look. 'If you imagine I will leave Lowena under your roof a moment longer then you are mistaken.'

Edward shrugged. 'Do as you like.'

Without another word he turned and went out.

Marcus watched him go, but the rage that distorted his brother's face was hidden from his view.

Marcus was unaware of how Edward cursed him, how his heart was dark and full of hate. Lowena's beauty tantalised him, and knowing the jealousy that would consume him if he saw the woman he had decided would be *his* mistress bestowing her favours on his brother, returned from the war in America, he had decided it was not to be borne.

Plagued by what Edward might have done to Lowena, Marcus was impatient to see her—to see for himself the changes his brother had wrought on a girl he remembered as being as sweet and pure, with the smile of an angel and an unspoiled charm. As a child she had been shy as a woodland creature, her manner as graceful, with none of the world's callousness to cause her heartache and pain. Time after time he had been drawn to her, but he had not explored his feelings because he had felt it wrong to do so.

She had been just sixteen when he had last laid eyes on her, when he had returned home on a brief spell away from his military duties. Her childhood had been behind her, and at that age she'd been old enough to be kissed. It shamed him to remember that the half formed young woman had aroused desires within him that, although perfectly natural, had made his sexual urge immense. But he was only human, after all, and a healthy and willing lover to any young girl.

Of course her age had mattered back then, and because she was who she was, and because he had had Isabel's affair with Edward occupying his thoughts, he would not have touched her. And Izzy would not have taken kindly to him toying with the girl who was as dear to her as her own daughters.

Edward's vitriolic insinuations and the dark shadow of the large part of Lowena's life without him, which he knew nothing about, concerned Marcus more than he cared to admit. His heart twisted in fury at the image of her lying in his brother's arms.

In angry frustration he turned his mind from his tortured imaginings and tried concentrating on the joy of her instead, determined not to let Edward's words sour his memories of her.

When she appeared at the top of the stairs he found he had to test the accuracy of his memory. The sight of her stunned him. The young woman who descended, with her softly curving form, her glorious wealth of shining red-gold hair, its tendrils coiling like serpents down her spine, her stormy amber eyes shaded by long, curling lashes, and soft pink lips, possessed a full-blown beauty certainly more vivid and lively than he remembered.

Lowena seemed to exude the very essence of vitality and life.

It had taken Lowena all of five minutes to dress and pack her few belongings into a bundle. She had paused for a moment at the top of the stairs to look down at the man pacing the hall with long, impatient strides before moving gracefully down the stairs.

As she watched him she was conscious of a sudden tension and nervousness in her. Apart from their brief encounter earlier, she had not seen him for almost four years, and she did not know how to behave towards him.

Suddenly he looked up and saw her. Her face, pale and tense, was exposed.

She wasn't to know about the acrimonious meeting he had had with his half-brother, but she sensed that he knew more about her involvement with what had happened in the cove earlier than she was comfortable with. Everything about him exuded an unbending will, and that in turn made Lowena feel even more wretched and helpless.

Reaching the bottom of the stairs, she walked towards him. For an endless moment their gazes locked as they assessed one another. She looked at him with the same bright, intelligent gaze he remembered.

'I apologise for waking you at this hour,' he said, and there was a touch of irony in his tone. 'After speaking to my brother and being made fully aware that you are the person I encountered on the cliff earlier, it has become my opinion that it is more appropriate for you to reside at the cottage. I trust you have no objections?'

Even in her dazed state, having been woken and told to pack her things, Lowena was shaken to the core by the bewildering sensations racing through her body. Captain Carberry—Marcus— was home at last. Home and as handsome and strong as he had been when he'd gone away. She wasn't sure why it mattered, but in the deep, un-explored places inside her she knew it did. She'd kept the image of him in her heart, like a flower pressed between the pages of a book, and now she could open it and look at it once more.

She lowered her eyes, but his extraordinary eyes drew her back. 'None that I can think of,' she replied, thankful that her voice was calm and did not betray her inner nervousness. 'You must forgive me if I appear somewhat vague, but I am not used to being woken in the dead of night.'

He lifted a well-defined black brow in question. 'No? Not even when my brother requires your assistance on the cliff on certain nights? You little fool! I thought you would have more sense than to let him implicate you in his nefarious activities. It doesn't matter how he persuaded you. The facts speak for themselves.'

He noted her bewilderment and apprehension, the way she looked about her as if searching for a hole down which to disappear.

'Never mind,' he uttered crisply. 'We will speak of it tomorrow.'

'There is nothing for me to say,' she said with underlying desperation. 'Because of my situation, and with no family of my own to go to, I cannot afford to offend a man like your brother. He is my employer. It is impossible for me to disobey him. You have no idea what it has been like for me since Izzy died…'

A smile of understanding tempted Marcus's

lips. 'Maybe I should have, had I not been absent for so long, but I assure you, Lowena, that I have a good idea now.'

Hearing the gentleness behind his words, she looked at him and felt her heart skip a beat. Her eyes devoured him, worshipped him—his hair, his eyes, his face were all more attractive than any she had ever seen, and if what she felt for him was love, then she loved him absolutely, devotedly. With a love that had bonded her to him when she had been sixteen years old and was stronger still now, even with no hope of ever having her love returned.

She would be content to exist in the same space as he did.

His eyes were on her face, gauging her, watching for every nuance of emotion in her. He could have no notion of her wayward thoughts.

She flushed and drew herself up proudly. The spectre of his brother rose between them, intangible but strong, and an unexpected sense of pain filled Lowena's heart that Marcus might have listened to his brother and judged her unfairly. Her heart beat a tattoo in her chest and she was afraid he would hear. There was still so much of the girl in her, at war with the young woman this man was capable of bringing to the surface.

'All I ask is that, whatever Lord Carberry has

told you, you do not judge me too harshly. Remember that I am not the girl I was when you went away.'

'No, I realise that. If my brother's words are to be believed, then I can only assume that your conduct has been reprehensible, that you haven't an ounce of sense or propriety, and that your behaviour would have been an embarrassment to Izzy had she been alive.'

The unfairness of his words brought a gasp to Lowena's lips. 'How *dare* you say that to me? I have never failed to respect Izzy—but I suppose if I hadn't, the name I bear does not permit any offence to go unpunished,' she bit back, bristling with indignation at being wrongfully accused. 'You said *if* your brother's words were to be believed. Do you believe them?'

His eyes refused to relinquish their hold on hers as he sought the truth. 'He implied that you and he are lovers.' He arched a dark brow, his eyes quizzical, probing hers. 'Should I believe him?'

Lowena stared at him in stunned, hurt disbelief, and in a blinding flash of sick humiliation she saw he really did believe that his brother spoke the truth. Anger welled up in her heart, draining the blood from her face and bringing a furious sparkle to her eyes.

'I should know better than to speak against Lord Carberry, who has the power to dismiss upon a whim, but I have the right to speak in my defence. Do you think I *invited* his attentions somehow? Do you think it has been my ploy to lure him in the hopes of gaining some special privileges for myself? If so, you do me an injustice. I work at Tregarrick because I have no choice. I am not intimidated by Lord Carberry, and nor am I awed by his attentions—which are most unwelcome.'

'Are you telling me that I have misconstrued what he told me—that is if I believed it in the first place?'

Forcing herself to remain calm, she raised her chin defensively. Her eyes were scornful and she spoke in a controlled voice. 'Believe what you like. I do not feel that I have to justify myself to you or to anyone else, for that matter. Perhaps it would make you feel better if I admitted to everything your brother has said about me—regardless of the fact that it may not be true.'

Marcus gazed at her from beneath his lowered eyes. He could see how tense she was, and that her eyes were shining with a pain he wondered at. He was touched, despite himself, by her youth— and also by some private scruples. Whatever the truth of the matter, she still had a virtuous innocence and a warm femininity that touched a deep chord inside him.

'Enough. Enough of this for now. The hour is late and it is not the time.'

'Enough, you say? How dare you be so judgemental? You have been away a long time and know nothing of what has been happening in my life. I find your inquisitorial and aggressive manner both unreasonable and unacceptable. You are playing the role of an outraged father whose honour has been besmirched a little too well for my liking—casting accusations and demanding explanations. A lot has happened to me in your absence. I am no longer the complaisant, naïve, pathetic young girl you remember.'

'You were many things, Lowena, but you were never pathetic,' he countered softly.

She stared at him, momentarily thrown by the sudden softening in his eyes. 'Oh—thank you. But you see I am my own person now, and I answer to no one.'

Looking at the tempestuous young woman standing before him, her eyes flashing like angry jewels and her breasts rising and falling with suppressed emotion, Marcus felt a stirring of reluctant admiration for her courage and daring to speak out so plainly.

'Thank you for that edifying piece of information.'

'Think nothing of it,' she retorted.

Drawing a deep, suffocating breath, she fought with all her strength to keep back the tears which had started to her eyes and to ignore a heart beating hard with a mixture of so many emotions that they almost overwhelmed her.

'Am I to reside at the cottage indefinitely?' she ventured to ask, when she was confident she could speak calmly. She was bewildered by the night's events and did not really know what she wanted to do at that moment.

'For now. I'll speak to my mother in the morning. Now, come along. The hour is late and I think we could both do with some sleep.'

Clutching her bundle close to her chest, Lowena followed Marcus out of the house and down the drive in the direction of the cottage. She stared at his broad back. Silly, girlish tears pricked her eyes. She blinked and set her mouth in a determined line before they reached the cottage.

They were not surprised to find it in darkness. Marcus hammered on the door and after a few minutes a woman in her night attire, carrying a lighted candle, opened it a crack.

'Who is it?' she enquired, clearly afraid that it might be someone up to no good.

'It's me, Mrs Seagrove—Lowena,' she said quickly, in order to allay the housekeeper's fears. 'Mr Marcus is with me.'

Mrs Seagrove opened the door to let them in. Marcus quickly explained the situation, and in no time at all Mrs Seagrove was showing them to their rooms. Marcus insisted that he did not want his mother disturbed. Time enough for her to welcome him home in the morning.

Chapter Two

The cottage was tucked away within its own hollow, the house and its gardens concealed by a protective planting of beeches. Anyone who had never been to the cottage before would have the impression that the house was a small establishment—and in comparison to Tregarrick it was—but it was of considerable size. It was beautifully proportioned, with large windows looking out onto a terrace and the lovely gardens. Marcus had always been fond of the cottage. His paternal grandmother, whom he had loved dearly, had spent her last days there.

The following morning, Marcus's mother, Lady Alice Carberry, welcomed him warmly, unashamed of the tears of overwhelming joy and relief that he was safely home at last which filled her eyes as she embraced her son. They sat across from each other as they ate breakfast, and she told

Marcus the details of her husband's heart problem that had resulted in his death. The lingering sadness that shadowed her eyes told him how deeply the loss of her husband affected her, and he knew she would quietly mourn him until the day she died.

Tall and slender, with silver-grey eyes like her son and a shock of dark brown hair streaked with grey, arranged neatly in an array of curls by her maid, Lady Alice led a full and happy life despite her sorrow. She was a woman highly thought of and respected in the area. She was also a strong woman, renowned for her ability to maintain her composure even in times of stress. She had run Tregarrick with precision and with perfect etiquette, demanding perfection from all who worked in the house. She could appear autocratic at times, but this was tempered by the softer side to her nature and her ability to balance the two perfectly.

'You have seen Edward?' she asked after a while, knowing the subject of his half-brother could be avoided no longer.

Marcus nodded. 'Last night. He had no right to turn you out.'

'Why not? It is his house now. I was thinking of moving out before Isabel died, but—well, it was such a sad time that I put it off.'

Marcus shifted uneasily. He had loved Isabel deeply, and found her betrayal of him with Edward still painful to deal with. He had no wish to discuss it now.

'I do wonder what will become of Edward,' Lady Alice said. 'There is something terrible about him—not only terrible, but merciless and self-destructive, and it will eventually destroy him. Unlike before his marriage, his smuggling is no longer the adventure he was seeking but a distraction. Perhaps from his grief—which is an emotion unknown to him—or from the guilt that chases him…misplaced guilt over Isabel's death. He blames himself for that. Isabel had told him she was to bear his child. He believes that if he had forbidden her to ride with the hunt things might have been different.'

Marcus's reply was abrupt. 'Isabel was headstrong. She would have found a way to defy him.'

'Yes, I think you're right. It saddens me when I think how Edward has always resented me for marrying his father. And I regret to say nothing has changed. It was best that I came to live in the cottage.'

'But Father made provision for you to remain at Tregarrick until your death.'

'I know, but I will not live in a house where I am not wanted.' She smiled. 'Try not to worry about me, Marcus. The cottage is a lovely house. Your grandmother lived here when your grandfather died and your father brought Edward's mother as a bride to Tregarrick. That is what it is for—to house the dowager mistress of Tregarrick when a new bride arrives. I have always loved this house and I am quite content living here. It will be even better now that you're home. I also gave some thought to you and what would be best when you came back. The two of you are better apart.'

'I have to agree, but I wish things could have been different.'

'So do I. Edward's behaviour towards me and then you hurt your father deeply. But he left you and Juliet well provided for. He was not a frivolous man, and as you know he made shrewd investments in coal mining in the North and banking in London. He died an extremely wealthy man.'

'Nevertheless, Edward deeply resents the fact that Father left me the mine.'

'It's what you always wanted. You won't mind living here, will you, Marcus? When I have gone to London you will have the cottage to yourself.'

'You are going to stay with Juliet?'

'Your sister is always asking me to go to her. I miss Juliet and the little ones. I would ask you to come with me, but I know you have no liking for the city.'

His mother was right. London held no delights for him, but he was impatient to see his sister. They had always been close. Now she was married to Lord Simon Mallory and had left Cornwall to live in London. They had two children Marcus had not yet seen. He was impatient to rectify this.

'You are right. London is not for me, but I would dearly like to see Juliet again. I will consider accompanying you—although if we are going then we must do so soon if we are to return to Cornwall before winter sets in. The roads—which are bad at the best of times in Cornwall—will become unpassable. I hope you don't mind Lowena coming to the cottage too?'

'Not at all. There's always room for another pair of hands in the house.' She gave Marcus a thoughtful look. 'According to Mrs Seagrove, you didn't arrive until the middle of the night. What made you bring Lowena with you?'

'You may not know about it, but last night there was a smugglers' run. Edward had her on the clifftop, manning the beacon, and I came across her. Edward also has an eye for her. I thought she would be safer here at the cottage with you.'

'Oh, dear!' Lady Alice said, deeply troubled to hear this. 'I didn't know—but then her duties are as a kitchen maid, so I rarely see her. Tregarrick is large, and we have such a large number of servants it's difficult keeping track of them all. I leave that to the housekeeper. Edward has his own ideas, and it suits his needs as a gentleman to employ a large number of staff.'

'It is also common practice for the gentry to take advantage of young women in their employ. My brother is no different—but why must he cast his eye on Lowena, who is little more than a girl?'

Lady Alice laughed softly. 'If you think that then your eyesight is sadly impaired, Marcus. Lowena is a beautiful young woman.'

'She is also a rare jewel and quite unique—as Izzy was always telling me.'

Marcus fell silent, recalling the night before and how Lowena had so boldly stood her ground and spoken her mind. Marcus cursed beneath his breath as he realised what those impressions had extracted from him—admiration and desire.

His awareness of the latter left him both outraged with himself and shaken by its swift encroachment on his life at a time when he had vowed never to become enamoured by another woman. But, try as he might to dismiss them, those thoughts gave birth to an impractical possibility that he would not let himself consider just then—for to do so would unleash the pain and heartache he had locked away when Isabel had betrayed him with Edward.

But he would not allow himself to think for another moment that the young girl he had teased and laughed with, who had enchanted and amused him, was romantically entangled with Edward. Such an idea was insane. It was obscene. He would not believe it—because he couldn't bear to believe it.

But if there was no truth in it then why had she not come right out and said so?

'When I said she is a girl,' he went on, 'what I really meant was that she is a child compared to Edward and his vast experience with women.'

'Then we must keep an eye on her and keep her away from him.'

'Yes, I intend to do just that. Much as I applaud Edward for his good taste, I can't help thinking that if we let Lowena find herself in his clutches it would be like feeding her to the wolves.'

'I think you underestimate her, Marcus. I strongly suspect that she has the courage to pit her will against any man—including you,' Lady Alice said quietly.

Marcus's face tensed and he gave his mother a sharp look. 'Rest assured, Mother. Lowena is quite safe from me. Now, tell me what you have been up to since you were removed from Tregarrick.'

'I've been to Devon to stay with my dear friend

Anne Holland and her family—she thought some time away after the funeral would be a comfort to me. But never mind that. We must make arrangements for Lowena.'

'Very well. What do you suggest?'

'I shall see that she is given responsible work. In fact Dorothy, my personal maid, is not as young as she was, and I have noticed that she is slowing down of late—not that I would say anything…the last thing I want to do is upset her. Lowena is a bright young thing, and if she is in agreement— even though I think her talents would be wasted— I will train her as a lady's maid. I'll give her a few days to settle in and then I'll discuss it with her. Leave it with me. I will deal with it.'

'Thank you—that is a relief. Although I worry about what will happen to her when we leave for London. Would you think of taking her with you?'

'Certainly, if she accepts the position I offer her. Without Izzy, and with Hester and Kenza married now, and Annie having gone to live with Hester, she is quite alone in the world, poor girl. I often wonder about her—who were her parents and where did she come from?'

She sighed.

'I've always had a fondness for her—and I know you have too, and that because you were the one who found her you have always felt responsible for her. However, for all her provincial ways, I feel she is not of the servant class. My heart goes out to her, for I cannot imagine what it would be like to be without family.'

'Lowena always considered Izzy's family her own.'

'I know, but it's not the same, Marcus. After all this time I don't suppose we will ever know where she comes from. She's such a bright girl, with an intelligence I have not witnessed before in a young lady. Not even Juliet. Izzy taught her well—although a great deal of what she has learned she's gleaned from the books she borrows from the library at Tregarrick. Izzy was disappointed that her own girls did not have the same enthusiasm for learning.'

Gazing at her son she smiled.

'You really do look very handsome in your red coat, Marcus, but I imagine you'll have to discard it now you're no longer a soldier.'

'I intend to. But I've worn uniform for so long that I've outgrown most of my clothes. I thought I'd ride into St Austell and visit the tailor. I intend to call at the mine on the way.'

Sheltered in the protective folds of low hills was the Tregarrick estate. It dated back several centuries, and each generation of the Carberrys had made its mark on the house with some addition or alteration. It was a beautiful house, with an air of permanence and importance about it. Built of Cornish granite, its very solidity gave it an air of solemnity. Large mullioned windows allowed light to pour into the interior, the gardens were beautifully landscaped, and the high surrounding walls and tall iron gates concealed the private lives of those within.

Lowena put her hand on the gate at the same moment as a skein of geese left the lake and took to the air overhead in a V formation, and she did not see the curtain that was let fall to cover a window as the watcher moved to follow the girl.

Once through the gates, Lowena headed towards the sea. When it reached the coastal path the land sloped down towards the village, which had clung to the Cornish cliffs for centuries. Life there was something of a challenge, fishing, farming and mining being the bedrock of the community, but the village was not to be Lowena's destination today.

Heading west, she followed the coastal path. Lady Alice had been kind enough to allow her a day to settle in at the cottage, so she had taken advantage of the fine weather to walk by the sea. She was grateful to Mr Marcus for removing her from Tregarrick. At least now she would be free of the predatory attentions of its owner.

As she walked along she took delight in the wild flowers that grew in abundance, along with the overgrown prickly gorse bushes, ablaze with yellow flowers, and the brambles and honeysuckle running rampant in the hollows and thickets.

Having walked some distance, she suddenly had an eerie sense that she was being followed. Halting her step, she turned and glanced back. Apart from the distant faint rhythm of the sea breaking gently upon the shore she could hear nothing, and there was no one in sight, but she had an unsettling feeling—as though someone was watching her. After a moment she carried on walking, thinking that perhaps she was imagining it.

Focusing her attention on the endless miles of sea, she saw that today it was calm, the waves breaking lazily on the soft smooth sand. A small fishing boat heading towards the village sailed slowly by on the calm water, followed by squawking gulls. Ahead of her, about half a mile away, was the cursed cove, and beyond that the Carberry mine, Wheal Rozen. Its tall chimney was clearly visible.

Below ground its shafts stretched right out beneath the sea. A shudder made its way down her spine, as it always did when she thought of the men who toiled in cramped, hot and airless conditions, working in fear of rock falls and many suffering chest conditions which would shorten their lives.

At nineteen, Lowena was in the uncertainty between being a young lady and a woman. Since Izzy had died she had been cast adrift, alone in a world she did not understand. Before, she had been an orphan too, she supposed, but she had never felt like one. Izzy had loved her family and sacrificed so much for them, and Lowena would be eternally grateful to her for making her a part of that family.

They had been a joyous family—full of fun and laughter—and throughout Lowena's childhood they had shaken their heads and teased her whenever she'd studied too long at her books, laughingly saying—not unkindly—what a cuckoo it was that had arrived in their nest from nowhere.

The description hadn't concerned her, because the fact was that she *was* different. Izzy's teachings and encouragement to advance herself had inspired Lowena. She had often reflected on her future, and before Izzy had died she had considered following the same path she had taken and becoming a governess. Her world and her aspirations for the future had fallen apart when Izzy had died, and her passing had left her bereft until Lady Alice had been kindness itself and taken her on as a servant at Tregarrick.

But Lowena was a restless soul, with a yearning to be free of all constraints, and her spirit was as wild as the moor to the north. With a sudden release of energy she broke into a run as if the Devil himself pursued her. Her skirts flapped about her legs and her unbound hair streamed behind her like a ship's pennant.

Not until she reached her destination did she slow her step.

Cornwall had hundreds of coves along its coastline, many of them ideal for smuggling. Protected by high ragged cliffs, giving shelter to the east and west, the cove below her now was small in size. The tide was out, but at high tide it was inaccessible. Hidden from the cliff path, making it completely private, this cove was Lowena's favourite, and she did not fear it as she did the cursed cove, which she always avoided.

Breathless from her exertions, she left the path and pushed her way through a narrow opening in the gorse bushes. Her cheeks were flushed pink, the colour heightening the intensity of her amber eyes. With care she climbed down to the beach and walked to the edge of the surf, taking in deep breaths of clean air. The sun was sitting on the distant horizon and the sky was an azure blue. Last night the sky had been red. Sailors said a red sky at night meant sailors' delight. How she hoped that was true.

She was snatched from her preoccupations when she heard a sound behind her. Spinning round, she saw Edward Carberry swaggering towards her. She shuddered, and felt herself shrink as he approached her. She hated him with a vengeance, and distrusted his presence now as she had distrusted it many years ago, when she had become aware of him as the future Lord Carberry and he had so cruelly called her 'that foundling bastard'.

But that had never stopped him looking at her, watching her, biding his time until Izzy or the servants she now worked with were not there to protect her.

When Edward stopped in front of her there was a sneer on his mouth—and it was a cruel mouth, twisted in perpetual contempt for those who, in his opinion, were beneath him. His eyes were heavy-lidded, beguiling, gloating and hungry. He looked at her with impudent admiration, letting his gaze travel from her eyes to her mouth and then, after lingering on its soft fullness, moving down to the gentle swell of her breasts beneath her bodice.

'Well, well, Miss Trevanion! They do say as how, if one is patient enough, one will get what one wants in the end. My half-brother may have removed you from the house, but you are not out of my reach.'

As she tried to force words to her lips Lowena hated the smile which twisted his mouth. Standing stiffly, every nerve of her body tense, she knew her eyes were wary as they watched him.

'I cannot imagine what you mean, Sir Edward,' she replied, her look one of pure innocence even while she knew perfectly well what was in his mind. 'Please be so kind as to step aside.'

'Not yet, Miss Trevanion.'

Lowena stared at him with fear-filled eyes. Lord Carberry was a powerful man, and if he attacked her she would not be strong enough to fend him off. All she had was her determination to escape him and two good legs. Fair-haired and blue-eyed, his features handsomely wrought, his bold gaze swept over her once more, taking in every detail of her flower-sprigged blue dress, and all the while he continued to smile that hateful twisted smile, so much more suave and slippery of manner than any man she knew.

In the depths of his cold eyes something stirred, and she felt a strong desire to push him away. There was an air of menace about him that entered her heart like a sliver of ice.

Realising she was in terrible danger, she backed away, feeling sea water fill her shoes but uncaring at that moment. 'I asked you to let me pass. I have to get back to Lady Alice.'

'Oh, such a proud beauty,' he said, laughing softly. 'I'll be happy to let you pass…for the price of a kiss.'

'I will not. You—you followed me—'

'I thought that was what you wanted when I saw you turn on the cliff path and look back. At any rate, I am at liberty to seek you out whenever I please.' Tilting his head to one side, Edward cocked a smooth, elegant brow, the glint in the depths of his eyes needle-sharp. 'You *did* know I was following you, did you not, Lowena?'

He was taunting her, as he invariably did when he managed to waylay her, and she stiffened, half with anger and half with apprehension at being alone with him. She met his eyes, so bold, gazing down at her, taking in every detail of her fear-filled face.

With his handsome looks and the merry twinkle in his eye, it was hard to believe he was anything other than a gentleman, and she could understand why all the girls she knew in the village, even those who had been born to rich families, made eyes at him and vied for his favours—but she was not one of them.

'I did not,' she said sharply in reply to his question, hating the nervous tremor she was unable to control in her voice. She knew what had happened to his wife, and had always felt sorry for him, but she found it both annoying and distasteful that he paid her so much attention. It did not go unnoticed by the people she worked with and she was embarrassed by it. It was uncomfortable to be singled out.

'Had I known, I would not have come to the cove.'

'No?' he murmured, his face and voice expressing a disappointment he did not feel. 'I wanted to thank you for standing watch last night. You did well.'

'I was obeying orders. I didn't want to do it, but I was left with no choice.'

'There will be other nights I shall call on you.'

'I will not do it again. Your brother—'

'Will *not* stop you when I send for you,' he was quick to inform her, anger flaring in his eyes. 'It is me you answer to—not my brother. He knows better than to interfere in my affairs. Anyone—and I mean *anyone*—who informs on me or meddles in what I do—be it Marcus or anyone else—will rue the day he was born.'

Lowena remained silent. She found the implication of his words and the threat he posed towards his brother deeply troubling.

His sudden surge of anger had diminished and, reaching out, Edward touched the thick tress of her hair which hung over her breast. She recoiled sharply, and her eyes still blazed in her lovely face. His own eyes narrowed when he saw the expression in hers, and there was a moment of silence—intense, burning...

When Lowena failed to lower her eyes he recognised in that moment that Lowena Trevanion possessed something quite rare. Whatever it was that he saw he wanted a part of it, and he was prepared to be patient, to wait for it, secure in the knowledge that it would be his.

'Ever since you came to work at the house,' he went on, 'I have waited for this. I thought the opportunity to get you alone would never come when my stepmother watched my every move. You are looking very lovely today.'

His voice was thick and seductive—a trick that had always proved irresistible to the many ladies of his acquaintance. His eyes rested on the soft flesh at the base of her neck, where a pulse throbbed gently, before lowering to the soft swelling of her breasts.

Instinctively Lowena put her hands to her

throat, angry with herself for having inadvertently led him to this place where she had no defence.

'Please do not speak to me like this. I have to go. Lady Alice will have need of me. I said I would not be long.'

'To hell with my stepmother. Let someone else do her bidding.'

'Let me go...' she breathed, her eyes flashing angrily.

She made a move to pass him, but his hand shot out and he seized her arm. Snatching it away instantly, she backed further into the foaming surf.

'Take your hands off me and let me pass at once.'

Edward stared at her for a moment, and then the mocking smile was back. 'What spirit you have, Lowena. You remind me of a horse that is unbroken—a horse that is in need of a master. *Me.*'

It was not a threat he uttered—more a statement of fact. Lowena went cold, the blood draining from her face as she saw sudden fire leap in his eyes.

'What do you want?'

'You,' he answered smoothly, moving closer. 'Come, Lowena, why so hostile? I have done nothing to justify it. As lovely as you are, you know how much I like you.'

Words fell from his gilded tongue effortlessly, as if they carried no weight or conviction.

Lowena's face flushed hotly with indignation. 'Please—do not speak to me in this manner, sir. It is not proper. I am nothing to you.'

'You *will* be. You are a servant in my house—or you were until my brother whisked you away to wait on his mother. However, since I pay your wages it means I have certain rights.'

Lowena's eyes blazed with anger. How dared he treat her in this manner, as if she were nothing at all? 'Where I am concerned you have *no* rights. I do the work I am paid for and nothing more.'

Her remark made him laugh, throwing back his head and letting his laughter ring round the cove and echo through the caves beneath the cliff. 'You are so lovely, Lowena, and delightful when you are angry. At least you are not indifferent to me.'

Before Lowena could react, his hands shot out and he drew her towards him. Too late she realised that he had succeeded in slipping through her guard and arousing her to an expression of her personal feelings, forcing her to a trembling awareness of him when all she wanted was to avoid him and put him from her mind.

Raising her hands, she tried to fend him off, to escape this nightmare she had fallen into. She began to fight him, blindly thrashing in his iron grip, but his arms became bonds. His mouth ground down onto hers, silencing her cries of outrage. Inwardly she seethed, finding his assault disgusting. His mouth was wet, hot and hard, and she hated it. It revolted her senses. She struggled and fought but he held her easily.

He was behaving like a depraved beast, intent on ravishment, without tenderness or decency. He must be aware of the force he was inflicting on her. He wanted power over her, but she would resist to her dying breath. She struggled fiercely, convinced that this sexually excited man had but one objective.

'Let me go...'

'Don't fight me,' he whispered. 'I don't like it and I am in no mood to play games.'

He fastened his mouth on hers once more and Lenora's fear turned to cold fury.

Not until she bit down sharply on his lower lip did he relinquish her mouth.

Angry about her lack of submission, and too aroused to let anything get in the way of what his body wanted, Edward lifted his head and looked down into her angry, upturned face. A faint line of blood trickled from the corner of his mouth, which he casually wiped away with the back of his hand.

'I've thought of this moment many times, and I mean to enjoy every moment of it. Indeed, Lowena, I would heartily like to hear you plead for mercy.'

'Never!' she bit out. 'You will never hear that from me.'

Edward's eyes narrowed dangerously. 'Ah, such defiance. Such spirit. Don't fight me. Don't resist me. It will be better for you if you don't.'

'Let go of me. You may be an important man in these parts, but there are better men than you in Cornwall.'

His eyes narrowed dangerously. 'I warn you, Lowena, do not mock me. Have a care lest I turn you out without a penny piece.'

'I *do* mock you,' she flung back at him tauntingly, uncaring that he was Lord Carberry of Tregarrick as she found the strength to extricate herself from his hold. 'And turn me out if you so wish, but do not touch me again. Ever.'

Edward reached out to capture her again, and without giving her next action any thought, other than to save herself from his assault, she raised her hand to fend him off. He caught it and flung it back at her in anger. He was not accustomed to having anyone stand up to him—let alone a female servant—and certainly no one who would dare raise her hand to him in anger.

'You little hellion! I'll teach you not to use your hands on me,' he snarled. 'How dare you—?'

'I *do* dare, your lordship. Don't you ever touch me again!' she flared defensively, too incensed to realise the implications of what she might have done had he not stayed her hand.

Unbeknown to her, she came from a long line of proud ancestors who had endurance and courage running through their veins—ancestors who would allow nothing to stand in their way and certainly not a man like Edward Carberry, who was the epitome of all Lowena deplored.

When Edward recovered his equilibrium he almost retaliated in kind, for he was outraged that this girl would not submit to his will, but Lowena was looking beyond him, an expression of shock having replaced the fury on her face.

A flash of scarlet had caught her eye, and then her gaze became riveted as she saw it was a man—a soldier. *Marcus Carberry.* She stood perfectly still, her face drained of all colour. Feeling cold shock run through her, she realised how what had happened must have looked to him.

He stood unmoving on the edge of the cliff, looking down at the cove, watching them. Suddenly she came alive. The distance between them was too great for her to see his features, but she could imagine his anger.

Edward saw the change in her and turned, following the direction of her gaze. His face froze on seeing the scarlet-clad figure who had interrupted his dalliance. His smug reaction on seeing his half-brother was in his eyes and in his arrogantly curling mouth.

'It—it's Mr Marcus,' Lowena said quietly.

For once Edward's bland, inscrutable face dropped its guard, and it was as though a mask had been stripped from it. He made no other perceptible movement but, watching him intently, Lowena was aware of an indefinable change in him.

A hardness settled on his face, and then he was striding off across the sand in the direction of the cliff and his brother.

As if recollecting himself, he glanced back at the girl he had assaulted. 'You will be sorry for this, I promise you,' he ground out. 'No woman gets the better of me—especially not a servant—so I advise you to have a care, Lowena Trevanion. Have a care…'

Alone and unmoving, Lowena watched him go, her eyes drawn back to the magnetic force of the scarlet-coated soldier on the cliff. At the sight of him all thought of Edward Carberry and his unwelcome amorous advances had vanished. She'd told herself that things would be different now he was home and she no longer lived at Tregarrick.

She watched Edward climb back up to the cliff top and speak to his brother before disappearing from sight. Slowly she made her way across the sand and turned her thoughts back to her own predicament and what had just transpired. It had been but a kiss, but the nature and force of the kiss, and the way Edward Carberry's arms had held her in a vice-like grip, making it impossible for her to move... At that moment it seemed that her innocence had vanished—that Edward Carberry had taken her far beyond the apparently safe bounds that had sheltered her until today.

A conflict raged in her mind between shock and anger. Shock that a man she hated should take such liberties with her, and anger that he had done so. However Marcus interpreted what he had witnessed, she thanked God he had arrived to put a halt to his brother's assault. She felt sick at the thought of what Edward might have done to her.

Marcus had ridden to Wheal Rozen shortly after breakfast. It had given him a peculiar feeling of continuity to see old friends and all the people who worked at the mine whose faces were familiar, even though he had been away so long. Instead of going overland on his return to Tregarrick, which was the quickest way, he had decided to take in the longer coastal route.

Following the winding path along the cliff edge, ahead of him he'd seen a flutter of blue skirts disappear through the gorse. He'd thought nothing of it until he'd seen his brother appear, leaving his mount tethered to a branch and disappearing through the gorse after the girl.

Unable to quell his curiosity, Marcus had followed, moving to stand on the cliff edge. Below him the water had reflected the colour of the sky, and the beach had glistened with newly washed sand. He'd watched Edward walk towards a woman who had been looking out to sea...

Now he waited for Edward to reach him. Marcus's eyes were colder than ice when they met his brother's, his face dark with anger. There was scorn in his eyes, and a contemptuous curl to his strong mouth. They faced each other, squaring off, poised to fight.

Every time they met merely served to stir emotions Marcus did not want to feel, produced memories he wanted to avoid. Edward's pride was at the core of it, along with anger and a need to blame.

When he'd seen Edward take hold of Lowena, every colourful oath Marcus had been able to think of had run through his mind. He'd wanted to cross the distance that separated them and strike his hands away from her, to thrust him away from that sweet girl. His brother was a dangerous man, and Marcus would make certain that Lowena was far removed from him.

In fact he'd been about to act—to scramble down to the beach, stride across the sands and separate Lowena from his embrace—when Edward had suddenly released her.

'Damn you, Edward. I asked you to leave her alone, and yet here you are. If you want a woman there are plenty in St Austell to accommodate your needs, without forcing yourself on a virtuous young woman.'

Edward's brows lifted imperturbably. 'Virtuous? If you think that then you don't know her,' he scoffed with a malicious grin. 'You've been away from Cornwall a long time, Marcus. I told you how things were last night. You will never be certain that the relationship between me and Miss Trevanion has not already gone beyond the bounds of respectability—despite how many times she proclaims her innocence.'

His face darkening, something snapped inside Marcus, shattering his emotions almost beyond all rational control.

His jaw hardened. 'What did you say?' he asked, in a tone that had suddenly turned ominous.

Edward's smile was pure evil. He was satisfied that Marcus had read into his words exactly what he'd meant—even though there was no truth in them. 'I said that Miss Trevanion is not exactly the chaste little puritan you seem to think she is.'

Marcus stepped closer, a compelling steeliness in his eyes. 'I am undeceived by your base attempt to slander Lowena. There is no credit to your assertions. In other words, Edward, you are lying.'

'Lying, am I? Well—you'll never know how unchaste your precious Lowena has been in your absence. Will you? If you ask her she is hardly likely to confess to it, now, is she?' Edward smirked, triumph lighting his eyes and showing in every line of his body. 'And if she denies it you will doubt her word—no matter how hard you try not to.'

'Damn you, Edward! It's not as if you intend to marry her.'

Edward laughed—a laugh full of contempt and mocking cruelty...a laugh that was peculiarly his own—and when he spoke again his voice was low and intense. There was excitement in the straining cords of his throat and a bright glitter in his eyes as he leaned slightly forward.

'Marry her? A gentleman does not *marry* girls of her ilk. When I marry again it will be to someone of note—not a mere *servant*.'

Without another word Edward gave his brother a look of biting scorn, before mounting his horse and riding away—but not before Marcus had noted the thin streak of blood at the corner of his mouth.

He knew the power of his brother, the evil that inhabited him and the deadly consuming hatred Edward felt for him—a hatred which would surely grow now that he had come home. Edward had known how deeply he had loved Isabel and had immediately honed in on her, determined to have her for himself.

Isabel had been easily persuaded, and Marcus had felt his pride and self-respect stripped from him. There had been no deliverance from his seared vanity and the wound had continued to fester. The military had been his salvation.

Looking down to the cove, Marcus watched Lowena walk across the sands and climb up to where he stood. When he had least seen her, she had been barely more than a child, but he remembered only too plainly her quiet, serene beauty, the passion combined with hidden laughter that had been so much a part of her.

And all of a sudden there she was, walking slowly towards him, her head held high and her hair—the red-brown colour of a fox's pelt and just as thick—falling about her shoulders and down her spine in shining coils.

She was looking at him, tall, lissom and lovely. Her breasts had grown into curving, firm shapes, and her mouth was wide and soft and generous. Her facial bones were striking, and her eyes—

an unusual warm shade of amber, with tawny flecks—sparkled with a devil-may-care look.

She was watching him, aware of the searching intensity of his gaze as she favoured him with a melting smile which made his blood run hot in his veins and the heat of it move to his belly.

When he had seen her last night, after his unpleasant encounter with Edward, he had been angry and impatient to leave Tregarrick. Now he took in every detail of her body and her hair, which the sun had turned to a living flame as fiercely bright as it had been when she was a child. Lust hit him with such unexpected force that for a brief moment he could not move.

Standing before him was the grown-up Lowena, a woman whose body was a hidden treasure. Little wonder Edward was so taken with her. The way she looked, she must draw all men's eyes.

He had seen the way Edward had taken hold of her, and the remembrance of such familiarity sent a sudden surge of cold fury through him. Her loveliness would arouse lust in any man. Did she *have* to look so damned lovely?

Chapter Three

Lowena watched Marcus as she advanced towards him. He looked calm, unperturbed and supremely unaware, she thought, of the tumult raging within her breast. Her heart almost ceased to beat as she gazed on that incredibly handsome face, bewitched and still disbelieving that this god-like man had come home at last.

Joy exploded in her heart with such violence that it almost sent her to her knees. And, meeting his eyes, she found the sheer, concentrated power of his presence disturbed her, making it difficult for her to regard him as a member of the family that employed her.

She had worshipped him for as long as she could remember in her own childlike way, wanting to feel his eyes upon her and hoping to be the cause of their animation and admiration. But she was not foolish enough to think the feeling had ever been reciprocated, and nor was she naïve enough to believe she knew how to make him happy.

Besides, he had been in love with Isabel Morgan, the daughter of a local gentleman, and she had broken his heart when she had turned her attentions to Marcus's half-brother and married him.

Because of Lowena's lowly station in life, her unsuitability to form any kind of romantic relationship with a gentleman of his standing was without question. When he married it would be to a woman of his own kind, from a well-to-do family.

Standing before him, slightly breathless after her climb up from the cove, Lowena faced Marcus with her head held high. What his thoughts were she had no way of knowing. He was just standing there, looking at her, with a faint smile lingering on his firm lips. He had been too far away for her to hear what he had said to Edward, but no doubt he believed she had arranged to meet his brother at the cove. She was hurt that he might think that and that he would judge her.

'Please don't think I'm neglecting my work,' she said, throwing him a cautious look. 'Lady Alice said I could take the day off before starting my duties tomorrow.'

'I don't think that. I'm more interested in knowing why you came to this cove.'

Lowena saw that his eyes were on her, gauging her, watching for every shade of thought and emotion in her. She was conscious of a sudden feeling of embarrassment. There was still so much of the girl in her, at war with the young woman she had become, and this man had the knack of bringing it quickly to the surface.

'Why do you look at me like that?' she asked, meeting his eyes.

'I was watching you on the beach—with Edward. Are you all right?' he asked, looking at her more closely.

He'd noticed redness and slight bruising on her lips—the kind of marks left when a man had forced his attentions on a woman with little regard for the sensitivity of her flesh.

A fierce anger against his brother surged through him. 'Did he hurt you?'

She shook her head. 'No,' she murmured, having no wish to discuss his brother. Averting her eyes, she said, 'Lady Alice will be pleased—and relieved—that you are home at last.'

'She is.'

As he spoke his eyes dropped down to the wet skirts falling about her legs and feet. Lowena instinctively looked too, and sighed.

'I stepped into the sea,' she explained. 'My shoes are none too dry either.'

'Perhaps you should have removed them before you took a paddle.'

'I had no intention of taking a paddle, only— Well—Lord Carberry came…and…'

Marcus studied her with concern. 'Are you sure you are all right?'

She nodded, gnawing at her bottom lip as the full impact of what she had done hit her. 'Yes— But your brother is Lord Carberry—and—well, he made me angry and I almost slapped him. I should not have done that. Only what he did— forcing himself on me like that when I was most unwilling—it was inappropriate.'

Marcus frowned down at her. 'Maybe it would be better if you did not walk alone, Lowena.'

Lowena's face became tense. 'Perhaps you are right, but I have always come to this cove. I come here to seek solitude, and if your brother was any sort of a gentleman he would not have followed me. He would have left me in peace. I was angry when I almost slapped his face. He was furious. I cannot imagine him not retaliating in some way.'

'Did he threaten you?'

'He—he said that I must have a care,' she murmured, keeping to herself the threat Edward had made against Marcus, which caused her deep concern.

'Did you make it plain that you do not welcome his attentions?'

'Yes—at least I did try.'

'I imagine you did. He should know better than to force his attentions on an unwilling girl who is almost young enough to be his daughter.'

'I'm no longer a *girl*,' Lowena retorted, with an audible gasp of indignation.

In the bright sunlight, as she turned her face towards him, Marcus could see that behind her defiance there were unshed tears shining in those eyes that looked into the very heart of him. She was truly lovely, and the time they had been apart had brought an added enchantment. She looked older, more grown up—indeed more a woman than a girl.

Her remark brought a curve to his lips. 'My dear Lowena, I can see that. You are transparent. I may have been away for a long time, but I can still read you well.'

He looked at her thoughtfully, touched by her innocence. She possessed a tender femininity that touched a deep chord in him, and once again the urge to protect her that he had felt when he had found her that day abandoned in the wood over-whelmed him.

'You have friends among the staff?'

'Some of them. There is Nessa—Nessa Borlase.'

'I remember Nessa. She is still with us?'

'Yes. She was brought up not far from Tregarrick. When her parents died she came to Tregarrick in the hope of being taken on. I think I was about two years old at the time. She was fortunate that there was a vacancy in the laundry. She's worked for your family for many years, and now works in both the house and the dairy—or wherever she is needed. Nessa looks out for me. She is always kind, and several times she has come between Edward and me when he has accosted me when I was working. I have always rejected his advances, so I can only assume that in anger he might try to malign my character to you, to besmirch my reputation. I beg you not to listen to him.'

'I know my brother well enough, Lowena, so don't worry. I won't.'

She looked up at her companion, a serious expression in her eyes. She was no match for Lord Carberry physically, but Marcus was. Now he was home she was confident that he would protect her from his brother.

'You've been gone a long time,' she said quietly. 'It is not my place to speak against your brother, but I am aware of something in him that should not be pushed too far.'

'Do your fear him?'

'Sometimes, yes. I feel him to be dangerous in some way.'

Marcus became thoughtful, clearly troubled. After a moment he took the reins of his horse. 'Come, we will walk together to the cottage. I was on my way back from the mine and decided to take the longer route. It's a good thing I did. I've spoken to my mother,' he said as they walked side by side. 'She will ensure your safety now you are no longer at Tregarrick.'

'There is to be an annual get-together of the local gentry tomorrow night,' Lowena said. 'A large gathering is expected and I am to help out. I shall make sure that I am never alone. I imagine you were sad to hear about Izzy?'

'Very much so. I was extremely fond of her—she played an important part in my childhood. Mother wrote to inform me of her passing. I'm sorry, Lowena. You must miss her.'

She nodded. 'Yes, I do—and her girls. Hester and Kenza are married now, and living in Padstow. And Annie has gone to live with Hester and is to marry very soon.'

They walked together in companionable silence. Lowena was conscious of Marcus's closeness—in fact she was very much aware of everything about him, and still could not believe he was home at last. It was like coming face to face with a stranger. Long of limb, the whole six foot three of him was lean, hard muscle—a military officer tailor-made.

Their long separation made her awkward and shy with him. She was uneasy, especially when those heavily fringed silver-grey eyes locked on hers. She had forgotten how brilliant they were. His hair was black and tousled, his flesh bronzed from long periods in the sun.

Quite suddenly she was conscious of an overwhelming impulse ask him to stop, and to reach out and touch his face, to thread her fingers through his thick hair, to draw his mouth down to hers and touch his warm lips with her own. Ashamed of her wayward thoughts, feeling her cheeks burn, she lowered her head, almost having to run to keep up with his long strides. After a moment she glanced sideways at him. He appeared to be relaxed, his manner casual, in fact he was treating this meeting with a cool nonchalance that seemed inappropriate, considering what he had just borne witness to in the cove.

'It—it is good to see you back,' she murmured, unable to stand the silence a moment longer as they neared the cottage.

'It would appear not a moment too soon.' Marcus gave her a troubled look, and his voice, for the first time, was uncertain. 'Edward is an attractive man. There are few young ladies who would shun him as you have done.'

Acutely aware of her dishevelled appearance, Lowena ran an ineffectual hand through her hair, which hung down her back in a shining tangled cascade. 'I know, and you are right. I have seen them—rich and poor alike. But I am not one of them.'

Marcus glanced at her gravely. 'I can imagine how your rejection must have battered his pride, and it will make him even more determined in the future.'

'I've been too busy trying to avoid him to spare his pride.'

'Set your mind at rest. I will speak to him. He may be lord of the manor, but that does not give him licence to go around molesting the servants—or anyone else, for that matter.'

Lowena was deeply touched by his obvious concern for her well-being, and it would be a relief if he *did* speak to his brother and ask him to leave her alone. However, she didn't like being reminded of her lowly status. Thanks to Izzy's teachings she could read and write, and converse in French with the best of them, but sadly that didn't alter her station in life.

Marcus looked at her. With her hair floating like a cloud about her shoulders and down her back, she walked beside him with the sunlight gently caressing her form, the folds of her skirts falling and forming a circle round her feet. Her face was flushed from the heat, and with her head turned towards him her eyes were watching him closely. She looked breathtakingly lovely and stunningly arousing. He could feel himself responding—a fact that caused him some unease.

'Do you like your work, Lowena?' he asked, in an attempt to take his mind off her closeness.

'Being a servant, you mean?'

He nodded.

'It's all right, I suppose, but I would like to think there is something more. I was told in the beginning that it was my good fortune to be given a place at Tregarrick, and that with good fortune came responsibility—that my conduct would reflect directly on the family and I must do the family justice at all times, keep their secrets and deserve their trust in all things. Which, I was given to understand, meant doing as I was told on the nights when your brother....' She sighed. 'Well, you know all about that. Izzy had such plans for me, and sometimes I fear those hours of learning were wasted.'

'Come, now, Lowena, that is defeatist talk. Time spent learning is never wasted. We are what we make of things, and given your start in life you have done remarkably well.'

'Izzy was a good teacher. If women are to have a future then they must be educated—that was what she told me early on in my life. I told her that surely all women had a future.'

Marcus laughed. 'And what did Izzy say to that? Being the educated woman that she was.'

'She told me that this is a male-dominated world and that if women are to be in charge of their own destinies then they have to do it through education. She said that women are as intelligent as men, but because learning is not as accessible to them they are looked upon as inferior. Why should women meekly accept the menial work in life when all they need is to be taught so they can do the same jobs as men? Izzy taught me so much—not only how to read and write, but the principles of mathematics, and to speak French and a little Latin.'

'All of which will offer you more opportunities.'

'Precisely. I am sure I am qualified to work with figures or books—or even to teach as a governess, or something of that nature.'

'Then why are you working here at Tregarrick as a maid?'

They had reached the point where they must go

their separate ways—he to the stables and Lowena to the cottage. She sighed dejectedly. 'Because the right opportunity has not presented itself.'

'If you wait for the right opportunity to come to you, you may find yourself waiting for ever. Why not go out and look for it? Take the bull by the horns, so to speak, and make your own destiny?'

She looked at him, at the laughter in his eyes. 'You are laughing at me. No doubt you think I'm getting too big for my boots.'

The humour melted from his eyes and his expression became serious. 'I don't think that, Lowena, and I would never laugh at you.'

'So if I am to better myself I have to help myself. Is that what you are saying?'

'Something like that.'

She stopped and looked at him. 'Someone like you—born into a wealthy family and with all the advantages that brings—will have no difficulty doing exactly what you want with your life. You know who you are, you see, and so does everyone else in these parts.'

'That's true—although I have been away for quite some time, so there will be many who do not remember me.'

'That's not true. Once met, you are a hard man to forget.' Looking past him into the distance, she let a wistful look come into her eyes, and when she spoke again her voice was quiet. 'I know who *you* are. What I don't know is who *I* am. That's the problem.'

'And that troubles you?'

She nodded. 'Yes—yes, it does. More than anything else I want to know who I am, where I came from. I want to know who my parents were—are. Perhaps they still exist. I wish I knew.'

'I can understand you wanting to know,' he said gravely. 'I wish I could help. That day when I found you in the woods I had the feeling that I was being watched. Although I could not be certain. I believe that if I had left you there, whoever it was that was watching would not have abandoned you.'

'I hope not. Surely nobody could be so cruel as to abandon a baby so callously. Izzy kept the clothes and the shawl I was wrapped in. She said they were quality, which led her to believe that my mother was of the gentry.'

'You still have them?'

Lowena nodded and looked up at him with an air of resignation. Her lips smiled, but the sadness in her eyes remained. 'Much good it will do me. But please don't look so concerned. It's not sympathy I seek. I don't suppose I'll ever know who I really am—I don't even know the date of my birth—so I will have to treasure and make the best of what I have.'

* * *

Marcus watched her walk away. He would have liked to talk to her for longer. He had not wanted their conversation to end. He had not wanted her to leave him, and he was reluctant to analyse where that feeling was coming from.

Since Isabel had betrayed him with Edward, he had merely tolerated the women who had wanted him, treating them with nothing more than amused condescension. Not once had he looked at them with the sort of gentle warmth he'd shown Lowena in the last half-hour. When he was with her and she was smiling into his eyes some of his old warmth and the need for a closer relationship with a woman returned.

Lowena was heading for the cottage when she saw Nessa walking down the path towards her. On seeing her Lowena widened her lips in a warm and welcoming mile.

'Nessa! How nice to see you. What are you doing here?'

'I came to see if you are all right. Cook told me you have moved to the cottage. I missed you. It was sudden.'

'Yes, I'm afraid it was.'

'I know there was a run last night, and that

Captain Carberry has come home. Did your leaving have anything to do with that?'

Lowena nodded. 'He saw me on the cliff and was angry with Lord Carberry for involving me in the smuggling. He insisted that I move out of the house right away.'

'Then I thank the Lord for it. At least under Captain Carberry's watchful eye you should be safe.'

Lowena glanced at her sharply. 'Safe? Why do you say that, Nessa? Am I in danger? If so, in what way?'

'Heavens, Lowena, I am not blind. It's no secret that you've caught Lord Carberry's eye. You certainly have the ability to attract him, even when you've done nothing to provoke it. As I said, you'll be safe at the cottage—which will make it easier for me when I leave Tregarrick. I would like to know you're settled in your work.'

Lowena stared at her in alarm, thinking she must have misheard. Nessa couldn't possibly leave. 'You're going away?'

'Yes, love. I'm going to Saltash to take care of my aunt. She's had a nasty turn and has taken to her bed. She needs someone to care of her.'

The news that Nessa was to leave Tregarrick hit Lowena hard. Nessa had *always* been there. She couldn't imagine her not being there. 'I'm sorry about your aunt, Nessa, but—I shall miss you.'

'I know you will, love, but I have to. You'll be all right. I'll worry about you—but then, when haven't I?'

Nessa's voice was soft, but very sure. There was an air about her that Lowena knew well. She had seen it many times before in the past, beginning when she had been a small child and Nessa had come to call on Izzy and taken tea with her. She had also seen it at those times when Izzy had died and when she had gone to work at Tregarrick. She had always seemed to be there when some seemingly insurmountable barrier had stood in her way. There was something steadying about Nessa's calm presence and it made her work easier.

Of course Lowena couldn't know that Nessa didn't mind scrubbing floors and scouring pans and lending a hand in the dairy if she could be near Lowena, somewhere she could watch her grow and protect her if need be.

'I'm deeply touched that you should worry about me so, Nessa. But I'm all right—truly.'

'Since Izzy died I have been concerned about you. You are always in my thoughts, Lowena.'

Lowena's heart swelled with the warmth she felt for Nessa. 'I know that, Nessa. But be assured that I shall be all right now I've moved to the cottage with Lady Alice and Mr Marcus. I start my duties after the party tomorrow night. There will be a great deal to do, but I will be over to help whenever there's entertaining.'

'And what are your duties to be here at the cottage? Are they to be the same as they were at the house?'

'No—no kitchen duties for me. I know it sounds very grand, but I'm to be trained up as Lady Alice's personal maid.'

'I see.' Nessa gave her a sideways look. 'But Lady Alice already has a personal maid.'

'I know, but I am to help her.'

'You don't seem thrilled about it.'

'I know I should be, but I'm not—not really. It's—it's just not enough, Nessa.'

'Then what is it you want?'

'A more worthwhile occupation. Something to stretch my mind. I want a *purpose* in my life.'

'You want to leave Tregarrick?'

Lowena glanced away as she considered Nessa's question. She did want to do something more with her life, to expand on what Izzy had taught her, but if she left Tregarrick then she would also be leaving Marcus.

'The truth is, Nessa, at this time I have nowhere to go and there is nothing I can do.' Laughing lightly, she made to move on. 'In the meantime we have tomorrow night's party to prepare for, so I will see you in the morning, Nessa.'

Nessa stood and watched her go. Lowena was a decent, respectable young woman. She had been gently reared by Izzy, in ignorance of what went on in the wider world beyond Tregarrick. Besides that she was lovely to look at—not unlike her mother in features, but her hair and those strange amber-coloured eyes of hers were her father's.

There was a quality about her that stirred the senses of everyone who met her, and Nessa had feared from the moment she came to work at Tregarrick she would attract the attention of a man like Lord Carberry. He was a dark, perverted man, and Nessa felt sorry for the woman he would eventually make his second wife.

Meanwhile he had his sights set on Lowena. It wouldn't matter to him that she no longer worked in his house. If he wanted her he would find a way to have her.

Over the years Nessa had struggled with her conscience. Living close to Tregarrick with her parents, before their demise, had enabled her to know what happened to Lowena. It had been a great relief and comfort to her, knowing she was being brought up by Izzy. Many times she had been tempted to tell Izzy about Lowena, but seeing how happy and content Lowena was, living with a family she loved—a family who loved her unconditionally, which was much more than her grandmother had—right or wrong, she had decided against it.

But now, since Izzy's death, things had changed—they had changed in another way, too. She had received the letter from her aunt in Saltash, informing her about her illness and recalling Nessa's time at Beresford Hall and the unfortunate circumstances that had ended her employment there. Her aunt had also written that she thought Nessa might be interested to know that Sir Robert Wesley was *not* dead after all. Apparently he had been seen recently in Saltash, visiting friends…

Nessa had kept her secrets all these years. Now she was to leave Tregarrick she felt it was time to reveal the past to Lowena. She had every right to know about her father, and she could not keep the secret any longer.

Edward Carberry might have many faults, but setting aside the traditions that the Hall was known for was not one of them. Every year since his great-grandfather's time Tregarrick had entertained a host of glittering guests from the Cornish gentry in an evening of dancing and dining to mark the end of the winter months.

The long drive bordered by lime trees was lined with the fancy coaches and carriages which had deposited their well-to-do occupants at the door. Tregarrick was a large house, capable of putting up the many guests who had some distance to travel, and tonight the stables were full to capacity with coaches and horses, grooms and footmen.

Lowena looked down from her vantage point at the top of the stairs, where she crouched to watch the dancers below through the gaps in the bannister. The party was larger than usual—about seventy guests in all—because of the presence of Captain Marcus Carberry. Most of them had heard he was back from the war in America and wanted to welcome him home.

The numerous tapers in the huge chandelier reflected off the crystal pendants, bathing the ballroom in an amber glow. Gentlemen in powdered periwigs and embroidered waistcoats led their ladies in the dance. Every guest was like a carefully cut jewel, representing the splendour and vanity of the privileged classes. It was a beautiful event, with the entertainment spilling out into the gardens, where the trees were hung with lanterns and garlands of flowers, creating a wistful atmosphere.

Her eyes were directed to the door when someone new entered. Marcus Carberry. He was the last to arrive. She recognised him the moment she saw him. Of course she had known he would be present, along with Lady Alice who, despite her removal to the cottage, would continue to act as hostess at any social event held at the house until Edward found himself a wife.

For the moment no one else was aware of Marcus's presence as he stood tall and dark and proud, his face grim and unsmiling, his silver-grey eyes smouldering with many conflicting emotions as he surveyed the happy scene in the great hall of Tregarrick.

Lowena hadn't seen him since he had escorted her from the cove, but she had not stopped thinking about him. Her eyes sought him out at every opportunity. On seeing him now, she felt her heart seemed to have stopped beating, checked by the potency of his mere presence. In a moment she took in his attire. She had only seen him in his uniform red jacket since his return, and his transformation into a gentleman took her breath. He was wearing midnight-blue satin knee breeches and a matching frock coat, and his white satin waistcoat was delicately embroidered with pale blue. A fine lace jabot spilled from his throat and wrists.

Then there was the shrill noise of a bow passing over the strings of a violin and the spell she had been brought under upon seeing him was shattered. A hot wave of horror engulfed her that she had allowed her thoughts to wander so, but that was immediately replaced with interest once more, for she was unable to look away from him.

She smiled to herself and a dimple broke out in the curve of her cheek as she watched him move a little further into the room with an air of utter assurance. Highly conspicuous, he seemed oblivious to the ripple of curiosity and excitement that swept among the guests, and the admiring feminine glances and appreciative whispers from behind unfurled fans. His eyes did a quick sweep of the gathering, coming to rest on his fair-haired half-brother, lounging against one of the pillars on the edge of the dance floor.

The expression on Lord Carberry's face was one of intense boredom—which altered dramatically when he met the eyes of his half-brother. Casually pushing himself away from the pillar, he waited for Marcus to join him. After exchanging a few words with Edward Marcus, aware that the guests were looking his way, coolly excused himself and began to mingle among them.

Exuding a strong masculinity few women could resist, he had the ability to charm his way into most of their rapidly beating hearts with merely a look and a cynically humorous smile. His tall, lean and yet athletic stature had a splendour to it with which few other men present could compete.

Lowena watched her fill as he casually took a glass of wine from the tray of a passing footman and moved among the gathering with ease. She was brought out of her reverie when Polly, one of the kitchen maids, suddenly appeared beside her.

'What are you doing?' she whispered, sitting down beside her on the stairs.

'Just looking. I wanted to see the gentry and the dancing. What a sight, Polly. It's all so grand. I'd love to dress like they do.' Her voice was wistful, rather sad.

Polly looked at her. 'I'm sure you would—and wouldn't we all?—but for all their grand finery they are just like us, only richer and snootier, and we are here to wait on them. Mrs Bradshaw has sent me to find you. You're wanted in the kitchen so you'd best get a move on.'

With one last look at the refined gathering, Lowena followed Polly to the domestic quarters to take up her duties in whatever capacity Cook demanded.

The kitchen was a hive of activity. Every surface was so highly polished it reflected the light, and there was an enormous table bearing bowls filled with all manner of ingredients and chopping boards. There was a tumultuous frenzy among the servants as food was carried to and fro.

Halfway through the evening Lowena managed to slip back into the brilliantly lit hall to take another look at the dancing. Watching through a crack in the door, saw caught her breath at what she saw. A pang of envy wrenched at her heart as she watched the swirling and twirling as the ladies were spun around in the gentlemen's arms in a lively country dance.

'Heavens…' she breathed. How she wished she could go to the ball, laugh and have fun—dance in Marcus Carberry's arms.

But it was not for the likes of her.

Several of the servants had also found their way to where she stood, to take a peek over her head at the gentry enjoying themselves. Catching sight of Marcus dancing with a pretty dark-haired young lady, Lowena felt her heart sink. His dark head was bent close to the lady's beautiful face—he was whispering pretty compliments, no doubt—and she was simpering and pouting and fluttering her eyelashes with all the vivacity of a born flirt.

Lowena felt a pain in her chest where her heart lay—a bitter pain caused by the malevolent pangs of jealousy.

He doesn't even know I'm here, she thought.

Abruptly she backed away and made her way to the kitchen, ignoring her sinking heart.

Later, when all the food had been served, she couldn't believe her luck when Mrs Bradshaw told her to go to the dining room, where the buffet had been laid out, and collect any dirty crockery and glasses the overstretched footmen had left.

Removing her apron and smoothing her skirts, Lowena stepped into the spacious hall where the guests were once again dancing—with a flourish now they had eaten and drunk the sparkling wine. Walking past the elegant rooms set aside for those who fancied a game of cards or dice, she made her way to the dining room.

The house was very grand. As a child she had often been in the domestic quarters, and had taken the occasional peep into the hallway when the servants had left the door open, but she had ventured no further until Izzy had died and she'd taken up employment at Tregarrick. She had entered a different world from the one she knew.

The kitchen, with its huge range and table and its shining utensils, had seemed very grand to her, but the interior of Tregarrick was beyond anything she could have imagined. The furniture, the oriental carpets and the sumptuous curtains and the beautiful paintings on the walls were hard to take in. This was a life that would never be hers and she was sensible enough to accept that.

In the dining room people stood around or sat gossiping. Lowena tried to keep her mind focussed on her work as she listened with amused fascination to three gentlemen bewailing their losses at cards. As she flitted about the room, collecting glasses and china plates and piling them onto a tray, she was totally unaware of the stir she was creating among the guests, and that her hair shone beneath the glow of the chandeliers like a bright beacon of light.

One or two of the gentlemen tried to draw her into conversation, but she smiled and, keeping her eyes lowered politely, told them she was working. One of them even went so far as to offer her a pinch of snuff from his gem-studded snuffbox. With her natural exuberance, and forgetting the housekeeper's strict instructions not to converse with the guests, she laughed and shook her head and told him she didn't dare because she might sneeze and drop the tray of pots.

This caused much hilarity—which drew the attention of Lord Carberry, who was passing by the room. He merely scowled and walked away.

Suddenly Marcus Carberry appeared in the doorway. For Lowena, all the other guests faded into the shadows beside him. His presence was like a positive force. His glance idly swept the room until, drawn by her beauty, his eyes met hers, wide and direct. There was a cool impertinence on his face when he looked at her, and his eyes were bold with a twinkle of appraisal in their depths. His lips curved in a crooked smile.

Lowena caught her breath, and for a brief moment experienced the same pleasurable feminine sensations as all the other women upon whom he had bestowed his enigmatic gaze during the evening. She favoured him with a slight smile before turning away to collect more glasses, but he had no intention of letting her escape so easily.

'I see Cook has allowed you out of the kitchen.'

Turning round, Lowena noticed how one of his dark brows arched and how his eyes glittered down at her with warm humour. Glancing up at him, she was unaware of the gentle flush that mantled her cheeks. She tried to ignore the aura of confidence that surrounded him, the impact his closeness was having on her, and the way his potent masculine virility was making her feel altogether vulnerable. When she spoke she tried to sound assertive, which wasn't easy—especially while she was trying to balance a tray full of glasses.

'Yes—it makes a pleasant change. Although for the life of me I cannot think why you would want to converse with one of the servants when you have all these ladies present impatient for you to dance with them,' she dared to venture, remembering how Mrs Bradshaw had instructed her to be politeness personified in her dealings with the guests.

She found it hard to abide by that when those silver-grey penetrating eyes provoked in her a welter of disturbing emotions that threatened to discompose her completely.

Marcus had been an interested observer, watching Lowena going about her duties. In fact he had watched her to the point when everything and everyone else had become a blur around him. Always a disciplined man, he never allowed himself to be encumbered by distractions of any kind—especially not a woman—but from the moment he had set eyes on Lowena again he'd found it hard not to think about her.

Her image was implanted in his mind as if carved there. He put his preoccupation down to surprise that in his absence an innocent girl had grown into a beautiful young woman who had the face of an angel and the body of a goddess.

He had noticed as she flitted among the guests that when she walked her steps were light and she had an unconscious swing to her body, a natural grace, making the material of her dark grey dress fluid. Darting shafts of light moved with her, making him imagine her rounded hips and the long slender legs beneath the flaring skirts.

He'd found her pleasing to watch as she smiled and laughed with the gentlemen in the dining room, throwing back her head and laughing delightedly at something one of them had said, the long slender column of her throat arching like the curved white neck of a swan.

She had moved about the tables with a mysterious grace and a sensuality that had the power to set a man's soul on fire, he thought, and her eyes shone with a brilliance like sunlight on water. He thought how radiant she looked—how, dressed in the right clothes, she would outshine every other woman present.

'You are no ordinary servant, Lowena,' he uttered softly. 'Not to me. May I tell you how charming you look?'

'You may!' Lowena laughed, his comment causing her heart-rate to increase. Putting the tray down to cover her confusion, she picked up more empty glasses as the musicians began to play another country dance. 'But I suspect that flattery is not your forte.'

'I can flatter as much as the next man when I find myself in the company of a pretty woman.'

Lowena cast him a rueful glance. His manner was teasingly flirtatious. And because there was a familiarity between them and he had always teased her when she was a child she accepted it for what it was. But where his brother was concerned, his position of Lord of the Manor made any such familiarity unacceptable.

'I think, sir, you have had one too many glasses of wine.'

He laughed, his strong white teeth gleaming between his parted lips. 'I do not require wine to converse with a lovely young lady. If circumstances were different I would ask you to dance.'

She arched her eyebrows in mock reproach. 'What? With a *servant*? And create a scandal? Shame on you!'

He grinned. 'I know. It would be most improper—but I would be willing to take the risk.'

'You are right—it would not be proper and I would not be that brave. Naturally I would have to decline your offer.'

'There's not a lady among these guests who would refuse to dance with me,' he persisted, with a mischievous twinkle in his eyes.

Absolutely enthralled by this new, teasingly flirtatious side to him, and happy to be among so much frivolity, Lowena automatically matched his mood. 'I'm not a guest.'

He raised a brow, amused. 'No, but you *are* a lady, Lowena Trevanion.'

'I'm also sensible and level-headed—'

'And young and beautiful, with an engaging personality—'

'*And* aware of the consequences were I to accept your offer. You are out of your mind if you think I would.'

'You don't know what you're missing.'

She grinned up at him, her eyes twinkling with mirth. 'I think you should count your blessings that I *would* refuse. Believe me, you would suffer greatly.'

'With what?'

'Sore toes.' She turned her back on him. 'You see, Captain Carberry, I cannot dance a step.'

Marcus laughed, and Lowena felt light-hearted and joyous and exceedingly happy just being with him and exchanging light banter.

When she walked away, balancing her tray laden with glasses, the gentlemen who watched her go laughed and told her to hurry back.

Lowena was immediately brought down to earth when Edward seemed to appear from nowhere as she entered the passage that led to the kitchen. Instinctively she shrank against the wall. A strained smile played on his lips and she could tell he was irritated by her popularity.

Edward had watched her going about her duties, thinking that not one of the women present could match her beauty. They were cold, colourless objects when compared to Lowena. Now he studied her creamy skin, so flawless and translucent, especially taking in her demurely arranged hair, the warm colour of ripe chestnuts streaked with honey-gold, and noted her trim figure with its tiny waist, the dove-grey dress with a thin edging of lace around the high neck of her bodice that did little to conceal the gentle swelling of her breasts.

Edward's mouth went dry and he wiped his moist palms down his coat.

'Since when was collecting pots one of your duties?'

'Mrs Bradshaw asked me to help since the footmen are so busy.'

'So I saw. You are employed to work—not to socialise with the guests.'

Looking at her lovely face, and the bright eyes upturned to his, he felt lust stir inside him. As the night wore on the more he drank the more dissatisfied he felt.

His voice was low and silky, his eyes sultry. 'Leave it for now and go to the stables. Lady Barrymore would like to take a walk outside, and it appears she has left her shawl in her coach. One of the grooms will direct you.'

Thinking this rather odd—for Lowena thought Lady Barrymore's maid would have been better instructed to carry out the request for her mistress—she stared at him, trying hard to conceal her dislike. Knowing Edward, she felt certain that something was afoot—and she didn't like the feel of it.

After a moment she lowered her eyes, reminding herself that such was Lord Carberry's power as the owner of Tregarrick over his servants that it was not her place to refuse him. However, she didn't trust him in the slightest, and would ask Polly to accompany her—just in case.

'Is there a problem, Lowena?' he asked, his voice low and silky-smooth.

Meeting her forthright stare, he was disappointed to see her antagonism towards him. The unconcealed hostility in her eyes and her lack of deference aroused his displeasure. She didn't behave as a maid should.

'No, not at all,' she answered, brushing past him. 'I'll just take these to the kitchen.'

It was unfortunate that when she entered the kitchen, where everyone was still rushing about to get the work done, Polly was nowhere in sight. On a sigh, she let herself out of the door into the yard at the back of the house and headed for the stables. The wide track leading to the large stable block was dark, but she was guided by the moon and the golden light streaming through the stable gates. A sudden breeze disturbed the trees and she could hear the sound of joyful music on the air.

She hurried on, glancing right and left into the shadows, breathing a sigh of relief when she finally entered the stable yard.

One of the grooms directed her to Lord Barrymore's carriage, but when she looked inside there was no sign of the shawl Edward had ordered her to fetch. Angered because she had been sent on a fruitless errand, she left the stables, picking up her pace as it was not a night for sauntering.

On seeing a shadowy figure ahead of her she stopped. The light from the house some distance away silhouetted him against the dark, and when he moved slowly towards her and she saw who it was she became quite still—like a young animal that sensed a trap.

Angered that Lord Carberry had engineered this, and knowing that she had been right not to trust him, Lowena drew herself up straight, tossing her head and facing him with all the indignation she could muster. She was not ready to spar with him tonight. She had had a busy day helping with the preparations for the festivities and she longed for her bed.

'Lord Carberry! I could not find Lady Barrymore's shawl. I'm afraid she must have left it elsewhere.' When he moved to take hold of her she stepped back. 'Please don't touch me.'

Dropping his arm, he moved closer to her, his eyes glittering with purpose. 'Why do you persist in fighting me all the time, Lowena?'

'Oh, but I *will* fight you,' she said with undiluted anger.

In the silver moonlight she saw that around his eyes and at the corners of his mouth there was a hint of weakness, of self-indulgence and depravity.

'I will fight you with every ounce of strength I possess.'

Edward's jaw clenched and his cold eyes glared at the young woman standing proud and defiant before him. 'Have a care who you are talking to, Lowena. I could turn you out on a whim if I chose to do so. You cannot go on avoiding me for ever.'

Chapter Four

On seeing Lowena leave the house shortly followed by Edward, and suspecting that his brother had not heeded his demands to leave Lowena alone and had sent her on some fruitless errand to get her alone, Marcus ran every colourful oath he could think of through his mind.

He following him outside and saw him waylay Lowena on her return from the stables. When he was close he saw the way Edward was looking at her, and the sight sent a sudden surge of cold fury through him. The intoxicating beauty before his brother would arouse lust in any man. Even dressed as a maid, in her plain dove-grey dress, she looked so damned *lovely*.

His voice low and menacing, Marcus said, 'Touch her at your peril, Edward.'

A perplexed look crossed Edward's face, and then he turned to find Marcus towering over him.

'Oh, it's you, Marcus. I might have known you would follow me.'

'Yesterday I asked you to leave Lowena alone. Apparently you didn't take my warning seriously. What in God's name is the matter with you, Edward? You hound her like a rutting beast with no intention of using decent restraint.'

Edward stepped aside, arrogant in his demeanour. 'There is nothing wrong with me, Brother. I feel what any red-blooded male feels when faced with a wench as comely as Miss Trevanion.'

Turning to Lowena, his jaw set in a hard line, Marcus glanced down at her pale face, seeing pain combined with fury at what had occurred in her eyes.

'Go back to your guests, Edward. You may resent my interference, but you will not touch her again.'

Edward looked at his brother with contempt. In his eyes Marcus had humiliated him, despite the reason for the humiliation. Without another word he turned on his heel and walked away.

Now Edward had gone the two of them were alone in an atmosphere bristling with tension, holding none of the light-heartedness of their earlier meeting.

Lowena was staring up at him. Beneath the fullness of her fringed lashes her amber eyes glowed with their own light, the colour in their depths shifting and deeply hued. Her nose was elevated and her gently rising cheekbones were touched with a light flush of colour. Her curving lips were expressive and soft, and Marcus was sure that no man could come within sight of her and not be fascinated by her. Edward's aggressive approach was deplorable, but it was little wonder he was entranced by her.

'Why did you come out here? You know what he's like, and that one way or another he is determined to get you alone at any opportunity. Why did you? Was it because he asked you?'

'No,' she answered. 'It was because he *ordered* me to. There's the difference. He told me Lady Barrymore had left her shawl in her carriage and asked me to fetch it. I know now it was a ruse to get me alone. There was no shawl when I looked.'

Hearing the music and the laughter of the guests resplendent in their finery drifting out through the open windows reminded Lowena of her position—that she was a servant, that she was here to wait on them, to pander to their needs.

Suddenly she was ashamed of her dishevelled appearance. But then something began to stir within her. Straightening her spine she lifted her head in an act of defiance. 'Thank you for trying to protect me. I will try harder to avoid him.'

'I know you will,' Marcus uttered on a softer note.

Lowena sighed dejectedly. 'All my life I felt content in the quiet, comfortable existence which was Izzy's home. And it has only taken her death to set the wheels of fate in motion, precipitating me from that tranquil, familiar world into the future, whose far-reaching horizons are hazy and unknowable and often frightening.'

'Frightening?'

She nodded. 'I have no illusions about your brother. He is one of the most dangerous and feared men I have ever met or heard about. There are many in his gang of smugglers who are in awe of him and fear him. Only the most hard-bitten defy Edward Carberry and, brave though I try to be, I am not one of them—especially on the nights when he orders me to watch the cliff path.'

'I have spoken to him. You won't be doing that any more, Lowena. He can't go on doing what he does for ever.'

'I saw the fire in his eyes when you appeared and exchanged angry words with him. But you are brothers,' she reminded him, with a hint of irony, 'and brothers can forgive each other anything, can't they?'

'Most brothers, yes. I wish it could be like that between Edward and me. Unfortunately he is not the forgiving sort.'

'I think you are right. Does he not realise that what he is doing is sheer wickedness?'

'Edward is aware of that. He simply does not care. I can't fathom what goes on inside that head of his…what makes him like he is. Perhaps it has something to do with his losing his mother at a young age and his father marrying my mother so soon afterwards—then my birth and that of Juliet,' he murmured with a resigned shrug. 'Or maybe it is some unknown flaw inherited from his mother's family that has made him like he is—she was a highly strung woman, I believe, and given to fits of intense rage. It is a question I have asked myself many times.'

Turning her head to look at him, all of a sudden Lowena thought he looked vulnerable—vulnerable and hurt. He was a good, decent man—she knew that. It was always the good men who agonised this way, always the good ones who suffered.

'Things should be easier for you now you no longer work at the house,' he said.

'I hope so. But I fear it will make little difference to Lord Carberry.' Lowena sighed. 'I miss Izzy so much. Nothing has been the same since she died.'

'She was a fine woman. I miss her too.'

'She was very fond of you, and she always looked forward to your visits.'

'And you?'

'Now you're fishing for compliments,' she said, smiling up at him. 'It's a pity Lord Carberry isn't more like you. At first when he began taking an interest in me, appearing when I was alone, I tried to cultivate an attitude of indifference—perhaps contempt—but I did not succeed. My fear of him comes not just from what I know about his smuggling activities, but from an intuitive understanding of his nature. For a start, I know that his charm—when he cares to use it—is not spontaneous but manipulative, and that if he seems amenable it is only because he wants to use me. I have spent several nights as his lookout when there is a run. He is my employer and he leaves me with no choice—I have a duty to do as I am told. It's either that or dismissal. I find it increasingly difficult to keep out of his way—and yet I cannot spend my life avoiding him.'

'You shouldn't have to. Try not to dwell on it tonight. Come, I'll walk with you to the cottage. They can do without you at Tregarrick for the rest of tonight.'

In the orange glow from the lamps hanging in the trees they walked in the direction of the cottage. The night was gently warm, the moon bright and casting a silver sheen on the water spouting gently from the fountain.

Marcus was attentive, holding out his hand to guide her lest she stumble when they walked through the shadows. And, walking beside him, Lowena was in heaven. She dared not speak in case she broke the spell. Seduction was in the air as couples strolled along the garden paths, their arms entwined and whispering to each other. Lowena looked at them with envy. A gentle breeze lifted her hair and caressed her face.

She turned her head and looked at her companion, glorying in his presence, casting her mind back to the ball. The way he had been with her— teasing, almost flirtatious—could it mean that this man who affected her so bewilderingly, so strongly, might feel the same way about her? She was blinded by what she felt for him, and the thought that he might filled her with such promise, such joy and hope, that it brought added sparkle to her eyes.

He was staring straight ahead. Uncertain of his mood, she remained silent. In the moonlight his profile was harsh. He looked like a man in the throes of some deep internal battle. Suddenly it seemed colder and she shivered.

On reaching the cottage they stopped and faced

each other. Marcus looked down into her upturned face, tracing with his gaze the beautiful lines, the soft roundness of her cheeks and the delicate hollow of her throat where a strand of red-gold hair had come to rest against her creamy flesh. Moonlight caressed her face, and the lips that were parted in repose. She really was extraordinarily lovely, with an untamed quality and a wild freedom of spirit that found its counterpart in his own restless nature.

Among his fellow soldiers he had been known as a hard man—a stubborn, iron-willed man, but always fair. But here he stood before Lowena Trevanion, who was making him feel more than he should feel.

Now that he was alone with her he found her even more compelling as their eyes held. Her dress clung in fluid lines to her body, moulding itself against her as if reluctant to be parted from her, showing the womanly curves of her breasts and the graceful curve of her hips. She looked composed and serene—not in the least like the angry young woman who had thwarted his brother's attentions.

He had returned home thinking of her as the girl he had known. Now he had ended up thinking of her all the time. He could see her vulnerable side and he found that endearing. She had a way of overturning his thinking, his emotions that was worrying. He never ceased to be amazed and fascinated by her enticing blend of innocence and boldness. Each trait was wonderfully intriguing, and he had never been more aware of his growing infatuation than at this present moment.

'You are too tempting by far, Lowena. Little wonder my brother is so smitten.'

His words acted on her like a douche of cold water.

'I swear that apart from the kiss he forced on me in the cove he has never touched me. I could *never* love a man like him.'

'Can you know yourself as well as that?' he said quietly, watching her, his silver-grey eyes unfathomable.

Looking into his lean face, for some strange reason she could not explain Lowena found her colour mounting. There was still so much of the girl in her, at war with the young woman she had become, and this man had the knack of bringing it quickly to the surface.

'Yes, I can.'

Her eyes darkened as the feelings she carried in her heart for him overwhelmed her. She found it impossible to conceal them.

Encouraged by his attentions earlier, and because she thought he might feel the same way about her, she managed to hold his gaze as she quietly and shyly admitted the truth. 'I can because I love you, you see—quite desperately, in fact. Oh, it's quite all right,' she said quickly, when she saw his eyes widen with astonishment, 'you don't have to say anything. I don't expect you to. But please don't laugh at me and say I'll get over it—because I won't. Any kind of commitment is out of the question because of my circumstances—my lack of birth and breeding—but I shall love you all the days of my life. So, you see, there it is.'

She was looking at Marcus with eyes as large as her soul and as dark as midnight. Her sincere, heartfelt declaration of love had hit him hard, like a punch in the gut. It also struck a chord of intense feeling deep inside him. How could she be in love with him? She was too sincere. It would be too difficult to heartlessly deny her. But could he cope with her love?

After Isabel's betrayal he had sworn that never again would he believe a woman's claims of such a debilitating emotion. To do so would leave his emotions wide open and vulnerable. And yet Lowena was not Isabel. She was nothing like her, and she was drawing on emotions and feelings he had believed long since buried.

Slowly something awakened in him—longings

he had not felt in a long time. A huge, constricting knot of tenderness and desire tightened his throat and he wanted to pull Lowena into his arms. His body was sending him all sorts of messages his brain didn't want to accept.

His face remained strangely expressionless while a myriad of feelings raced through his mind, among them doubts and uncertainty, while tenderness and desire throbbed through every nerve-ending in his body. His feelings were disturbing, strong and dangerous. Reaching out, he tenderly brushed her temple. The feeling became a desire so strong it was like an intense pain—urgent, needing to be fulfilled.

Lowena watched his gaze drop to her mouth in a state of anticipation that was reaching dizzying heights as she waited. Marcus took two steps to close the distance that separated them, his gaze still focused on her lips. She caught her breath. She could feel his warmth, the vital power of him. The size and heat of him still had the power to shock her. Sensations of unexpected pleasure flickered through her. She was powerless to prevent what she hoped with all her heart would happen next.

Taking her arms, he drew her to his chest. Their faces were close together, his breath warm on her lips. Her trembling hands reached up to hold him. Beneath her clutching fingertips the muscles of his shoulders beneath his coat coiled and quivered reflexively. Placing his finger beneath her chin, he tilted her face to his, lowering his head and covering her mouth with his own.

The contact was exquisite.

Relinquishing her lips after a moment, he slowly reached up to run his finger gently along her full bottom lip, tracing its curving outline. He slipped a hand behind her neck, his touch light and sensual as he drew her against his hard body.

'I shouldn't be doing this,' he murmured, his mouth hovering close to hers.

'Please don't stop,' she whispered.

Gleaming whiteness flashed briefly as Marcus smiled down at her. He took her hand in his and looked deep into her eyes. His skin was warm to the touch and somehow reassuring. But he seemed too much of a man—too knowing and strong, too able to bend her to his will. She was dizzy with conflicting emotions and the turmoil made her momentarily speechless.

She desperately wanted him to kiss her again.

She was not disappointed.

Tentatively he took her lips once more. They were as soft and gentle as a butterfly's wings and as sweet as newly extracted honey. If he had previously had any doubts about her innocence they

vanished now. She was cool and virginal and unlike any woman he had kissed before—sensual
and inexperienced, urgent but unschooled. His
lips began to move on hers, his tongue to explore.

Lowena was experiencing the most wonderful, warm feeling. She pressed into him, answering his passion with the same wild, exquisitely
provocative ardour, feeling a burgeoning pleasure and an immense joy that was almost beyond
bearing. Half stifled, she found her head reeling.
Waves seemed to be running through her body,
but there was also another far more disturbing
sensation—a deep, primeval passion.

She gasped, totally innocent of the warmth, the
passion he was so skilfully arousing in her, that
was pouring through her veins with a shattering
explosion of delight. It was a kiss like nothing she
could have imagined, a kiss of exquisite restraint,
and she was unable to think of anything but the
exciting urgency of his mouth and the warmth of
his breath.

Soon she felt herself falling slowly into a dizzying abyss of sensuality. She longed for him to kiss
her more deeply. But almost urgently he pushed
her back, breaking the spell.

What in God's name was he *doing*? he asked
himself. This was all wrong. To take advantage
of her like this made him no better than Edward.

When she had pressed herself against him, becoming a living spell, a temptress, a triumphant siren in his arms, he had very nearly admitted defeat and had almost been tempted to strip her clothes away and make love to her.

He was shocked to discover just how close he'd come to losing control.

He seldom felt ashamed of his actions, but some devil inside him had goaded him to take her in his arms and kiss her. And what a kiss! He had felt her response to his kiss and it had fired his own need. Her mouth had been soft and yielding and moist. He'd savoured the feel of it, the taste of her. He'd felt as though he could have gone on kissing her all night and never got tired of it.

He drew a breath and looked away so she could not see the expression on his face. What was the matter with him? Why was he feeling this gnawing in his chest which her lips and the feel of her body pressed to his had caused?

He had always felt protective towards her—but that had been the kind of protection he had felt for her when she had been a child. Now she was grown, and these feelings were new to him.

He had left the war behind and his present way of life suited him. His family excepted, he had no ties and no emotional involvements.

Suddenly memories long-buried of eyes as blue as the sky began to stir. When this happened he always pushed them down. There wasn't enough fire in the world to thaw him out and make him feel the way he had for Isabel in those heady, golden days when he had loved her, and even if there were he was determined not to let it happen again.

When Isabel had transferred her affections to Edward she had hurt Marcus cruelly. He still found the memory of the hideous affair between them difficult and painful, and it had turned him irrevocably against allowing another woman to get too close.

He had made love to many desirable and beautiful women since, but none of them had touched his heart. He always kept himself detached, giving nothing of himself—which seemed to attract them to him even more. He tried to fight his overwhelming feelings of bitterness, but even so love wasn't on his agenda. Until he had come home and found Lowena—all grown up and telling him that she loved him.

He thought about what had just happened between them, turning it over and over in his mind, and suddenly everything—his life, his future—took on new dimensions. He could no longer deny even to himself that he had feelings for Lowena, and he could not ignore his ever-increasing desire to have her near him—but that did not necessarily signify love.

She was fresh and alive and unspoiled, and he was extremely fond of her, liked being with her. He had certainly enjoyed kissing her, and he wanted to lose himself in her, to cleanse himself of the past and rid himself of the memories of Isabel. But his instincts told him to hold back until he'd considered this new situation carefully.

Drawing a long, audible breath, he combed his fingers through his hair. 'I should not have kissed you. It was a mistake. It should not have happened. I should know better. I'm sorry, Lowena.'

'Why?' she said, her eyes clouded with bewilderment. 'It did happen and we can't take it back. Please don't say you're sorry,' she begged, 'because that means that you regret it.'

She saw Marcus's shoulders stiffen and he took a step back, resisting her, the slight smile that curved his lips a curious blend of withdrawal and self-derision.

'Did you not enjoy kissing me?'

'I did—I admit it. And there is nothing wrong in sharing a kiss,' he stated. 'But a mere kiss can be far more tempting than you realise. If you were anyone else I would think we might get to know each other better, so long as we resolved to be discreet. But I don't think either of us would enjoy the attention we would receive at Tregarrick. Do you know what I am saying, Lowena?'

Disappointed, and hurt that he did not reciprocate her feelings, she stared at him in disbelief at what he was saying. Her stomach clenched and she felt as if something were shattering inside her, but she could not deny to herself that she had liked the way he kissed her.

'Yes—I do. I had not thought… You are right. That is not the kind of attention I would welcome. I know perfectly well that I could never be anything to you other than your mistress, and I have too much self-respect for that.'

Their gazes linked and held—hers open and frank, his a blend of seriousness and frustration.

'I should not have said what I did,' she said quickly as all her anxieties about her feelings for Marcus churned inside her. He was trying to rid himself of her—she could feel it. 'It was my fault. I shouldn't have done that. I should have kept my feelings to myself. I can see it isn't what you want and that it has caused you some embarrassment. You are right to have reservations.'

Her words were sincere and heartfelt. Reaching out, she placed her hand on his arm. The gesture was spontaneous, but one she immediately regretted, for Marcus drew back, resisting her.

'I'm sorry.'

'Don't be—and don't blame yourself,' he said harshly. 'The fault was all mine. It was a moment of weakness, Lowena. Nothing more than that. Do you understand?'

Lowena understood because his expression made it clear—no tears, no recriminations.

Drowning in humiliation, she knew his casual statement had made her cheeks flame with embarrassment, but her pride came to the fore and she managed to raise her head and meet his gaze squarely. 'Yes, I do. I was foolish in opening my heart and caring too much for you.'

Marcus stepped back, making his voice condescendingly amused as he tried not to look too deeply into Lowena's wounded eyes, eloquent in their hurt and fixed on his face. 'I never intended you to do that. I think you are very lovely and very special, but in many ways you are still so young, Lowena—naïve and inexperienced—'

'And not the sort of girl men of your standing would look at twice—unless, like your brother, you have less noble intentions,' Lowena interrupted sharply, deeply hurt by what he'd said. His callousness was not to be borne. 'Please don't insult me by ridiculing my feelings, Marcus, or treat me like a child. It's cruel.'

'I apologise. I was about to say that at this time

I value your friendship very much—but that is no basis for a love affair. Contrary to what you may think of me, unlike my brother I am not in the habit of seducing innocent young ladies.'

Lowena's cheeks grew hotter at this. He still saw her as a child—a stupid, pathetic child who had a lot of growing up to do. How could she even begin to compare with some of the beautiful women he must associate with? How could she ever have assumed a man like Marcus Carberry would be interested in *her*? Never in all her life had she felt so humiliated.

Her wounded pride forced her chin up. 'Was I in danger of being seduced?' she ventured to ask.

'No, but I suggest you go inside before I'm tempted to change my mind.'

The silence that followed was long and heavy. The moonlight cast shadows over his handsome face, making his expression stern.

'Having no wish to play on your weakness, I will remove myself from your presence,' she said. 'There is nothing left to say—or at least nothing that you want to hear.'

'No,' he said. His face tightened and shut as if a door had been closed.

Lowena heard the absolute finality of that word and knew it would be futile to say anything else. Fighting desperately to hold on to her shattered pride, she said, 'Goodnight, Marcus. I think it's best if I go inside before I make an even bigger fool of myself.'

Dragging her gaze from his, she turned and walked with as much dignity as she could muster towards the door of the cottage. She could no longer look at him without giving her feelings away.

Marcus watched Lowena disappear into the house. He had read her every reaction in her expressive eyes and was satisfied that he'd done his utmost to kill any romantic illusions about love she might have. It was too soon. Everything was moving too quickly. But when she had uttered her parting words he had heard the catch in her voice and his conscience had torn at him.

He had done well, not letting her know how much he had come to care for her, how much she belonged in his heart. But it was hard, no matter how he tried, to still his emotional rebellion against the rational reason of his mind.

In her room, Lowena climbed into bed. By telling Marcus how much she cared for him she had overstepped the bounds of friendship and found herself in unfamiliar territory. She'd made no demands on him—how could she, a woman in her circumstances, without birth or breeding. But she'd made a gift of telling him something she'd never uttered to another human being—that she loved him.

She'd made a complete fool of herself. Like a child, she had indulged in a daydream and had fallen in love with a man who looked on her as a child. Misery and unhappiness folded around her like a shroud, and she wished with all her heart that she could go away, disappear to a place where nobody knew her.

Utterly overcome with emotion and shame, she drew the covers over her head and began to weep. For a brief time she had allowed herself to hope, and Marcus's rejection of her had diminished her in some irreparable way. She had not *asked* to feel like this—had not *chosen* to feel so deeply for him.

She closed her eyes tightly and with a sigh uttered a prayer. Only it wasn't really a prayer. It was a strengthening of her own will.

Two weeks after that night things took a turn for the worse. Rain had been falling from a leaden sky for four days without any let-up, and a crisis had arisen at the mine. Marcus had been there constantly. With all the rain that had fallen and poured through every crack and crevice, one of the lower levels of Wheal Rozen had become flooded, and the pump was struggling to cope with such a vast amount of water.

Mrs Seagrove had taken to her bed early that evening, with one of her migraines, and the girl from the village who came in daily to help clean the house had gone home. Lady Alice was also in bed, as was Dorothy, Lady Alice's maid, who, once asleep, wouldn't wake if a gun went off beside her head.

Lowena was about to go to bed herself. The only sound to be heard was the rain beating on the windows and the wind. She checked on the stew Mrs Seagrove had left keeping warm on the range, should Marcus come home from the mine hungry. Suddenly there was a tapping on the door.

Wondering who it could be at that time, she went to see. A tall man, dripping wet, stood in the shadows. She recognised him as one of the men who worked in the woods on the Tregarrick estate.

'What is it? What do you want?'

'His lordship wants you,' he said gruffly. 'There's a run tonight and no one to watch from the coastal path.'

'Tonight?' she gasped. 'But—in this weather?'

'It can't be changed. Revenue men were seen earlier three miles west along the coast, so we have to be quick and careful. You're needed.'

Lowena stared at him, hating what he was asking of her. 'But—no—*no*, I can't. I won't. I want nothing to do with any of that…'

The man ignored her protest. 'You've got to. No argument—and you're to hurry. It's all arranged. The cargo is coming in to the cove some time around midnight. We've got to be ready.'

'This has nothing to do with me any more,' she hissed vehemently. '*Nothing*. Do you hear me? There must be someone else who can do it.'

How could Lord Carberry ask this of her and go against his brother's orders? But Edward would know Marcus was occupied at the mine, and with no one else to watch the coastal path he had thought of her.

The man shrugged, water running from his hat and down his face. 'We're short-handed as it is—most of the men are at the mine, trying to stop the flooding. There's work to do. I've given you the message. Do as you will, but it doesn't do to anger his lordship. You should know that. He's the leader of this game and always has been. He's in a dangerous mood tonight, and it won't do to cross him. Shall I tell him you'll come?'

Lowena was tempted to say no, but remembering what Edward had said to her on the beach, the day after Marcus's return to Tregarrick, and fearing that Edward would remain true to his threat and would harm his brother in some way, made her hesitate. If she weren't there, sharply on the look-out, should the dragoons or the Revenue men come along Lord Carberry would be arrested or—should he resist—worse. No matter how deeply she loathed him, if trouble was to come to Tregarrick or Marcus it would not be by her hand.

Swallowing her fear, she nodded.

She watched the man hurry away, hearing his boots squelching on the sodden path. Life had suddenly become very complicated as far as her loyalties were concerned, but unless Marcus came home from the mine he would never know what she had done—would he? She sighed resignedly, knowing she could not keep it from him.

Pulling the hood of her cloak over her head, she ran from the house, disregarding the certain knowledge that the last thing she ought to be doing was helping Edward Carberry. Some surefooted instinct born and bred in her kept her from stumbling on the path made muddy and slippery with rain, but it was a wild night, the wind whipping her skirts about her legs. With the swiftness of a hunted animal she sped towards the cove, her cloak and the skirts beneath soon becoming coated and weighted down with mud.

Feeling as she did about Marcus—wanting to be near him, to feel him close—the last thing she wanted was to anger him. But he was not here to protect her. He could not really protect her, anyway—not from Lord Carberry. Not for ever.

She laughed a little bitterly, hearing the sound go out into the darkness and be carried away on the wind. She felt tears welling into her eyes—tears because she suddenly felt that everything about her life was hopeless. Never had she felt so lost, and she was lonelier than ever before.

On and on she ran, with shadows all around her, her heart beating in a tempo of fear as the rain penetrated her cloak and soaked her through to the skin. Eventually she reached the coastal path, which wound along the edge of the cliff. She knew it well, but it was dangerous in the dark. She realised she must keep all her wits about her, and tried to prevent herself thinking about anything except the urgency of what she had to do now.

But, whether she wished it or not, she kept seeing pictures of Marcus's face when he had walked with her back to the cottage after the party, almost feeling again his closeness and thinking of their conversation—and their kiss.

'Must I think of him now?' she whispered to herself, and then realised with a sense of relief that she had reached the spot above the cove where the beacon stood—the one she had to light should trouble come in the form of the Revenue men.

Fortunately it had been built beneath an over-hang on the cliff, which protected it from the rain.

Her heart almost ceased to beat when a fig-ure emerged from the shadows. Edward Carberry stepped in front of her, his eyes gleaming coldly. All the colour drained out of her face. When he spoke there was no mockery in his voice. He was already organising and planning the night ahead.

'You came.'

'This is the last time I collude with you in your evil business. No more will I do your bidding. You are mad if you think that.'

He smiled thinly, unconcerned by her argu-ment. The eyes that bored into hers were deadly.

'No, not mad. It takes a very sane person to plan the things I do—to make them perfect,' he replied with infuriating calm.

Lowena faced him with hatred burning in the depths of her eyes. 'You have a black heart, Ed-ward Carberry,' she said, her voice trembling with anger, 'and I despise you. It will be your own wickedness and greed that will bring about your destruction.'

'Perhaps,' he retorted coldly, unperturbed. 'However, we can argue about that another day. I must get back to the matter in hand.'

His hand shot out with the quickness of a snake about to strike, his fingers closing round her chin and his face thrusting close to hers. 'Understand this, Lowena. I require your full co-operation to-night. Do you understand me?'

Taking note of her pallor and the trembling he could feel in her body, his instinct told him she would do as she was told and his lips stretched in an odious smile of triumph.

'You really have no choice. Do as I require and nothing unpleasant will happen to you. But I promise you, Lowena, that you will regret doing anything to make me angry.'

Releasing his grip on her chin, turning quickly, he strode away from her, making his way down to the cove.

He was gone before Lowena could recover enough to reply. There had been an underlying warning in the lightness of his words, and she knew the seriousness of it. A new kind of fear stole over her when she realised he meant to do her harm if she did not comply with his demands.

Finding what shelter she could beneath the cliff, she waited, listening to the waves rolling and crashing to the shore, trying to penetrate the rain and the gloom to watch what was taking place in the cove. There was no horizon where the inter-minable stretch of sea met the sky, but as her eyes adjusted to the dark she could make out the rocks and the solidity of the cliffs, and the crouched, motionless, ghostly figures of men on the sand below, facing the sea, their eyes fastened on the rolling breakers.

After about half an hour she could make out a thin pinprick of light, which only just penetrated the curtain of rain and bobbed about like a cockleshell on the storm-tossed sea. Then the hull of the vessel everyone was waiting for appeared.

Lowena knew the risk Edward Carberry was taking to chance a run on a night like this. There was every danger that the vessel carrying the contraband would be washed up on the shore or, worse, driven onto the rocks where it would break up.

Suddenly everything seemed to happen at once. It was a scene Lowena had watched many times before. Each man sprang forward. They knew precisely what to do. There was method in their work which they accomplished quickly, their actions hurried. They were mere shadows in the dark of the night, coming and going between the boat and the sands, wading through the freezing water, moving with precision and urgency, their minds set on their purpose—humping kegs and packages up the beach to the packhorses and wagons that waited like phantoms to carry the booty to a safe hiding place or to travel across the moor before dawn.

Not until the last man and horse had left the cove did Lowena turn and head for home.

Apart from the glow of the lamp Lowena had left burning in the kitchen, the house was in darkness. Weary and impatient to get out of her wet clothes, she let herself in and removed her cloak, unaware of the man standing close to the range to feed off its warmth.

Having stirred the fire into life and removed his shirt and boots, he was rubbing his wet hair dry with a towel. Not having slept or eaten properly in two days, his face was taut with strain, and there were dark circles around his eyes.

When Lowena entered he turned to look at her, unable to conceal his surprise. 'Lowena…'

Stopped in her tracks, all Lowena could do was stare at him. For an endless moment their gazes locked as they assessed one another. Slowly the dawning of understand filled his eyes. His entire body tensed and his jaw clenched so tightly that a muscle began to throb in his cheek. His granite features were an impenetrable mask as he threw the towel into a chair and moved towards her, staring at her, his chest bare and his silver-grey eyes piercing through her even though he wasn't really seeing her at all.

In frigid, trembling silence she waited for him

to speak, desperately wanting to justify herself for what was to come.

'Where have you been—or do I really need to ask?' he demanded.

Shaking her head, she tried not to look at him too closely—at his tangled wet hair and his naked body above his waist, gleaming in the fire-light. Through an ache in her throat, she whispered, 'No—no, you don't. I think you know well enough. There was a run tonight.'

She stared searchingly at him, not quite certain of his mood, but sensing his anger. As he continued to look at her his face was so bitter that her chest was filled with remorse.

'I can't believe you have done this,' he flared, fighting the urge to wrap her in his arms until her shivering ceased and she grew warm again. '*Why*, Lowena? After all that has been said, why did you go?'

'Because there was no one else.'

'But why *you*?' he demanded. 'Did Edward come here and drag you to the cliff top?'

Swamped in her own misery, she shook her head. 'No—he sent someone. I told you. I went because there was no one else. I know what he is doing is wrong, but if your brother is caught it will not be by my doing, Marcus.'

Marcus's eyes narrowed. 'You little fool. Perhaps he *should* be caught. At least that would put an end to this cloud we're all living under, caused by his illegal activities.'

'Then it is up to you—his brother—to do something about it. But have a care. When you came home from America he—he threatened to harm you should you stop me watching the cliff path on the nights when there's a run or interfere in his affairs in any way.'

Marcus stared at her. The mere thought that Edward had made Lowena his pawn once more in his illegal venture, putting the fear of God into her that he would do him harm if stopped her, almost sent him over the edge.

'And was this the reason you went tonight—because you thought he would harm me in some way if you didn't do his bidding?'

She nodded dumbly. 'I was afraid he would carry out his threat.'

'Edward will not harm me—and, besides, I fight my own battles. Tell me, Lowena, if I had not seen you come back just now, did you intend telling me?'

Lowena actually flinched at the cold, ruthless fury in his eyes. 'I—I don't think I could have kept it to myself, knowing you would be bound to find out.'

'How vastly obliging of you,' he growled.

'Please, Marcus,' she implored him, drowning in agony. 'I didn't want to go—I swear it.'

She shook her head, the tears she could no longer contain spilling down her cheeks. Feeling the damp chill of her wet clothes, she shivered. Her skirts felt like dead weights about her trembling legs. She stretched out her hand in a gesture of mute appeal, then let it fall to her side when it got her nothing but a blast of contempt from his cold eyes.

Her tears failed to move him. 'Pray, continue. I am listening.'

'When I came in and saw you I was ready to admit where I had been. I'd never willingly displease you. Now you have berated me as you saw fit, and I deeply regret that I have angered you, that you think I have failed you. But I don't think I can bear your scorn and contempt.'

'After all I have done—after threatening my own brother for continuing to involve you in his nefarious schemes—I thought that would be an end to it. Only to find that the minute he tells you to jump, you do so without argument. Do you expect me to act as if nothing has happened?'

She shook her head dejectedly. 'No, of course I don't—and whatever you might have thought when you discovered what I had done I cannot blame you. But what I did I did not do willingly.

In trying to protect you I have made you angry. You have no idea how I hate myself for not being brave enough to refuse your brother.'

Her statement was made simply and came from the heart, and for a moment Marcus felt his resolve weakening. Her head was bent forward, her hair hanging like a wet curtain on either side, concealing her face from his view. She looked so small, so vulnerable, that he felt a twinge of conscience.

'Listen to me, Lowena, and listen well. If you believe Edward will not do you any harm if you do his bidding then you are foolishly mistaken. He is not that noble. He will do exactly as he wants as long as it suits him to do so. Now, there are two things I have to say to you. Firstly, you are not to go near the house under any circumstances. Secondly, any message that is delivered to you passes through me. I say this because, unlike my brother, I am deeply concerned for your safety.

'I do not blame you for what you have done tonight. I only regret that I wasn't here to stop you. God knows what would happen to you if the Revenue men came along and you were caught with the rest of them. I wish to keep as much distance between Edward and myself as is possible. When something like this happens it only serves to deepen the animosity we already feel for each other, which is something I wish to avoid.'

He looked at her and saw afresh the state she was in. He drew in a breath. With her hair hanging loose she looked pale and bedraggled, even pitiful as she stood there, shivering on the point of collapse.

Something in his chest tightened. 'Look at you,' he murmured. 'You're soaked through. You should get out of those wet clothes.'

Placing a gentle finger under her chin, he compelled her to meet his eyes.

'Yes,' she whispered, her teeth chattering. 'I suppose I should.'

He had already noted that she was chilled to the bone. But it was more than the cold that was causing her body to tremble. She was only now realising, he guessed, how afraid she was of Edward and his threats.

Opening his arms, he said, 'Come here,' and when she came into them he could feel her body trembling. 'There's nothing to fear. Edward can't hurt you now,' he said, gently stroking her wet hair before pressing his cheek against it. 'Promise me you will avoid Edward.'

Edward's persistence in getting close to Lowena worried him more than he wanted her to know.

'I do promise.'

Marcus supressed a smile, suspecting her do-cility was a measure of her cold and fatigue. 'I think we've got to get you out of those wet clothes before you catch your death.'

Scooping her up into his arms, he carried her out of the kitchen and up the stairs to her room.

Chapter Five

Pushing open Lowena's bedroom door, Marcus sat her on the bed while he quickly lit the candle on the bedside table. It soon cast a warm orange glow about the room.

Kneeling on the floor, he hesitantly raised her skirt and pulled off her sodden boots and stockings, almost without being aware of what he did, so concerned was he to get her out of her wet things. Getting to his feet, he raised her up as he would a child and unfastened the buttons down the back of her dress, peeling the icy garment off her shoulders and down.

Like an obedient child she stepped out of it, standing in her petticoat and looking up at him, her arms covering her breasts. She continued to shiver.

His gaze was drawn to her face, to her cold, trembling lips. Her eyes, which had avoided looking at him directly, now clung to his, sending a message that was easy for him to decipher. The room was a warm and intimate place to be. Suddenly there was a different quality to the atmosphere between them. And they were completely alone.

Marcus felt heat flare in his belly. He raised a finger and gently brushed a remaining tear from the sweet curve of her cheek. She did not speak or move, but her eyes darkened almost to black as her pupils dilated. At that moment, more than anything in the world, he wanted to take her to bed and make love to her. Had she made the smallest seductive gesture that she was willing he might have taken her there and then, quickly, in the heat of the moment.

But this was Lowena, innocent and inexperienced in the ways of men, not a mere body to be used quickly and cast aside. But with her amber eyes darkened and the soft creaminess of her shoulders and the firm mounds of her breasts straining against her damp petticoat, their nipples chilled and rigid, how could any man with blood in his veins withstand her?

'Tell me,' he murmured, tracing his finger along the line of her shoulder, 'how does a woman who has done what you have done tonight, and returned soaked to the skin, manage to look as lovely as you do?' His finger continued slowly up the slender column of her neck. 'You have wonderful eyes—did you know that?—and your skin is as soft as velvet.'

Lowena opened her mouth and drew in a deep, quivering breath, letting it out against the palm of his hand which cupped her cheek. She lifted her gaze to his, and somewhere in the depths of those silver eyes looking down at her she saw something deep and profound and silent, holding her captive, promising her something inviting, something exciting.

'I—I cannot say.' The touch of his finger on her flesh made her shiver with excitement.

'Can you not?' His voice was low and seductive, his fingers curling round her nape and drawing her head closer.

'No…' she breathed. His lips were perilously close.

Suffused by the scent of her, and finding her too bewitching to resist, slowly he covered her mouth with his, warming her. He heard her sigh and felt her shudder, and when her hands tentatively came to rest against his chest he deepened the kiss. He realised with a surge of desire that her demureness and naivety hid a woman of passion and courage—and he wanted her. He wanted to lie her down on the bed and draw those inviting hips beneath him, to have her long, lithe legs wrapped around him and to fill his mouth with the taste of her.

The fierceness of his wanting startled him.

Relinquishing her lips, he looked down at her upturned face. 'Lowena…' the word was husky '…any minute now and I am likely to forget I shouldn't be here alone with you.'

'I know—but please don't leave me,' she murmured, moving closer, seeking the warm haven of his arms and solace from the turmoil of her emotions.

She could not bear it if he did not stay. This man she had adored all her life represented safety and security, and his concern was making her feel cherished and protected.

Immediately Marcus's body responded to her plea. He tried to remind himself of who she was— who *he* was—but all he could think about was losing himself in the sweetness of her. All he could see was the quiver of her tantalising mouth, urging him to kiss her into insensibility.

Aware of all this time of being around her, watching her, of the fatigue of the past few days battling with the water at the mine and the unrelenting rain, he sighed deeply. All he was conscious of at that moment was the woman in his arms, the self-denial and frustration that was driving him beyond restraint.

'I know what I am doing is wrong,' he said hoarsely, with his last vestiges of reason, 'and that this is insane...' But his words were lost as he lowered his mouth and then, like a fire, came the sudden abdication of all common sense.

Lost in the exciting, exotic beauty of her, he groaned as her lips opened and he tasted her warm tongue. And then, with a long, shuddering sigh, he felt their bodies fuse together. His fingers threaded through her hair, drawing her closer. Without releasing her he somehow managed to divest her of her petticoat, and anything else that got in his way, and she emerged creamy white and gloriously beautiful. Her arms clung to him and her mouth to his. Only once, in exasperation, did she assist him in his task, obsessed with having his mouth on hers without delay.

His hands found her breasts, the nipples hard between his fingers, before moving on to span her small waist and the full curve of her hips. Her arms were about his neck, drawing him to her, and her mouth was like a living flame as he removed what clothes he had left. Only now, when they were both naked, did he lay her down on the bed, but then, instead of joining her, he knelt before her, placing his hands on either side of her waist.

Through half-lowered lids Lowena watched

him, and shivered at the marvellous perfection of his body—earthy, muscular and splendidly virile.

Marcus saw where her mesmerised gaze had settled, and the touch of it sent raw need quaking through his body. His hand slid up her inner thigh, making her gasp, and proceeded upwards to cup her breasts before he leaned forward and with exquisite tenderness pressed his lips where his hands had gone before.

She gasped with shock beneath his assault. He was stirring such sensations in her—desire and heat and unbelievable pleasure. A small, insidious voice whispered caution, reminding her that to take this relationship further would bring her nothing but heartbreak, but another voice was whispering something else—not to let the moment pass, to catch it and hold on to it.

Only this moment existed. His mouth, his hands, the scent of him and his hard male body, insistent and eager. The fact that he was there, that he wanted her, superseded any reflection on the possible consequences.

Marcus brushed back the damp tendrils of her hair. In a moment of sanity he paused and looked down at her face, flushed with passion, suddenly swamped with self-loathing for taking her innocence.

'You are a virgin, Lowena. You don't have to do this. I will not force you.'

She gave him a little smile. 'I know, but don't stop—not now.'

'For what reason do you surrender your virginity to me when I have nothing to offer you?'

'It's all right—it doesn't matter…' she whispered as his lips moved to her throat, her mouth.

And then slowly he drew her against him.

She moaned and strained beneath him, her response arousing him even further, and he fought for control, his corded muscles contracting into hard knots. He found her trembling innocence incredibly erotic, and suddenly he was without sight or hearing as his manhood quested between her open thighs.

Lowena's eyes were soft, warm and dazed, unfocused with the loveliness that came when a woman was deep in the pleasures of the flesh. Marcus's kisses acted on her like a balm, blotting out the hostile world, annihilating her fear and loneliness, and his fragrance and his lips filled her mind and her soul.

A detached thread of thought warned her that there would be no lasting future for her with Marcus, but she didn't care. All she cared about was *now*, this moment. She wanted him to love her and she felt a wild surge of excitement and anticipation.

Desire, primitive and potent, pounded through Marcus's veins. Her sighs caressed him as he touched her, and little gasps escaped her throat when his fingers penetrated that most secret place. He gloried in her, and knew the soft yielding of her body was redolent of his passion.

He took what she was offering, took it mindlessly, driven by a violent compulsion to have her. He took her with urgency and hunger and an ungovernable surge of dominant desire that stunned and aroused him, and he used all his sexual experience to knock down the defences of an inexperienced young woman who hadn't any idea how to withstand it.

When he entered her she wrapped her legs about him and they both experienced an explosive mass of emotion that was unlike anything before. His penetration was long and slow, carefully allowing her body to accept his manhood, and all the while he was watching her face, the way her breath quickened and her eyes widened with startled desire.

Lowena was as ardent as Marcus. All rational thought had flown from her head. With an abandon that shocked her, she melted against him. Yielding to the exquisite pleasure of his touch, she soon realised that Marcus Carberry was a man of extraordinary skill and power. She could feel the strength of him, the force of his arms and his firm thighs, the soft hair on his chest brushing against her.

In his eyes she saw the flame that had been lit—a bright, consuming flame of passion that spread and licked about their naked bodies. Her soft flesh began to glow and throb, and the throbbing spread throughout her, into her blood, her bones. It was a wonderful kind of torture that continued to grow until she could feel a warm fountain within, soon to run over, soon to drown her in a flood of pleasure, and then the sound of their joy was heard by no one but each other.

Marcus collapsed upon her, barely remembering to protect her from his weight as he lay against her, sated and spent. Whatever the reasons that had brought him to Lowena's bed, they were forgotten as he wrapped his arms around her back and pulled her with him on to his side. She was exquisitely soft. In the flickering light of the candle they lay together on her narrow bed, not speaking.

Lowena smiled. There was no shame, no guilt, only peace—perfect peace and tranquillity. She sighed and nestled against him, closing her eyes.

Later—when Marcus's breathing had eased,

when he could think again—he realised how still Lowena had become. Looking down at her flushed face, he was amazed to find she had fallen to sleep.

He held her close, feeling strangely protective of her. He had made love to many women, but not one of them had given him what Lowena had. Her responses had been real and uncontrolled. The pleasure he had experienced was a wonder to him. He had not, until now, held a woman in his arms who was innocent, untouched and pure. A woman who had never known the hands of a man on her.

Beauty was moulded into every flawless sculpted feature of her face, but her allure went much deeper than that. It was in her voice and her graceful movements. There was something inside her that made her sparkle and glow, and she needed only the proper background and situation and elegant clothes to complement her alluring figure and exquisite features.

But, he thought on a more sober note, with an abrupt descent into reality, this was where it must end.

He couldn't continue living in the same house with her if he was to have any peace. She was too much of a threat to his sanity. Everywhere he turned she would be there, ready to ensnare him, and when she was absent his need to see her would make him seek her out.

He had not realised that his sexual desire for her would become a complication. It was a situation he could not ignore and he could not let it go on. Better that she was away from him altogether, before she disrupted his whole life. There was no middle ground. There never would be a time when he would be safe from what he felt when he was with her.

His decision would hurt her—he knew that. Would hurt the one person whose feelings he didn't want to hurt. But he could not let this beautiful, intelligent, idealistic girl waste one more moment of her precious life believing she was in love with him, and while ever she remained at Tregarrick, then her infatuation—for he believed it was just that—would deepen.

Now was the time for her to expand her horizons and put what Izzy had taught her to some use—but not immediately... Not until he was certain she was not carrying his child.

Lowena awoke and stretched with a pleasant feeling of well-being and contentment. Marcus was gone. Only the familiar scent of his body lingered on the sheets, drugging her senses.

Blinking the lingering slumber from her eyes,

she felt a host of conflicting emotions roil within her. There was a lingering sultriness in her eyes, a deep flush of colour across her cheeks, a full pulsating softness on her lips, and the blood was still hot in her veins as she relived the moments she had spent in Marcus's arms.

She flushed hotly, remembering precisely what had occurred in her bed. But she was unable to summon an appropriate sense of shock when she realised that she was still naked beneath the covers.

It seemed impossible to her now that not only had she allowed Marcus to make love to her but had practically encouraged him to do so. She had thrown away her virtue without a thought. Stretching out her young body, she ran her hands over her smooth white flesh, feeling her nipples spring to life as she recalled the unbelievable responses of her virgin body—responses Edward Carberry could never arouse.

When she had returned from the cove she'd had no idea that the night would hold such unexpected pleasures. Marcus had known full well what he was doing to her, and that he was capable of annihilating her will, her mind and her soul, and that she would hunger for that same devastating ecstasy. He had made her feel sensual and beautiful and full of life.

But she would not allow herself to become caught up in a romantic dream. Even at the height of their lovemaking he had told her he had nothing to offer her. She already knew that. Marriage between them would be unacceptable.

So what to do?

Lowena was going about her duties with a lightness to her step. Marcus had clearly risen early again and gone to Wheal Rozen, which had taken up most of his time for the past week—a week during which Lowena had not seen him again.

She was passing the drawing room, where Lady Alice was writing letters at her desk. She paused on hearing a masculine voice. It was Marcus, having just returned from the mine. As she listened to his voice the mere sound of it made her heart sing. She was about to move on, for she was not one to listen into other people's conversations, but on hearing her name mentioned she paused, her curiosity aroused.

The tragic thing that had caught her attention was Marcus, saying the time had come for Lowena to leave them. She stood there, frozen, trying to take in what she was hearing.

'But why?' asked Lady Alice, sounding not at all pleased with what her son had decided. 'Why must she leave? What explanation can you possibly give?'

Lowena could have no idea how tormented Marcus had been since he had left her bed. He wondered how someone as innocent, as pure and devoid of guile as she, could drive him half-mad with desire. His passion for her was torn asunder by guilt—for taking her to bed when he should have exercised restraint. What had she done to him? What might she do to him if he let her?

In the past, hard logic and cold reason had always conquered his lust—with Lowena it was different. He would have to purge her from his mind before he was completely beaten—and if she continued living in the same house he would lose the battle. He was in danger of losing his heart to her, and he would not permit that. The stakes were too high. He had no choice but to send her away.

'I think she is wasted here,' he replied in response to his mother's question, concealing his inner struggle. 'It is time she left. It would be for her own good.' His voice was determined.

'I don't see that,' Lady Alice protested. 'Lowena is happy helping Dorothy, and I am very fond of her.'

'I know you are, Mother,' he said on a softer note, hating himself for what he was doing—for hurting not only his mother but ultimately Lowena. 'But she is intelligent. She deserves better than to be a lady's maid.

'I absolutely agree with you, but what kind of employment are you thinking of?'

'A governess. She is well taught.'

'She is extremely intelligent, I grant you—which is all down to Izzy's teaching. Although I don't know how she will react to finding herself in unfamiliar surroundings. That does concern me. It's no easy thing for a woman to acquire the necessary training to lift her station in life.'

'Perhaps *you* could raise the matter with her and help her to overcome any issues she might have on being employed in an establishment where she can realise her potential.'

As Lowena listened to Marcus's voice, quiet and persuasive, she knew Lady Alice would be swayed by his suggestion and agree.

'I will talk to her,' Lady Alice said, confirming Lowena's thoughts, 'although she may not want to leave. Have you not considered that? She trusts you implicitly.'

'I realise that, and in return I am about to abuse that trust by sending her away.'

There was something in his mother's face—a speculative, thoughtful expression Marcus did not attempt to interpret. Feeling satisfied that all the important considerations had been resolved, he began to relax and to divert his thoughts away from Lowena.

But why did what he was doing leave him feeling so wretched?

It was such a dreadful thing for Lowena to hear him say that her heart was in shreds. Her head spun and for a moment she thought she was going to faint. She stepped back in an instinctive search for support, groping behind her until her hand met the warm, comforting wood of the hall table.

Marcus wanted her to go. He wanted rid of her. Tears of hurt and humiliation burned the backs of her eyes. She felt as if she was dying by inches.

The memory of how she had offered herself to him, only for him to take that offering and use it to his satisfaction, and then reject her, and compound that rejection by telling her she must leave, made her want to crawl away and hide somewhere dark until she had ceased to be—so she could no longer feel the hurt, the agony and the shame of having been so stupid, so unlovable—so childish.

But could she blame him? After all, she had already known that he wouldn't marry her.

Nevertheless, life at that moment seemed impossibly cruel.

Suddenly the door to the drawing room opened and Marcus emerged, closing it behind him. At once his gaze settled on her pale and graceful figure. Her beauty caught him like an unexpected blow to the chest. He knew immediately that she must have overheard his discussion with his mother. There was a stricken look on her face, and her eyes were wide, hurt and staring accusingly.

Her world was tilting crazily—there was no room in Lowena's sights for anything except Marcus. She beheld the faint widening of his eyes as he looked at her, but otherwise his expression was as inscrutable as a marble mask. She found it difficult to endure his gaze, but she did, the conversation she had overheard sounding inside her head like a death knell.

'You heard?' he said, the words simply stated.

It was plain to Lowena that he was unprepared to refute it, which was no consolation. Why did he adopt this remote attitude towards her? Was it possible he was ashamed of the way he had behaved towards her? Or was his desire for her so great that he could not bear to be close to her? She hoped it was the latter, but the way he was looking at her made her discount it.

She met his eyes proudly. 'Either I am mad, sir, or you are, if you think you can dispose of my life at will. How dare you discuss my future in that way—as if you were discussing a common business arrangement—without any feeling or emotion?'

'Because that's the way I am, and that's the way it is. I'm sorry, Lowena. I would rather you hadn't overheard. I wanted to tell you myself.'

'Why? What difference would it make? You're sending me away, aren't you?'

Marcus's jaw tightened and, turning from her slightly, he nodded his head. 'Yes.'

Lowena heard the absolute finality in the word, telling her that it would be futile to argue. Looking at him now, she was struck by his stern profile, outlined against the golden glow of the sun slanting through the windows. She saw a kind of beauty in that face, but as quickly dismissed the thought. It was out of keeping with what was taking place.

Displaying a calm she did not feel, she took a step towards him, managing with a painful effort to dominate her disappointment and accept the slap fate had dealt her. She must blot from her mind the events of that night they had been together...the pleasure, the exquisite sweetness of what they had done.

Jerking her mind from such weakening thoughts, she fixed him with a hard gaze. 'If the chivalrous feelings you say you possess towards me are genuine—the feelings that made you act as you did when you found me that day in the woods—then this is a poor way of showing it. What if I do not wish to leave?'

He shook his head slowly, and even though his voice was soft it was steady and resolute. He had to be strong if he was to send her away from him, no matter how hard it was for him to do so.

'I think you should, Lowena.'

'Why? Because I embarrass you and you want rid of me?'

'No—never that. I admit that by taking you to bed I behaved in a manner for which I am ashamed and regretful. It is difficult to explain. For many reasons it would have been better if our tryst had never happened, because you are forcing me to recognise and reflect on things I have kept locked away in my mind for a long time— things I would prefer not to analyse just now. I want nothing more than to know you are safe.'

Suddenly he looked at her with unexpected softness.

'You have to go, Lowena. You must. I want you to go. There are some things you cannot understand. You told me you want to better yourself—'

'Yes, I do. But I do not belong to your privileged class—I will never be a fine lady who can sit all day embroidering samples, waiting for her lord and master to come home.'

'Maybe not, but you said you want to make something of your life and to put into practice everything that Izzy taught you. Well, this is your chance. I desire only your peace and happiness. Do not forget that. We have no intention of simply turning you out this instant. There is no immediate hurry. We will help you find employment—the *right* employment.'

'If it's because I told you that I l—?'

Moving quickly towards her, he covered her lips with his fingertips, silencing the words she was about to utter. 'Don't,' he said fiercely. 'Don't say it. And please don't tell me you expect me to marry you because of what happened. If that is what you think then you have misled yourself. Tell me you aren't that naïve.'

Flinching from the sting of his words, Lowena looked at his hard, handsome face, at the cynicism she hadn't recognised in his eyes before.

'Or that stupid,' she retorted sharply.

The injustice of his words increased her anger. But it was the way he retained his arrogant superiority that was hardest for her to take.

'I certainly did not expect an offer of marriage from you, but do you mind telling me why you are dismissing me as though I were an untouchable?'

'Now you are being ridiculous,' he said.

'*Am* I?' She stepped back.

Her cheeks burned with disillusionment, with the after-burn of confrontation. She had perceived a closeness where none existed. May God forgive her, but in the dark corners of her mind she had begun to imagine he might want to spend more time with her. How foolish she had been to have taken what they had done for greater feeling.

'What I gave to you, I gave from my heart. Can you not remember how it was between us?'

'Of course I remember. And I would be grateful not to be reminded of how I allowed my desire for you to carry me away. I've since had cause to reproach myself.'

Lowena threw back her head, her eyes meeting his proudly; a raw flame of anger springing to life in their depths. 'Why?' she taunted, smiling contemptuously. 'Was it so awful?'

'Damn you, Lowena. You know it wasn't. But it was a mistake—*my* mistake,' he said, his voice strained. 'The moment was one of weakness, for I did not seem to have the strength or the inclination to resist you. Seducing a gently reared virgin—one who happens to be in my family's employ—violates even *my* code of honour where women are concerned.'

'I see. But you are mistaken if you think I expected more of you. I work in your house, but you are not my lord and master. We spent the night together—a pleasurable night. It meant nothing more to me than that. I would like you to understand that not for a moment have I thought of claiming anything more than an acquaintance with you.'

Drawing herself up proudly, she showed him that she too could be hard and cold. He would never know how much he had hurt her.

'I agree with you when you say it was a mistake—that it shouldn't have happened—but I did not offer any resistance. You might say that I encouraged you. I'm afraid that I was unseemingly forward—wanton, even. I should have known better than to reveal my feelings as I did—which, on reflection, I too have reason to regret,' she told him.

It was not the truth. She would go on wanting him until the day she died.

'Are you saying you regret having feelings for me—or for revealing them?'

'Both. I should prefer to forget the whole episode. I hope you will too.'

'I doubt I can forget, Lowena, but we will put it behind us.'

'Thank you. You need not trouble yourself that I will take advantage of what happened between us. I am a servant in your house. Nothing more. Nothing less.'

'Good. I should hate there to be any misunderstanding between us. You are young, inexperienced and naïve, Lowena. You don't know the difference between infatuation and love.'

Stung by a sense of injustice, Lowena glared at him. Her pride and her love were both suffering very badly. She now realised with cold clarity that she must count for very little in Marcus Carberry's eyes. But perhaps his concept of love was different from that of a nineteen-year-old girl.

She looked at him with fresh eyes, allowing her gaze to dwell upon his handsome face, on the mouth whose kisses she had long dreamed about. A pain in the region of her heart told her that her anger and disappointment were not enough to kill the feelings she carried in her heart for him. But now she saw it as some kind of deep-rooted growth, unwholesome and ugly, which she was determined to rip out by the roots, even if her heart was rendered in the process.

'I am not a child. Please don't treat me like one.'

'I'm sorry. I don't mean to. Please don't make this harder for yourself than it is.'

Lowena wondered how it could possibly be

harder, but she bit back that futile protest. She felt devastated, but her wounded pride brought her chin up. 'Why? Because I'll make an even bigger fool of myself?'

'The only foolish thing you are guilty of is caring too much for me,' he said with unexpected gentleness.

Feeling bewildered, ill-used and deeply angry, still fighting back tears, she turned her head away. 'I thought you were different—different from your brother. I was wrong. All things considered, you are cold-hearted and cruel just like him. You make a noble pair. Now. please excuse me. There is nothing else to be said or done and I have work to do.'

Lowena's face was a pale, emotionless mask as she turned from him and crossed to the door. Her heart and mind felt empty, and she was chilled to the bone. Even now, when she was desperate with the thought of leaving him, her head was held high as she left the room.

Marcus watched her go, hating himself for hurting her, for abandoning her as if she were nothing at all. He could not escape the fact that she was a woman as alluring and desirable as any he had ever known. When he had kissed her on the night of the party he had known it might be the prelude to all the delicious imaginings in his mind—imaginings that would compromise his honour and her innocence. Even now, when the consequences of what he had done were so grave, he wanted her again. She had become a passion to him, a lovely, vibrant young woman, and he had wounded her very badly.

He was a soldier and a gentleman—something that had never been hard for him to remember. Over all the years of fulfilling the obligations and duties of his military position, of obeying the strictures of an upbringing of discipline, no matter what his rank, he had known that true gentlemen did not corrupt an innocent young woman—especially not one in his brother's employ. He should have stepped back.

For the first time in years he felt the pain of uncertainty. It was unfortunate that honour had not dictated his actions when he had taken her to bed.

Driven by a need to feel less wretched and alone, Lowena hurried away, her face empty of all expression. A huge desolation spread over her. The very thought of leaving Tregarrick and Marcus devastated her. But no matter how much it hurt she would go, even though in all probability she would never see him again.

She had never thought she could feel such pain. Somehow she found her way to the door and let herself out. She walked away from the house, uncaring of the direction in which her feet took her, her only thought to put as much distance between her and Marcus Carberry as possible. She was shaken momentarily mindless that he could do this to her. It was not just anger and resentment she felt, she realised, but humiliation, shame, hurt pride—and an awareness of her own foolish naivety.

In a cold and cynical manner he had calmly discussed with his mother how to get her off his hands. Her jaw tightened and her resilient spirits stretched themselves as they had done once before, when Izzy had died and she had come to work at Tregarrick.

Straightening her back, with a new determined gleam in her eyes, she lengthened her stride as she tried to put her thoughts into some kind of order. In no way did she resemble the innocent young girl who had plunged headlong with such blind infatuation into the fantasy of calf love. Yes, she felt hurt, and disappointed, and terribly let down, but her overriding feeling was one of intense anger. Marcus had betrayed her—disposed of her in the coldest manner.

Without conscious thought of where she was going, she found herself close to the dairy. Nessa, taking a break from her duties, was sitting outside. The rain had at last stopped falling, and although it was still cold the sun shone and she was happily gossiping with some of the other women she worked with.

On seeing Lowena she got up and came towards her, frowning with concern at her pallor and the troubled look in her eyes.

'What is it, Lowena? Is something amiss?' She scowled as an unpleasant thought occurred to her. 'His lordship hasn't been bothering you again, has he?'

'No, Nessa.' Lowena sighed, looking beyond her to the women gathered outside the dairy, watching them, straining their ears to hear what was said. 'Can I talk to you, Nessa? Do you have time?'

''Course, love. I've nearly finished for today, so let's walk a little way down the lane away from the house. I was going to come and see you before I leave for Saltash anyway. There's something I want to talk to you about.'

Walking beside Nessa, Lowena sighed deeply, unable to still the confusion of the thoughts in her head or calm the emotions that had torn her apart when she had overheard Marcus telling his mother he wanted her to leave. And, to make matters worse, Nessa had only a few days left to work at Tregarrick before she left for Saltash to take care of her aunt.

'I wish you weren't leaving, Nessa. First Izzy and the girls and now you. Everyone I care about is disappearing. I'm going to miss you terribly. It won't be the same without you.'

'I know, love, but now you're working for Lady Alice at the cottage, and to train as her maid— well, things will be different. There's talk of her going to London. She's bound to take you with her.'

'London? I've never been further than St Austell.'

'Look on it as an adventure.'

Lowena sighed. 'I don't think that's going to be possible.'

'No? Why? Has something happened?' Nessa turned and looked at the young woman walking beside her, her head bowed with dejection. 'What is it, Lowena? Something's happened, hasn't it? I am not blind. If it isn't his lordship then what is it?'

'They want me to leave here, Nessa. Captain Carberry and Lady Alice want me to leave Tregarrick for good.'

Nessa was aghast. '*Leave?* What are you talking about?'

Lowena quickly told her of the conversation

she had overheard between Lady Alice and Marcus. Nessa listened, unable to believe Lady Alice would send Lowena away if she didn't wish to leave.

'What am I to do? Izzy always hoped I would find employment as a governess, but I'm beginning to doubt my own capabilities. I suppose some would blame Izzy for putting such grand ideas in my head. The only employment I am good for is to be a servant. The world is divided into masters and servants, Nessa. And I am tired of being a servant. How I wish I could make my own way.'

Nessa looked at her, wrestling with her thoughts and the knowledge she had kept to herself for such a long time—and her new-found knowledge that Lowena's father was alive. All these years she had held the key to Lowena's future. She could withhold it no longer. It was time to tell the truth that she had put off telling for so long—she had made up her mind to do so before leaving Tregarrick.

A look of pain appeared on her face—not physical pain but emotional pain. Taking Lowena's hand, she drew her towards a fallen log at the side of the lane. Seating herself, she patted the wood beside her. 'Come, sit down beside me, Lowena.'

The sat close together. Deep in thought, Nessa bowed her head, wondering how to tell Lowena what she had withheld for so long.

'Nessa, what is it?' Lowena noticed her face was moist. She pulled out a handkerchief and gave it to her. 'Are you unwell?'

Shaking her head dejectedly, Nessa wiped her eyes. 'It's the weight of distant memories that bring tears to my eyes—of long-held secrets. There have been many times when I've considered unburdening myself.'

'Secrets? Unburdening yourself? What do you mean?'

'I have something to say to you—something that should have been said a long time ago. I only hope you can find it in your heart to forgive me when you know what I have done.'

Bewildered, Lowena stared at her, slowly sitting down beside her, facing her. 'Nessa? What is it? Is it so terrible?'

At length, Nessa nodded. 'Yes—yes, it is. But you deserve to know the truth. I have lived with it so long it has almost destroyed me, and I am weary of the conflict that I have never ceased to battle with. It was me who left you in the woods that day—hoping Mr Marcus would stop and take you in.'

Lowena stared at her, incredulous. 'You? But—

Nessa, I don't understand.' Her heart beat rapidly as a thought suddenly occurred to her. 'Are—are you saying that you are my mother?'

'Good Lord, no, Lowena! Not that. But I do know who your mother was—*and* your father.'

Chapter Six

Lowena continued to stare at Nessa in amazement. 'You do?'

'Yes. Your grandfather was Sir Frederick Beresford. He died before you were born, leaving his wife Lady Margaret and his daughter Meredith—who was your mother.'

Lowena was silent as she digested what Nessa had told her. *Meredith!* Her mother's name was Meredith. 'Where is she? What happened to her?'

'Sadly she died, Lowena, shortly after you were born.'

'I see,' Lowena uttered, feeling sadness tug at her heart. 'Where did she live?'

'Devon.'

'And my father? Do you know his name?'

'Sir Robert Wesley. I have only recently discovered that he is still alive—I did not know that at the time you were born. His family have been involved in the mining of silver and lead in Devon for many years. I believe your father had gone to Mexico—where silver is mined—to learn different techniques. While he was there something happened and he became wounded—fatally, I was told.

'My parents weren't married?'

'No.'

'So—I am illegitimate,' Lowena uttered softly. 'And my mother's family—my grandmother?'

'Your grandmother was a hard, unforgiving woman. As a girl she had fallen in love with Sir Robert's father. He rejected her for another and she never forgave him. When your mother fell in love with his son she did everything in her power to keep them apart. Not even when he got her with child would she relent.'

'But—that is terrible. They must have loved each other very much.'

'Where your mother was concerned, nothing else mattered. She seemed to lose all sense of right and wrong where he was concerned. Lady Margaret, feeding off her own bitterness, never ceased telling her that what she was doing was wrong. But no force on earth could have stopped them. Unfortunately your father knew nothing of what Meredith was going through, having left for

Mexico. After you were born your mother lived just three days before she died.'

At this point Nessa paused as the pain of that time became real again.

'What happened, Nessa? Tell me?' Lowena asked, her voice holding a restless urgency to know everything. 'What did my grandmother do?'

'She—she turned me out—you too. I could have refused, I know that, but I would not have left a dog to be looked after by that unfeeling woman. She even talked of sending you to the orphanage.' On seeing the shock this caused Lowena, Nessa nodded. 'Yes, she would have done that—even though you were her own flesh and blood. That woman had no humanity in her soul.'

'How dreadful it must have been for you, Nessa.'

She nodded. 'Yes, I cannot lie. It was. At the time I was too upset to think about what I was going to do. I took you to Castle Creek—your father's home, hoping he would be there—only to be told he had died of his wounds in Mexico.' She shrugged wearily. 'What could I do? I was out of work, with two elderly parents in Cornwall to look after. Without my money they would be turned out of their cottage.'

'So you had a hard decision to make?'

'Yes. But I knew I would not part with you if

I could help it. I wanted to remain close to you, and I had the idea to find a family who, in exchange for my help in the house, might allow me to keep you with me. Before crossing the Tamar into Cornwall I tried to get employment in several parishes, but no family would set me on with a baby to care for. Tregarrick is close to where I was brought up. When I saw Marcus Carberry riding towards the woods in a moment of desperation I set you down, where he couldn't fail to find you. When he stopped and picked you up I saw it as a blessing from God.

'I waited until he rode away before going to my parents' home. I was extremely fond of your mother, and felt duty-bound to look after her child, so when my parents died I sought work at Tregarrick. I was fortunate to be taken on in the laundry. You were settled with Izzy.'

'But—didn't anyone try to find out where I had come from?'

'Yes, but all enquiries proved fruitless.'

'What if they had sent me to the orphanage?'

'In that case I would have divulged your true identity or claimed you as my own. I was determined you would not be taken there. As it was, I found you were being well looked after, and as you grew it was evident to me that you were secure and happy and well loved. Izzy and her girls had formed an attachment to you and could not bear the thought that they might lose you.'

'And my father? How do you know that he is alive?'

'My aunt—who knew of the unpleasant circumstances that forced me to leave Beresford Hall—told me in her last letter that Sir Robert Wesley had been seen in Saltash recently. When he came back from Mexico some years ago I doubt your grandmother would have told him of your existence—not that she would have known where to find you. She would want the past to remain buried. I didn't know what to do, but when Izzy died and you came to work at Tregarrick, and his lordship began showing an interest in you, I started to doubt the sense of keeping the secret. Then, when I discovered your father is not dead after all, I knew I must tell you everything.'

'I wish you'd told me sooner, Nessa.'

'Yes—I know. You had a right to know. But at the time when your grandmother turned us out things were hard for me. I was just a year older than you are now, and was helpless in a situation that was beyond my experience and ability to deal with. I did my best at the time.'

'And I thank you with all my heart. I thought it strange, but never questioned why you always seemed to be there while I was growing up. You helped me—yes, you helped me a lot.'

'Can you forgive me, Lowena, for keeping the truth from you all these years?'

'Yes, I can—even though I wish you had told me, I can understand why you didn't. So—my father is a gentleman?'

'He—is, and your mother was a lady. Now you know, what will you do?'

'I will go to Devon to find my father. What do you know of my grandmother? Is she still alive?'

'I have often wondered, but in truth I don't know.'

'Who am I like, Nessa? Do I resemble my father or my mother?'

Nessa smiled. 'You have inherited your mother's features—and her sweetness. She was a lovely young woman, with a gentle and caring nature, but as I remember you have your father's colouring—his eyes and his hair. But before you go to Devon you will have to tell Lady Alice and Captain Carberry what I have told you.'

Lowena's eyes hardened. 'I will speak to Lady Alice, but no matter what she says I'm leaving, Nessa. My mind is made up. Marcus Carberry doesn't want me here. He—he told me so just now. He wants to find me employment as a governess, or something of that nature, but I prefer to make my own way. I have some money put by, so I should manage until I reach Devon.'

Nessa could see the hurt in Lowena's eyes when she mentioned Captain Carberry. She had always suspected that Lowena carried a torch for him—and who could blame her, handsome as he was? She wondered what he could have said to her to hurt her so.

'So you decision is to go to Devon?'

'Yes. I must. I must see my father—speak to him—even though he will be shocked at having his illegitimate daughter turn up on his doorstep and might reject me.'

'Lowena, I ask you to think very carefully about this. Don't go rushing off. As much as I want you to see your father, I want you to think twice about doing so. Consider what you have now—you live with Lady Alice, who is a good person and is fond of you. Perhaps that is what you should hold on to. If you were to tell her you do not wish to leave, then I am sure she would let you stay. This has been your life for nineteen years. The things you know are sometimes better than the things you don't know.'

Lowena looked at her, struggling with her inner self. Nessa could almost feel her anguish.

'But I *have* to go, Nessa.'

Nessa nodded. Lowena was old enough to

make up her own mind. 'Then write to Sir Robert. How do you think he would react if you were to turn up on and announce you are his daughter? The man might have a seizure on the spot. In a letter you can tell him about yourself and what happened when you were born.'

'I can't wait that long, Nessa.' Suddenly a sharp, determined light entered her eyes. 'I have the answer. I will go with you when you leave for Saltash.'

The idea had appeared fully formed in Lowena's head, the words uttered before she had thought about them.

'But I leave in a few days, Lowena. You cannot just up and leave Tregarrick without telling Lady Alice what you intend. I ask you to consider telling her what you now know about your family.'

Lowena shook her head. 'Until I have seen and spoken to my father I would prefer to keep it to myself—should I wish to return, you understand. I shall speak to Lady Alice and request some time away. Please say you will take me with you, Nessa. We could travel to Saltash together.'

Nessa nodded. It was the least she could do after keeping the truth to herself all these years. 'Yes, all right, but I can't say that I approve of you leaving without being honest with Lady Alice.'

* * *

As Lowena made her way slowly back to the cottage and the reality of this new situation dawned on her she was bewildered and confused by the sudden turn of events in her life. After a lifetime of wondering, at last she knew who she was. She also knew that her mother was dead, which saddened her deeply. Was her grandmother dead also? Lowena was angry with her for treating her mother the way she had.

Now her mind was made up to go to Devon, her attitude had changed dramatically. She knew who she was. She had an identity and—more important than anything else—she had a father. Now, for the first time in her life she had hope for the future…something to aim for.

What she would do if Sir Robert Wesley didn't want anything to do with an illegitimate daughter she didn't want to think about just then.

Lady Alice was both surprised and concerned when Lowena told her she would like to have some time away to accompany Nessa to Saltash, but she raised no objections. Unfortunately the same could not be said of her son. He had asked to speak to her in the library, which he also used as his study.

When she entered he rose from the desk where he was working and moved to the front, leaning his buttocks against the edge, his arms crossed as he stood and watched her enter.

His attention was drawn to her. Her hair was neatly pinned up, and her face all rosy from the heat of the kitchen, but it was tense, which told him she was under great strain. He was anxious to fathom her mood, but when he had known her before as a quick-tempered, provocative and passionate young woman, he now perceived in her an air of quiet seriousness. Perhaps the tribulations of the past few days had stripped the humour from her. She bore no hint of the happy, charming Lowena he remembered of old, or the feisty young woman who had so courageously shunned Edward's amorous assault.

'Close the door, Lowena. I think you know what I want to speak to you about.'

Lowena quietly did as he asked. She was still angry with him for wanting her to leave.

Why had he done this to her? Why had she done it to herself? How could she have allowed such a thing to happen—let herself be swept away on a tidal wave of passion? How could she have succumbed like some green girl to the coercive, compelling force of this man's masculinity? Yes, she had loved him secretly since she was sixteen years old—but why could she not have kept it that way, without humiliating herself and blurting it out like an overheated village girl, exposing her innermost secret to the scrutiny of another?

And then there was what had come after. If only she could undo what had happened in her bed. The memory of it and the pleasure she had experienced flooded through her again. She flushed with embarrassment, realising how forward she must have seemed and how it had ended a friendship she had cherished.

She moved further into the room, her eyes broodingly sad. Gazing up at him, noting his usual careless elegance, she waited for him to speak. Her heart beat madly as her eyes searched his granite features. She saw no sign of the passionate, sensual side to his nature, of the man who had held her and kissed her with such tender passion.

'I've spoken to my mother, Lowena. She has told me you are going away. I was hoping you would stay until we had discussed your future further.'

'But you have told me I have to leave.'

Pushing himself away from the desk, Marcus strode across the deep carpet to stand ominously in front of her. He looked at her hard, scrutinising her face, realising that their earlier conversation had prompted this. But he suspected there was something more that she wasn't telling him.

'Why don't you tell me the real reason why you are going away? I would advise you to think very carefully about doing so until you have somewhere definite and suitable to go.'

Lowena could feel her own ire bubbling up inside her, but she could not seem to find the strength to fight back. How dared he question her actions? How dared he feel that he had the right to do that—to order her about as though she were his to direct, as though he had a perfect right to do so?

She tried to hold in the resentment she felt, to be dignified, but it was very difficult and her expression was hard. 'As I informed Lady Alice, Nessa is leaving for Saltash to take care of an elderly aunt. I have decided to go with her.'

Marcus raised one thick, well-defined eyebrow, watching her. 'Why? Are you not well?'

Drawing herself up straight, and with as much pride as she could muster, she looked at him squarely. 'I am perfectly well. I have worked constantly for months—ever since Izzy died. I would like to go away for a while—to consider my future. When Nessa told me she was going to Saltash I thought it the perfect opportunity.'

Uneasy about being alone with him, she was conscious of a sudden tension and nervousness in her. She was uncomfortably aware of their last encounter, and the scene flashed into her mind with all its searing pain and bitterness.

'Earlier, you told me you want me to go,' she went on, 'to leave Tregarrick. I have given it some thought and I agree with you. I think it would be in my best interests. But I will make my own way—I am my own mistress. For the first time in my life I will take control of my future.'

Despite instigating this whole situation, and being furious with himself for doing so, Marcus wanted to argue, to tell her he *didn't* want her to go, to persuade her to stay. But his mind was made up. Besides, he would see her again when she returned from Saltash.

'I respect that. When will you go?'

'Lady Alice has been very kind to me, and has said I can leave with Nessa. In fact what I would have done without her when Izzy died I cannot imagine. But that does not mean that *you* can take me over. However, I shall be eternally grateful for all you have done for me.'

The strain of hiding the heartache she would feel on leaving took away all the anticipation of going to find her father.

Marcus's eyes had turned warm with concern. She looked tired, and behind that calm exterior he sensed she endured a turmoil of distress. Something was wrong other than what had transpired between them. He could sense it, but he couldn't work out what it could be.

He stood with his hands behind his back, his face carefully blank, while all the time he wanted to reach out and take her in his arms, kiss and soothe her and tell her he was going to make everything all right, that he could not bear to think of her where she was not under his protection. And yet, remembering the deep division that stood between them, how could he?

Lowena's face was pale as she turned from him but, unable to let her just walk away, he reached out and took her arm, spinning her round to face him.

She shook his hand off. 'Please don't touch me. My mind is made up. You've had all you're going to get out of me.'

Turning on her heel, resolutely she crossed to the door. Her heart and mind felt empty, and she was chilled to the marrow—and even now, when she was desperate with the thought of leaving him, she had to ask herself why it should hurt so much, and to question what was in her heart.

When the door had closed Marcus felt his heart move painfully beneath his ribs, aching with some strange emotion in which shame and sorrow were mixed. Of all the women who had passed through his life, not since Isabel had he wanted any of them as he wanted Lowena. What *was* it about her? Her smile? The touch that set his heart beating like a callow youth in love? Her innocence? Her sincerity? And why was he sending her away?

He hadn't expected her to want to leave immediately, and the fact that she was so adamant to go had both surprised and completely thrown him.

He frowned and went to pour himself a drink, throwing it back in one. Whatever was wrong with him, it was not love. He was immune to love. And yet Lowena affected him deeply.

The thought that she was walking out on him was a growing torment. But she had told him she would come back. He would hold on to that.

Lowena packed her possessions into a bag—not forgetting the baby clothes she had been wearing and the blanket she had been wrapped in when Marcus had found her. She left the house quickly. There was no point in delaying a parting that to her was unbearable. Marcus and Lady Alice had no reason to believe she would not return, but Lowena's mind was made up.

One of the grooms drove Lowena and Nessa to St Austell, where they joined the London stagecoach. When Lowena climbed inside, with a thousand emotions warring within her heart, she was holding herself erect, her head held high. Retaining such a posture was the only way she could prevent herself from losing control. Under no circumstances must she allow herself to cry.

Taking the southern route, the coach avoided the bleak and barren landscape of Bodmin Moor. As they left the West Country behind the scenery became greener. Never having travelled further than St Austell, Lowena was transfixed by everything she saw. They spent the night in the coaching inn at Liskeard and the following morning set off for Saltash, after taking on armed guards—for the open land between Liskeard and Saltash was an ideal place for highwaymen.

The journey was long, and rain, shrouded the landscape, making it murky and grey. It did nothing to lift Lowena's spirits. She was trapped in the coach with only strangers and Nessa—and she was soon to be parted from her.

Inside the confines of the coach, as it jolted over the rough roads, Lowena spent the entire journey telling herself she had done the right thing—that she couldn't have remained at Tregarrick any longer. And by the time the coach pulled in at Saltash she had convinced herself. It was better this way. There was no choice. For the sake of her sanity she *had* to break all contact with Marcus Carberry, she decided, even though it would break her heart to do so. It was no good waiting for fate to take a hand. Fate had never been an ally of hers.

Overwhelmed by the significance of the moment, she felt she was standing at a crossroads, with paths stretching out in every direction, each one leading to an uncertain future. Everything that had been before, everything that was yet to come, depended on what she decided to do now.

The closer she got to Devon, the more the sadness that had lurked in her eyes on leaving her beloved Cornwall faded, and was replaced by an eagerness that gave vitality and sparkle to her face. The die was cast. She had made her choice. What remained was a determination to see things through, whatever the consequences.

But images of Marcus Carberry—of his silver-grey eyes filled with passion, the curve of his lips as he kissed her—were so powerful they hurt and brought tears to her eyes. Of course deep down she had known nothing could come of it, and it was a relief now there was some distance between them, but it was no less painful for that. Her pride was battered and her heart was bruised.

Little by little self-consciousness and embarrassment at having revealed herself so openly and so unexpectedly began to give way to regret.

Lowena said a heartfelt farewell to Nessa at Saltash, where she left her, and then the coach crossed the Tamar into Devon. Following Nessa's instructions, and using the transport available between villages, she eventually found herself close to Castle Creek—so named because of the deep cleft in the cliffs on which it stood.

The weatherbeaten coastline and high, rugged cliffs were exposed to all the elements visited upon them from the sea. But, solid and steadfast, the large house with crenelated battlements stood high above the small village. It must be bitterly cold when the winter gales blew, with giant rollers crashing onto the beach, but on this drowsy day of late spring it was a beautiful place to be, with the gentle Devon countryside to the north and the shining emerald and sapphire sea facing south.

Seeing no one as she passed through the tall iron gates and by the gatehouse, she walked up a long drive lined on either side with beautiful lime trees. Her steps slowed as she approached the house. Not having given much thought to how she ought to proceed when she had knocked on the door, she was suddenly reluctant to go further.

Clutching the bag holding her few possessions, she stood and stared at the solid double doors, feeling an odd sense of unreality. Overcome with doubt she stood in an agony of indecision— whether to go forward or to retreat and return to Nessa in Saltash.

She was startled when a voice rang out behind her.

'Can I help you?'

Lowena swung round. A man was walking towards her. There was an air of authority about him. Tall and slender, he was middle-aged, with a good head of hair which was greying at the temples but might once have been the colour of her own. She felt an almost physical shock, for she realised that her eyes bore a startling resemblance to this man's. Despite the lines of age, his was a handsome face, and the eyes that looked at her were friendly.

He looked suspiciously at the young woman coming tentatively towards him. Despite her plain attire, she was very lovely. 'Will you be good enough to tell me who you are and what I can do for you?' he said, his eyes still fixed on her face.

'I would like to see Sir Robert Wesley.'

He was looking at her with the bemused expression of one who had seen a ghost. A thought had occurred to him that was so astonishing, so incredibly devastating, that his heart almost ceased to beat.

'For the love of heaven! Who are you?'

'My name is Lowena Trevanion. I believe you are my father.'

He stared at her as he tried to absorb what she

had said, and then his face seemed to crumple. 'Meredith!' he uttered in a shaky voice. 'Meredith...oh, my God! But—how is that possible? Meredith is dead.'

'Yes, I know. I am sorry. This is all so sudden. I realise it must be a shock for you, but look at me. Look at me more closely.'

He came closer.

'Look at my eyes and my colouring and tell me I bear no resemblance to you. I am your daughter. Meredith Beresford was my mother.'

He fell silent, all doubt as to who stood before him extinguished. He seemed completely overcome. There was something about her...something in her face that bore a strong resemblance to Meredith. How well and how lovingly he remembered her.

Still staring at her, eyes wide with perplexity, he smiled slowly, and an odd tenderness glowed in his eyes.

'Dear me! You must forgive me, but... Well, I am shocked. I did not know. You are so like her. I should not even have had to ask. Except for your colouring—and your eyes...'

'I believe my colouring comes from you,' she said softly, seeing a mistiness in eyes undimmed by age.

'But Lady Beresford—Meredith's mother—

she told me… Oh, my dear Lord. She deliberately kept your birth from me. *She* did this—and said nothing to me. That she could do this I find unbelievable. The woman was more loathsome than I thought. But—please—come inside.'

'Do you live alone?' she asked, wondering if he had a wife.

All the time she had been travelling to Castle Creek one single thought had occupied her mind—to find her father. It had not even crossed her mind that he might have a wife, perhaps other children. She found herself hanging back, unwilling to intrude.

'I have a wife. Her name is Deborah. She is the daughter of Lord Lerwick of the Admiralty. We met when she accompanied her father to Plymouth. At present she is in London—where she spends most of her time. I'm to join her shortly. She doesn't care for Devon or its solitude.'

'Unlike you, I suspect?' Lowena ventured a little shyly.

He smiled. 'Unlike me,' he confirmed. 'Now, come inside. I would very much like to hear what you have to say.'

'I hope you don't mind me coming to see you. This is a sensitive issue. We—we are strangers to each other.'

He chuckled softly. 'We needn't be. It's not

every day a long-lost daughter turns up on my doorstep. I have no intention of turning you away. Come in.'

Lowena let him escort her up a shallow flight of steps and into the house. She was so overwhelmed with the sense of occasion that she hardly noticed the grandeur of the house as he led her into a comfortable sitting room off the large hall.

'Please,' he said, indicating a chair across from his own, 'will you be seated?'

Lowena did as she was bade, sitting stiffly, perching straight-backed on the edge of the chair, and waited until he had settled himself.

'Tell me, Lowena, how long have you known I am your father?'

'I only found out a few days ago. I—I know I should have written before coming here, but— well—all my life I have never known who I am, where I came from, and now...'

'Now you do?'

Lowena nodded. 'Did you really not know about me?' she asked.

He shook his head. 'Had I known I would have tried to find you. You have my word on that. My greatest sadness is that I did not see your mother before she died. I was in Mexico at the time. When I was told about her death I believed it was quite impossible to go on bearing the pain of it and could see no way out. I'd give my life to see her one more time…'

Lowena almost wept at the unmistakable sincerity she heard in his quiet voice and the sadness she saw in his eyes.

'Believe me,' he went on, 'when I say I did not know she was with child when I went away. Had I known I would not have left her. I would have married her despite your grandmother's opposition.' He cleared his throat, then shook his head, for a moment seeming reluctant to speak. 'First I lost my father, and then Meredith. I immersed myself in my work. It was a relief, in a way. I had to get on with it—leaving myself no opportunity to dwell on my troubles.'

When he fell silent Lowena asked the question that was hovering like a spectre in the darkness of her mind. 'Is she still alive—my grandmother?'

He shook his head. 'No. She's been dead these last ten years.'

'I see. How did she die? Was she ill?'

'Not that I know of. Beresford Hall was devastated when a fire broke out. Your grandmother perished in the flames. I'm sorry. Would you have liked to meet her?'

Lowena looked down at her hands and shook her head. 'No, I don't think so. Even though she is dead, her treatment of my mother—and me—I find hard to forgive.'

'I can understand that. I felt the same. Time helps—and now there is you. Tell me how you found out. Who told you?'

'Nessa Borlase—she was my mother's maid. She was with her when I was born—and when she died.'

He nodded. 'I remember Nessa. Why did she not tell you before now? What reason had she for such secrecy?'

'She was very young and protective of me. She brought me here when my grandmother turned us out. She was told you had died in Mexico. Her parents lived in Cornwall, so she took me there.'

Lowena quietly told him everything Nessa had told her of how she had taken her to Tregarrick, omitting nothing. 'The only things I possessed of my family were the clothes I was wearing and the blanket I was wrapped in, embroidered with the letter B.'

He nodded. 'For Beresford. Were you happy?' Robert asked when she fell silent.

'Yes, I was. Izzy Trevanion took me in and raised me as if I were her own child and her daughters were my sisters. I loved them dearly. Izzy and her husband were good, hard-working people. No matter what else they were, their home was a happy place to be. There was no shortage of good food and love. Before Izzy married she was a governess. She taught me well.'

The door opened and a maid appeared, bearing a tray of refreshments. She placed it on a table between them.

'Thank you,' Lowena said with a self-conscious smile directed at the maid. With a slight bob she returned her smile and withdrew.

'Will you be so kind as to pour the tea?' Robert asked.

'Of course.'

There was silence as Lowena went through the familiar ritual of pouring the tea, all the while aware of her father's eyes watching her every move.

She was unaware, as she handed him a cup of the steaming beverage, of how his heart swelled with pride at this lovely young woman whom he sincerely hoped would remain in his life, and with a great bitterness and anger directed at the woman who had condemned them both to this life—Lowena's grandmother.

Settling back in her chair, Lowena smiled widely and dimples appeared in her cheeks.

Robert was transported back in time twenty years. She looked so like Meredith when she smiled. Sipping his tea, after a moment's thought, he said, 'I deeply regret not having known you,

Lowena. I find it hard to believe that while I was mourning your mother I had a lovely daughter growing up beyond the Tamar. Now you are here I want you to stay. When I go to London, should you wish to, you could come with me. In the meantime you can get to know what would have been your home—where I grew up and where I would have brought your mother as a bride. It's a lovely old house. It was a happy house once. It could be again.

With a multitude of emotions roiling inside her heart and mind, Lowena could see how he had suffered the loss of her mother. But his love had remained constant. It had endured despite her death and his marriage to another woman. She could see how he grieved for her still. His face spoke of deep loss and regret. '

'What was your reason for going to Mexico?'

'My interest in mining silver. Mexico has emerged as the world's chief producer of silver and it is expanding—although, like everywhere, mining techniques are precarious, be it mining for silver, copper or coal. I went to see and to learn, with intentions of investing.'

'I see. It sounds extremely interesting. The mining in Cornwall is mainly tin and copper.'

He smiled. 'Yes, I know. I would like to show you the mine here at Castle Creek—if you are interested?'

'I would like that. What happened to you in Mexico? How did you come to be wounded?'

'The party I was travelling with was set upon by thieves. We were badly beaten—two of our party fatally. I was wounded—it was thought I would not survive. But after many weeks I was fit enough to travel and took ship for home.'

'I am *so* glad you didn't die.'

He chuckled. 'So am I.'

'Tell me more,' Lowena said shyly, eager to know more about the father she had yearned to hear of for so long.

'Not only does the mine keep me busy, I am also a magistrate, and I spend some of my time working for the community—which is something my estate manager assists me in by organising my diary of responsibilities. When I go to London to visit my wife he will take charge of everything.'

Listening to him, Lowena realised how much there was to know. She realised that, even though her parentage had now been established, being an illegitimate child gave her no legal rights to anything her father owned. Not that she wanted anything from him—and she wanted him to understand that.

'Please believe me when I say that I have not come here to claim anything. I am not interested

in anything you might have. It's all meaningless
to me, and in all truth since I discovered who I am
I have never given it any thought. I have managed
very well on my own for a long time.'

'You work for a living?'

'I do.'

'Then I am grateful that you could take time
off to come here—to see me.'

'How could I not? I wanted to see you. And
I—I am between positions just now. It is my intention to find a position as a governess if someone will take me on.'

'You were employed by Lord Carberry. Why
did you leave?'

Lowena felt her cheeks burn at memories of
Edward Carberry's assaults and she lowered her
eyes. 'I was left with no choice.'

'Do you mind if I ask why?

'He—he was a difficult man to work for. Are
you acquainted with him?'

'No, but I know of him. I know his stepmother—
Lady Alice Carberry—through a friend of hers.
She was in Devon recently—a pleasant, likeable
lady. Speaks her mind, which is something I like.'

'Yes, she does.'

'And what was her reaction when you told her
you had found out about your past?'

He frowned when she lowered her eyes and

chewed on her bottom lip, her expression apprehensive.

'You *did* tell her, didn't you, Lowena?'

'No,' she said quietly. 'I—I had reason not to. I wanted to wait until I had been here to see you. I will write to her.'

'Yes, I think you should. And when you have done so will you abandon your intention to seek a place as a governess and stay here with me?'

'You—you seem to forget that I am illegitimate,' she said quietly.

'You are still my daughter.'

'You could say that I am your ward—perhaps the daughter of friends who are deceased and you have taken me in.'

'There will be no pretence, Lowena. You are my daughter—flesh of my flesh. If you stay, all that I have is yours—freely given. Come, what do you say?'

'Yes,' she replied with a little smile. 'I would like to stay. But will there not be gossip?'

'I care nothing for such things.'

'How will you explain my presence in your house?'

'By telling the truth, if anyone asks. You are my daughter and I shall be proud to introduce you as such.'

'And your wife?'

He frowned, becoming thoughtful. 'I have a great deal of admiration and affection for Deborah.' He smiled across at Lowena. 'She leads a life with no social restraint, whereas I like normality and order in my life. She will soon get used to the idea of having a stepdaughter. Indeed, I think the two of you will get on. She will enjoy showing you London and introducing you to our friends. Sadly we have not been blessed with children. And if you are worried about being thrown into society then don't be. When Deborah has become used to having you in our lives she will teach you all you need to know. I promise you. I will write to her and explain the situation.'

There was silence between them as their eyes locked together. The pain caused by the years they had had stolen from them was diminishing slowly, for now they had found one another and the joy of it was taking away the pain.

'I would like it to be a permanent arrangement, Lowena. I ask you not to dwell too much on the past and what might have been. You are safe, and that's all that matters. Whatever you decide to do, I know a young lady needs much in the way of clothes and other fashionable things. I will ask Eliza—my housekeeper—to arrange for a dressmaker to call and fit you out with all the finery necessary.'

Lowena gasped. 'That is most generous, but I don't—'

He raised a hand, silencing her. 'Please, my dear, indulge me. I can only hope that once you have considered the circumstances of your situation you will not let your pride prevent you from having the security my position can provide. There is no hurry for us to leave for London. We will travel overland, which will take several days. In the meantime we will have plenty of time to get to know one another. You know, I can't tell you how much you are going to change my life.'

'For the better, I hope?'

'I felt my life was over when I returned from Mexico, but you have given me hope.'

Chapter Seven

While Lowena was finding it hard to believe all that had happened to bring about such a change to her life, immersing herself in adjusting to her new home and getting to know her father, at Tregarrick Marcus went about his usual business at the mine.

When three weeks had passed and there had been no news of Lowena, his concern for her welfare—and the fact that he was missing her more than he would have thought possible—began to overshadow everything else. The thought that he had driven her away by suggesting she should leave still haunted him, and the fear that she had now disappeared completely from his life was replaced by a deeper, darker feeling of uncertainty.

It was a new emotion to him.

Before he had made love to her he had always believed that she could never belong to him, and had accepted the fact as permanent, but that night she had cast a lethal spell over his life that could never be broken.

He lived from day to day in a silent, barely controlled private rage at himself. He had to drag his thoughts from the tormenting memory of their last bitter encounter—he preferred the more refined torture of thinking about the joy of her. He thought of the way she had melted against him and kissed him with innocent passion, how warm she had felt in his arms, wonderful and loving.

How would she cope alone? For, knowing her determination to find suitable employment, he doubted she would remain with Nessa. She was proud and stubborn, and the very thought that he would never see her again was eating away at him with every minute that passed without word from her.

He was at his desk, going over the accounts for the mine and poring over a column of figures, when his mother entered.

'I have received a short letter from Lowena,' she said, coming straight to the point.

Marcus was unprepared for the sudden relief that washed over him. *At last,* he thought. Throwing down his quill, he leaned back in his chair. 'What has she to say?'

'Very little, as it happens,' she replied, anxiously studying the deeply etched lines of strain and fatigue at his eyes and mouth, and strongly suspecting it was Lowena's absence that troubled him rather than trouble at the mine.

Holding up the letter, she read the contents. 'She writes, *"I have moved on with my life. Please do not be concerned about me. I am well and in a good situation. I thank you for all the support you have given me throughout my life. I shall be grateful for ever. Please do not try to find me."'*

Marcus stared at her in disbelief. 'Is that it? Does she not say where she is—where she is working?'

'No—nothing. I don't think she wants us to know where she is.'

'So it would appear,' he said, trying to suppress his irritation that Lowena was being so difficult. He still felt responsible for her—why couldn't she understand that? Why couldn't she understand his position?

'I am deeply concerned about her,' Lady Alice said. 'I really did think she would return. It seems I was wrong. If only you hadn't told her she must leave... I feel she would still be here.'

'Lowena left of her own accord,' Marcus stated, even while admitting that his mother's words held the ring of truth.

'She was put in such an impossible position by you that she must have felt compelled to go.'

Marcus pushed back his chair and, standing up, stalked to the window, where he stood looking out, seeing nothing. 'Don't concern yourself unduly, Mother. Lowena is a clever, sensible young woman. I am confident that she will find a situation that suits her—if she hasn't already done so'

Lady Alice went to his side and looked at his stern profile. Her eyes worriedly scanned his drawn face. 'My instinct tells me there is more to this than you want me to know about—and my instinct is never wrong. Did something happen between you and Lowena? I know how fond of her you have always been. It cannot have been easy for you, having Lowena—young, attractive and desirable—living beneath your roof.'

'It wasn't,' he admitted tightly. 'Which was why I decided that she should leave.'

Lady Alice looked at him with a new understanding. She hadn't wanted Lowena to leave, and knew she should have spoken her mind sooner, but she had been reluctant to interfere in something Marcus clearly felt so strongly about.

'I see. So I think what I am now seeing goes deeper than mere fondness. Lowena is proud, and a young woman of principles—very special. She has a right to be treated with respect, without the master of the house—both masters, as it happens—pursuing her,' she said with gentle re-proach.

'I am not guilty of pursuing her. I merely want to know that she is safe.'

On a sigh, Lady Alice placed her hand on his arm, wishing she could ease his suffering and magic Lowena back to Tregarrick. 'Of course you do. I understand that. I know Isabel hurt you very badly, and I suspect that because of what happened with her you are fighting your feelings for Lowena. You want her, and you care for her, and you hate yourself for that weakness. But if you wanted her to despise you, then you have gone the right way about it by asking her to leave.'

Marcus's features tightened and he looked at his mother sharply. 'The way you speak, Mother, anyone would think you wanted me to *marry* the girl.'

She smiled. 'And why not? Would that be so terrible? Isabel is in the past. Yes, she humiliated you when she left you for Edward, and wounded your male pride, but it happened and she is dead. Nothing can change what happened. You can't go on dwelling over former grievances. In my opinion, Lowena is nothing like Isabel. Oh, I know she is poor and un-dowered, but she would make any man an excellent wife. You,' she stated, 'since I can see that you care for her very much.'

Marcus scowled darkly at her. 'You see too much,' he retorted.

'Yes—well, there is nothing wrong with my eyesight. I agree we know nothing about her background, but that is not her fault. Besides, does it really matter? I have every confidence that Lowena would make you a good wife. Not only that—if you were to marry her then Edward would not dare touch her.'

'Unfortunately that is not the answer, and I will not wed her for that reason. Edward is determined to cause me harm, and whilst he has not harmed me directly he knows Lowena is special to me. It is only a suspicion, but I fear he might try to get to me by harming her in some way.'

'It is unfortunate that the resentment he feels towards you is long-standing and unlikely to change.'

With this seed of an idea that marriage to Lowena would be worth considering to end this torment her absence from his life was causing, he said, 'Does it not concern you that society would never accept Lowena?'

'I think we are both secure enough in our positions in society not to be bothered by such old-fashioned prejudices. You are not the kind of man to allow convention to dictate what you do.'

'I am not thinking of myself.'

'No?' she said archly. 'Then whom?'

He shot her a look of annoyance and then sighed, his mood softening. 'I would not wish Lowena to become the victim of vicious tongues. Here in Cornwall social prejudices may very well exclude her from respectable activities—imagine how it would be if I were to make her my wife and take her to London. The society papers would rip her to shreds and accuse her of being some kind of gold-digger, an opportunist. I couldn't bear to put her through that.'

Lady Alice's smile was one of immense satisfaction. 'Well, well... Do I hear angels singing at last?' she remarked happily, making herself comfortable in a large winged chair. 'It seems I was right.'

Marcus glanced down at her sharply. 'About what?'

'You are in love with Lowena after all.'

Shoving his hands deep into his pockets, Marcus made no comment. With a brooding look he turned his back on his mother and stared out of the window. Thinking of Lowena.

He saw her as she had stood against him, courageous and lovely, and he saw her as she had looked when he had kissed her, her eyes filled with innocent passion. She was gentle and proud and brave, and with a surge of remorse he recalled how she had driven him almost mad with desire, how he had fought a mental battle against the insidious doubt and confusion that raged within him.

When Isabel had betrayed him he had erected a barrier around himself—and then Lowena had appeared, flinging it back with her unavoidable invasion into his heart.

Tregarrick and this house should have been places of safety—places where she could live and work unmolested by the people within their walls. But the greatest danger to her had been from the masters themselves. Self-disgust for himself and his half-brother almost choked him.

'I admit that I treated her very badly by telling her she must leave. I will have to find a way to remedy that.'

'Marrying her would be the perfect way to redeem yourself. *Will* you marry her?'

'Damn it, Mother,' he uttered hoarsely. 'I have to find her first.'

Castle Creek, the ancestral home of generations of Wesleys, comprised acres of woodland and fertile farmland and the silver and lead mine. The Wesley family had been making a good profit from the mine for decades.

Sir Robert took Lowena to see it working. It

was very much like the mines in Cornwall, where women and young boys worked in the ore sheds and men and older boys worked in the mine. She watched in fascination as men climbed down the perpendicular ladders which extended deep into the earth, their only light coming from candles fixed to their hats with clay.

Over the days that had followed her arrival Lowena had begun to learn about her ancestors and her father as she had never thought to have a chance to do. As a person she found him to be quite exceptional. He was fit, and still a very handsome man, self-disciplined and totally honest and fair in his dealings with others, which made him an ideal magistrate.

She had adjusted herself to the routine of living in this lovely house, and her father had insisted that she learn to ride and that he would teach her himself. This he had done, showing patience and consideration as her lessons progressed.

She rode with a natural style, and such was her enthusiasm she proved to be an excellent horsewoman, showing a confidence and expertise that made her father glow with pride.

Her days were busy, and she knew she still had much to learn. Only when she closed her bedroom door at night did her thoughts turn to Marcus. He haunted her dreams, and with a tightening twinge of pain around her heart she realised how deeply she missed him.

When she had left Tregarrick she had worried that she might be with child, but the arrival of her flux had dispelled her concern.

Remembering their kiss, she would often feel herself softening inside, feel a stirring of pleasure like a ray of sunshine peeping out from behind a dark cloud—and then she would abruptly pull herself together. She had only just begun adjust to her new life, to enjoy all it had to offer, and she didn't want to risk her fragile newfound tranquillity.

But her body could not be ordered to obey, and her mind would not let her be. Her flesh had not stopped wanting this man, longing for him to touch and kiss her. Her mind had not stopped yearning to see him, no matter how strongly she tried to push the memories away.

Already she felt close to her father. He had told her that her presence and her heart-warming smile brightened the atmosphere of the house. Her place now was warm and comfortable and secure, and she lacked nothing materially. She began to love the man. That love was returned. He loved her for herself—for who she was and what she was.

The house was more beautiful and impressive

than any place Lowena could have imagined, and equally grand as Tregarrick. The entrance hall was large, with a wide staircase running up the middle, and the floor was marble. The walls were hung with oil paintings of family members past, and beautiful white marble figures occupied arched alcoves.

Lowena began to understand what it would have been like living and being brought up in such a house, surrounded by luxury and being waited on by servants. How different her life would have been had her mother not died. Had her grandmother not turned her bitterness on them all...

They were about to leave for London when Lowena had a surprise visitor. It was Nessa. Her aunt had died shortly after Nessa's arrival in Saltash and, having nowhere else to go, she had come in search of Lowena to Castle Creek.

'I didn't know what to do,' said the distraught Nessa, gratefully drinking the tea a concerned Lowena had placed in her hands. 'I didn't want to go back to Tregarrick—not that they would have me, having found someone else to take my place before I left.'

Lowena knew that now her aunt had died Nessa was quite alone in the world. From a distance, Nessa had quietly watched over her all her life. Now it was her turn to take care of Nessa. Lowena felt a deep affection for her, and wanted to help her in any way possible.

'You did right to come to me, Nessa, and I'm so glad that you have. Having you here means I will have a friend from the past.'

'But I must work—in the kitchen or the laundry. I would be grateful to do anything. I'm not one for an idle life. I must have something to do.'

'You are more than a servant to me, Nessa, and it's time you put your feet up a bit. But I will have a word with the housekeeper and see what we can come up with—I know my father will be happy to have you here.'

Nessa glanced at her warily. 'Will he? Surely he cannot feel kindly towards me after what I did.'

Lowena placed her hand gently on her arm. 'He does not blame you. Naturally he wishes you had told me about my past earlier, but he understands why you didn't and that you always had my best interests at heart. He is a lovely man, Nessa. And I am glad you have come now, because we're shortly to leave for London. Would you like to come with us—as my companion or even my chaperone?' She laughed lightly. 'My sudden rise in status makes it necessary, apparently.'

'Oh, no, I couldn't do that. I've come far enough from Cornwall as it is. I would like to stay here if I may—close to the sea.'

Lowena smiled. 'Whatever you like. I want what is best for you. Now, drink your tea and I'll go and have a word with the housekeeper and have a room prepared for you. The important thing is to get you settled in. I want you to be comfortable and to look on this house as your home, Nessa.'

They travelled to London in Sir Robert's impressive coach, drawn by a team of four handsome horses. Coach travel was not exactly comfortable or relaxing. The road was frequented by highwaymen, and to alleviate the dangers of being held up they always stopped for the night at a coaching inn before the light faded and to rest the horses.

Much as Lowena had pleaded with Nessa to accompany her, she would not be persuaded. From the first she had been drawn into the busy life of the Wesley household, and accepted by all those employed there, and undertook any duties presented to her under the expert supervision of the housekeeper, Mrs Eliza Carstairs, who was a kindly soul and had taken to Nessa like a long-lost friend.

The closer they got to London, the more apprehensive Lowena became about meeting Lady Deborah who, secure in her immense wealth and popularity, was very involved in society, attending functions both in and out of the Season.

The Wesleys had their own London residence, in Mayfair. The sky was overcast as the coach got closer to the house, but Lowena devoured the sights and sounds of what some of the girls who worked at Tregarrick had told her was the most exciting city in the world.

On reaching Mayfair, she stared in awe when the door of an impressive house was opened by a servant meticulously garbed in white wig, a dark green coat edged in gold and white breeches. His face was impassive as he stepped aside to let them enter.

'Welcome back, Sir Robert. You are expected. I trust you had a pleasant journey?'

'Yes, thank you, Williams,' Sir Robert said, taking Lowena's arm and leading her inside. 'Is my wife home?'

'She is, sir—in the drawing room. Shall I announce you?'

'No, don't bother. I'll announce myself.' He turned to Lowena. 'I am sure you would like to see your room and freshen up, my dear, but Deborah would never forgive me if I didn't introduce you right away.'

Lowena was completely overwhelmed by the beauty and wealth of the house. Crossing the white marble floor, she looked dazedly about her, wondering if she had not been brought to some royal palace by mistake. She wasn't to know that, compared to many houses in Mayfair, this house was considered to be of moderate proportions. Craning her neck and looking upwards, she was almost dazzled by the huge chandelier suspended from the ceiling, dripping with hundreds of tiny crystal pieces.

Lady Deborah Wesley was a tall and statuesque woman. Her face was striking, with haughty, high cheekbones. Her eyes were dark, her light brown hair a braided coil on her crown, touched with silver. Over the years she had acquired a formidable presence, and her strong, handsome features bore down on any challenge with cool authority.

Draped in a deep blue gown, with a scooped neckline that revealed the swell of her generous bosom, she stood in the centre of the room. After embracing her husband, she turned her attention to Lowena.

Lowena was apprehensive about meeting her stepmother, but she held her composure. She knew that she must have received and read her husband's correspondence regarding the surprise arrival of his illegitimate daughter and would not know what to expect. Lowena wouldn't blame her if she believed she was an opportunist.

She kissed Lowena on the cheek, and Lowena sensed that she was summing her up in the same sort of way that Lowena in turn had summed *her* up.

Lady Deborah gave her a frank look, thinking there was something untamed and quite unique about this lovely young woman. Lowena remained quietly composed beneath the older woman's appraisal, lifting her chin and meeting her gaze directly.

'So, you are Lowena.' She smiled, and when she did so it lit up her face. 'Welcome to London, my dear. I am so glad to meet you at last,' she said, her tone warm with obvious sincerity. 'But what a surprise you have given us! Robert has told me all about you in his letters, so that I feel I know you already. I have been looking forward to welcoming you into the family and to getting to know you.'

'And I look forward to knowing *you*, Lady Deborah,' Lowena replied, speaking quietly. She had expected coldness and stiffness and was relieved to find there was neither—in fact there were no reservations at all in her welcome.

'Come and sit by me,' Deborah said as a young maid entered carrying a tea tray, 'and please call me Deborah. "Lady Deborah" is much too formal, and "Stepmama" would make me feel quite ancient.'

Beginning to relax, Lowena found Deborah not

at all as she had expected. Her tone was warm, and when she smiled it was quite entrancing. In her mid-forties, she was still at the height of her beauty, with a certain style, and it was not difficult to see why her father had married her.

'Robert tells me you have been living at Tregarrick in Cornwall. I am acquainted with Lady Alice Carberry. We have a mutual friend who introduced us when she was in Devon last summer. Her son Marcus is a military man—in America, as I recall.'

'Yes. He is home now. He returned to Tregarrick on the death of his father.'

'And is he to go back to America?' Deborah asked, handing Lowena and her husband their tea.

'No, I do not believe so.'

'And his half-brother? How do you get on with him?'

Lowena stared at her. 'Edward? You know Edward Carberry?'

'Why, yes. It's his practice to come to London once every year, and he always stays a few weeks. He brought his wife on one occasion—Isabel. She was very popular—exquisitely beautiful, elegant and clever—and attractive to other men. Together with her husband, her behaviour was quite scandalous when she was in town.'

'I—I don't know about that. I wasn't working at Tregarrick at that time, but I saw her on occasion. It was a tragedy when she died.'

'A riding accident, wasn't it?'

Lowena nodded. 'They had scarcely been married twelve months. She liked to ride with the hunt and her horse threw her. She died instantly. Lord Carberry was devastated.'

'I'm sure he was—but no one would have believed so when he arrived in London shortly afterwards. He's considered a catch—but it is his brother who used to command the most attention. I recall him being a private, reserved individual, which added to his mystery and charm. He was favoured for his looks, and every hostess in society tried to secure him for her daughter—inviting him to their homes and any other social event when he was in town. But he more often than not declined their invitations. They mourned his absence when he went to America.'

'I believe he is to travel to London shortly with Lady Carberry, to visit his sister Juliet.'

'And he is still unmarried?'

'Yes.'

'Then there will be many a female heart aflutter when he arrives. Robert told me *he* was the one who found you that day when you had been left in the woods?'

'Yes—yes, he was.'

'Deborah, my dear,' Sir Robert said, knowing his wife would keep Lowena talking all day if he didn't interrupt. 'I think Lowena would like to see her room. It has been a long journey and she must be exhausted.'

'Why, of course. I do tend to carry on. Do forgive me, Lowena. I will arrange for my dressmaker to fit you out with a new wardrobe at once. The clothes Robert has you in are adequate, my dear, but hardly fashionable if you are to be introduced into society.'

Alarm bells began ringing in Lowena's head, and she could see the excited gleam of anticipation at future arrangements in the older woman's eyes. She still felt a certain unease in making the transition from servant to lady, without being thrust into society quite so soon.

'Oh—but I— It is not my intention to appear rude. or to give offence, but I had not thought— I have no wish to go into society.'

'But of course you must.' Deborah smiled and her eyes twinkled with mischief. 'I know. Robert has told me you have no wish to socialise—considering your past—but have you not thought to do it anyway? Just for the fun of it?'

Lowena's expression became grave. 'It is a long time since I did anything "for the fun of it". Besides, I am illegitimate, which leaves me outside convention and outside society.'

'Oh, I grant you—you are not like the young ladies of my acquaintance. You're different,' she said, not unkindly. 'I can see that, and I should hate to see you get hurt. You are still young and innocent, and I understand that you do not altogether understand the ways of the world or society as we do. As someone who knows it only too well, I do not intend to let you stray far from my side when you attend events in the future.'

Lowena was strangely touched by Deborah's obvious concern for her well-being, and she smiled. 'I imagine what you are intending is a seriously expensive business, which I understand is undertaken for the sole purpose of procuring a husband.'

'That is so, but—well, whether you are introduced officially into society or not is immaterial,' said Deborah lightly. 'As the daughter of Sir Robert Wesley you cannot hide yourself away indefinitely, so it is imperative that you have a fashionable wardrobe. We have been invited to several low-key events over the next two weeks, which I think would be a good opportunity to introduce you to our friends and acquaintances. Do you dance, Lowena?'

Lowena shook her head, beginning to feel totally inadequate in every way. 'I'm afraid not. I can do the country dances, but nothing sophisticated. I'm afraid I have a lot to learn.'

For a moment Deborah seemed to be lost for words at this candid admission, and she wondered how this lovely girl was adapting to the recent changes that had taken place in her life.

'Then we shall have to do something about it. We will employ a tutor to instruct you on all you need to know. You are intelligent and have been well taught, Robert tells me—which is more than can be said of *some* of the vain young girls who are turned out year after year for the Season, so it will take no time at all. Now, I am sure you will need a rest after your journey—I've arranged for a personal maid for you.'

'I've never had a personal maid before,' Lowena confessed.

An indulgent little smile appeared on Deborah's face. No doubt she had decided her ignorance could be excused.

'Don't worry about it, Lowena. You'll soon get used to the way of things. The girl I have chosen for you is called Martha. She will see to all your personal needs—take care of your clothes, everything, really,' she explained, looking across at her husband, who was seated with his legs stretched out in front of him, watching the meeting between his wife and daughter with a good deal of interest. 'I'll show Lowena to her room, Robert, and then I promise you will have my undivided attention.'

And so Lowena was transported to another world. The house was an Aladdin's cave of sumptuous wealth, beauty and refinement, all paid for with the proceeds of her father's silver mine.

But was this what she wanted? she asked herself. Growing up, she'd spent hours and hours talking with Kenza and Annie, imagining what it would be like to attend the parties and balls that made up the lives of the elite, and the eligible young gentlemen they would meet. And now she had it for real. Her father was her entrée into this new life, into a society she had only ever imagined, into a more exciting life.

True to her word. Deborah arranged Lowena's wardrobe, employing the modiste who enjoyed her own patronage. And there followed hectic days, which passed into weeks, of intensive instruction in perfecting the intricate steps of numerous dances. She learned how to curtsey without wobbling, deportment, and how to utilise her femininity by learning the correct use of the fan—how to hold it, how to close it. Lowena thought it all quite unnecessary, but to humour Deborah went along with it.

She slept in a spacious room beautifully decorated and furnished with only the finest. She had a servant to dress her, to bathe her, and someone to educate her in the proper way to behave in society.

To alleviate the tedium, her father took her on some tours of London. He wanted her to experience and explore the delights of the vibrant and sociable city, with its big squares and monuments. Here were sights and sounds and smells that Lowena had read about in storybooks brought to life. London was a delicious assault on every sense—a living, breathing city that filled her with excitement and curiosity.

She loved the beautiful gardens and parks—in particular Hyde Park, where she would often ride with her father or parade with Deborah in the carriage. The park was a rendezvous for the fashionable and the beautiful, with their splendid shining carriages and high-stepping horses. In her new attire Lowena presented a new distraction, drawing the admiring, curious and hopeful eyes of several dashing young males, displaying their prowess on high-spirited horses.

Under the watchful eye of Sir Robert and his wife Lowena blossomed into an extremely desirable young woman, who was refreshingly unselfconscious of her beauty. The attention she drew when they were out delighted them.

On seeing how dazzled and confused Lowena was by this, Deborah laughed lightly. 'You see how the gentlemen look at you, Lowena? I think it is time to introduce you to some of our friends. Already people are asking questions about you and when they can be introduced.'

Lowena wasn't so sure that she wanted to be paraded before these elegant gentlemen, prancing about on their magnificent horses. Her thoughts on what going out in society would entail and the many difficulties she might encounter made her feel extremely nervous, but she knew she would have to face it some time.

And face it she did.

Lowena embraced London and London embraced her. Heads turned wherever she went and she was creditably besieged by impeccable young men who flocked to her side. Courted and sought after, she was surprised to find herself enjoying herself to such an extent that her life began to resemble an obstacle course—but she allowed none of the pressing young men to come too close...

There was still no word from Lowena, and the horrifying days ran into weeks without her, exposing Marcus to himself in an unforgiving light that he could not ignore. By asking Lowena to

leave Tregarrick he had hurt her very badly—
and himself.

This feeling of loss was so profound it filled
him with a hopeless sense of desolation that made
him feel as though everything was spinning out of
his control. Every day he forced himself to do his
work, trying not to think of her. It was difficult
when the house in which he lived echoed with images of her in every room he entered. There was
no escape from the whisper of memory of her—
from visions of that spectacular, magical, unfor-
gettable night when he had made love to her, from
the smell of her, the taste of her that still lingered
on his tongue.

She was in every part of him, haunting him
like a ghost. What had he done? He would have
killed for her—died for her—and yet he had let
her go. For what?

He didn't know where to begin to undo the
damage he had done—and he couldn't do that
until he had found her. The longer they were apart
the harder any reconciliation with her would be.

Two days before his departure for London with
his mother, he was riding home from the mine and
was concerned to find a squadron of dragoons
had arrived in the area unannounced. They were
camped half a mile inland. Before going to bed
he went to Tregarrick, to see if Edward was aware

of the soldiers' presence and to advise him not to risk any smuggling ventures while they were in the area.

He met Peter Grimes on the drive, one of Edward's trusted men, and asked him if he knew of the dragoons' presence.

Peter nodded gravely. 'They've had word that some locals have been flouting the law and involving themselves in smuggling—landing vessels carrying contraband in the cove. They are here to investigate.'

'Where is my brother?

'He isn't here. He left for Guernsey the day before yesterday. That is where the cargo is waiting. He doesn't normally go himself, but this time there was some negotiating to do with the French. He was certain it would all go well—that all he'd have to do was ship it aboard and bring it in. The wind direction is ideal for the journey. There is also a sea mist, which is in his favour—but it will mean nothing if he runs into an ambush in the cove.'

Marcus stared at the man. He didn't want to consider in detail what Edward risked by sailing into the cove tonight. He preferred the tension inside him to the risk of facing the potentially painful truth that what he had feared for years was about to occur.

'He doesn't know about the dragoons?'

'No. I have been wondering at the best way to warn him.'

'What time is he expected to arrive?'

'He should be coming into the cove some time around midnight. I've sent out word to stop the pack ponies. I can't stop the boat. I've also learnt that a Revenue cutter is in the area. Lord Carberry will be off his guard. He'll bring the boat into the cove and the dragoons will invade the beach at the very last moment.'

'Are the dragoons aware that my brother is involved?'

'No. He's always been careful.'

'And how do they know there is to be a cargo arriving tonight?'

'Someone talked—damn them.'

'Can the beacon be lit to warn him?'

'The soldiers are strung out along the coastal path—they're everywhere. There's no way we can light it without being seen and arrested.'

Marcus did not have the luxury of time to think about the two options and weigh the relative morality of each. He could only act or let Edward face certain arrest and death. Despite everything Edward was guilty of where he was concerned, death was not an option. He was still his brother.

He chose to act.

'Edward will have to be warned. Can we get a boat?'

'In the village. There are enough fishing boats.'

'Will you accompany me?'

Peter nodded. 'We'd better go.'

Marcus realised he must have all his wits about him, and tried to stop himself thinking about anything but the urgency of the task in front of him. But the closer he got to the village the more his anxiety grew,—as did his anger. Images of his brother being arrested, hot—hanged—manifested themselves.

It was an hour off midnight when they reached the village—a twisting collection of alleys. The air was pungent with the odours of fish and kelp. Making their way to the uneven cobbled landing, where lobster baskets and fishing nets were stacked high and fishing boats had been dragged clear of the water, they knocked on a couple of doors and managed to secure a boat from a local fisherman, who was a volunteer for the smugglers and happy to loan them his boat.

It was drawn up just above the waterline. Fortunately the tide had just turned, and it didn't take much effort to push it into the water. Taking an oar each, they pushed it clear of the shore. The night, dark and moonless, favoured them. The sea was calm, with only the slightest swell. Moving the oars rhythmically, they were soon clear of the village.

Not until they were well out to sea did they consider it safe to light their lantern. It was a lantern with a spout attached, which funnelled the light out to sea and was less likely to be seen by people on shore. The cutter would carry no lights, and Marcus knew it would be impossible to see it until it was almost upon them.

As he pulled on the oar Marcus asked himself why he was doing this. But he could come up with nothing more than a host of memories of how, as a boy, he had craved Edward's friendship—and he was his brother. This alone made its own demand that he try and save him. Although he did consider the wisdom of his actions. How he would explain his own presence to the Revenue men, should they be caught, was a difficulty he didn't want to contemplate.

After rowing for a further fifteen minutes they heard a sound ahead of them. It came again—the sound of oars moving in the water. The two men stopped rowing, straining their eyes in the gathering mist. Suddenly the cutter became visible, and the men at the oars. It was a ghostly silhouette against the sky.

'Who is it?' a voice shouted. 'What do you want?'

'There is danger,' Marcus called. 'Is Edward Carberry aboard?'

'Who wants to know?'

'His brother—Marcus Carberry.'

The cutter was ever closer to them now, and Marcus could see a man hanging over the rail. He held the lantern close to his face.

'Dear God!' Marcus heard his brother cry. 'What the hell…?' He gave some orders and then came back to the rail, the better to see Marcus. 'Come alongside and we'll take you aboard. How many of you are there?'

'Just me and Peter Grimes.'

The men on the cutter shipped their oars so the boat could draw up alongside. When they had climbed aboard, and the boat had been secured to the stern of the cutter, Edward scrutinised his brother's face in the dim light.

'What's wrong?' Edward demanded. 'What's happened?'

'You can't go into the cove. Dragoons are waiting for you there.'

Marcus watched the play of emotions on his brother's face.

'So you came to warn me?' he said, walking between the oarsmen to the bow of the boat, where a cabin was located, piled with cargo of every description. 'You mean to say you are prepared to sully your reputation—perhaps your life—to salvage mine? What a turn-out that is. What's it to *you* what happens to me?'

'What should I have done?' Marcus replied irately, standing with his brother in the cabin doorway, where the smell of tobacco and liquor and the fragrance of French perfume mingled with the stench of bilge water. 'Ignored them and let them take you?'

Edward regarded him evenly for a moment, before he offered a cool, mocking smile. 'So you have come to save my skin? How very noble of you.'

'Noble be damned. You are my brother.'

Uttered as a simple declaration of fact, the statement brought a tight smile to Edward's lips. 'This should be your moment of exultation, Marcus—an exultation that has its roots in revenge. Here it is. Retribution after all. Here is justice. If there has to be an accounting, surely this is it.'

Marcus wanted to say that their blood tied them inextricably together, that it was that same blood that had brought him here to warn him. But he did not mention that fact now. He didn't tell him that he had not expected to feel this way— not the desire to rescue Edward nor the need to protect him.

'Only if they catch you,' he said instead.

Edward's face was impassive. Each feature settled as he considered his options—as Marcus had done earlier. And then, for the very first time, he faced the inescapable reality of the dangerous and exciting life style he had chosen, and the fact that the justice system was about to catch up with him. It didn't seem so exciting now—it had not done so for a long time.

'Then there is nothing for it. We'll have to run for it. Put out the lantern. It might be seen. Although they will realise soon enough that we are not running into the trap they've set.'

They had not yet sighted a ship, so when the cannon shot sounded, missing them by a safe distance, Edward and the crew were shocked. Then suddenly there was a shout that seemed to shatter the stillness.

'Heave to! I command you to heave to in the name of His Majesty King George!'

'It has to be the Revenue men,' Marcus provided. 'They've been prowling about all day—no doubt tipped off by the dragoons. Can we outrun them?'

Edward had recovered quickly. 'We'll have a damned good try. The shot came from the east. The cutter's most likely from Saltash—not that it matters. What matters is they'll not know the coast as well as we do. They've clearly heard us, but may not have seen us. Take up your oars, men, and row for your lives. We'll head back out to sea and slip into the mist. Hopefully they won't be able to follow us. With strong oarsmen we'll be quick enough to avoid the Revenue cutter and any other ships that might be out looking for us.'

Marcus felt the boat move forward at a pace that he had never believed possible. For several moments all that could be heard was the rattle of the oar locks and the grunt of the oarsmen.

'If you were to jettison the cargo you'd be faster,' Marcus suggested. 'And then at least if they were to board the boat you could not be arrested for smuggling.'

'What?' Edward barked. 'I'm not that stupid. I've paid a fortune for this cargo. No, I have a better idea. When we've lost them we'll take it further down the coast to Wellan Cove. They won't be expecting us there, and we can store it in the caves until it's safe to be moved. Keep rowing!' he commanded. 'Hard at it!'

It was two hours later that the boat ground onto the soft shingle of Wellan Cove and Edward sprang out. The men worked quickly and quietly to empty the boat of its cargo and store it deep inside one of the many caves there. Not until the last cask had been stored did Edward come to stand beside his brother.

'What now?' Marcus asked.

'We'll wait until first light and then we'll sail the boat back to Tregarrick village—catch some fish on the way. That way nothing can be proved, should anyone in an official capacity be prowling around.' He looked at his brother. 'You'll stay and go back with us?'

Marcus shook his head. 'I'll walk to the nearest village or farm and borrow a horse.' He began to turn. 'Have a care, Edward. You're not out of the woods yet.'

'Marcus?'

He turned back.

'You risked a great deal coming to warn us. Thank you—on behalf of all of us. You didn't have to.'

'Yes, I did.'

'I am not your responsibility.'

'It has nothing to do with responsibility. Why do you *do* it, Edward? You are a wealthy, powerful man. What more do you want?'

At any other time Marcus would have stepped back, with no lowering of his defences, for any attempt to reach Edward in simple brotherly friendship had always condemned him to failure. But this time he didn't step back. His eyes were compelling as he looked directly into his brother's.

The effect was disconcerting. Maybe it had

something to do with what Marcus had risked for him tonight, or something else, but whatever it was it drew confidence—demanded truth from Edward when he wanted to avoid giving it. He had to speak.

'The spirit of adventure...the excitement.' He smiled cynically. 'Of late the pleasure smuggling has always held for me has been beginning to wane—no doubt you will be relieved to hear that. I've been sailing too close to the wind for a long time—especially tonight.'

Marcus nodded, digesting Edward's words. 'You're right. I am relieved to hear that. I hope you can find something more worthwhile to do with your time.'

Edward watched him go. Marcus's words had sounded with a ring of finality—the end of any possibility to put things right between them. His mind reached back over the years and he tried to remember the boy who had come home from school, eager for his older brother's friendship. But Marcus was that boy no longer. There was no way to go back. No way to make amends.

When he was a boy himself, it had been Edward's father's marriage to Marcus's mother that Edward hadn't been able to face. He had seen it as a betrayal of his own mother's memory. It hadn't mattered to him that his stepmother and his father had loved each other. He hadn't understood it. It just hadn't seemed possible to him, and he hadn't been able to abide his own ignorance. How *could* his father love another woman?

From the moment his mother had died he had forced himself to be brave—striving for indifference, making a show of the fact that at five years old he could stand the trauma, the devastation of loss that he barely understood. And so he had given himself over to hurting others. And in doing so he had achieved a revenge that in the beginning and over the years that had ensued was satisfying.

But now he saw the true attainment of such a twisted victory. The vengeance he had wrought upon Marcus for merely being the son of the woman who had intruded into his life, stealing the affections of his father which he had craved to be directed at him alone, had merely turned on *him*, wounding *himself.*

It was as if he were finally seeing how irreparable was the damage he had done to his relationship with his brother over the years.

He could not go back. That was impossible. But he would try to go on—to make some kind of restitution.

Chapter Eight

It was early afternoon. Marcus had arrived in London the previous day with his mother and now, arm in arm with his sister Juliet, he strolled along the paths of Hyde Park, which was a hive of colour and activity. A slight breeze skimmed his face. The fine spring weather had beckoned people from all walks of life. They came to enjoy themselves—some to walk and others to ride, Marcus to enjoy the company of his sister.

His attention was caught by a gentleman and a lady riding side by side. They had slowed their horses to a walk. They were some distance away, and he was unable to see their features, but they were clearly relaxed in each other's company and conversing happily. The two looked close, and the lady was laughing delightedly at something the gentleman had said.

Riding a spirited mare, the lady—for that was what she looked like…a lady—was fashionably and expensively attired, looking extremely fetching in a dark green riding dress, a short jacket trimmed with gold braid, and a matching hat cocked at an impudent angle atop bunches of delectable red and gold curls that bounced delightfully when she moved her head.

The lady sat her horse like a goddess...

Lowena couldn't say what it was that made her turn her head—perhaps the prickling sensation she suddenly felt on the back of her neck—but turn she did, and with a shock that tightened itself about her heart looked across the distance that separated her from Marcus Carberry.

She felt her heart slam into her ribs. She froze for an instant, her thoughts scattered. She was like a senseless inanimate object, mindless, and she thought she might remain that way for ever, with people milling all around them. Although there was noise and laughter, and the conversation of people who had come to the park to absorb the atmosphere and socialise, there was stillness and silence about them.

She could feel Marcus's presence with every fibre of her being and—despite the shock of seeing him again after so long—an increasingly comforting warmth suffused her. Her eyes were riveted on his beloved face, loving every line of his form. An ache touched her heart, because everything about him was so achingly, wonderfully familiar. Her whole soul reached out to him through her eyes.

A strange sensation of security at knowing he was close at hand pleased her. But the memory of their parting, of the pain and the hurt he had caused her when he had told her she had to leave Tregarrick, was still present. She had not forgotten their night together, nor anything else about him. Memories of him were etched in her brain like engravings on a stone...memories of how he had held her and kissed her and made love to her.

Sweet Lord in heaven, she knew she had committed a sin when she had let him take her virginity, but she loved him—hopelessly, enduringly and compulsively.

Across the distance that separated them she saw him standing with a woman she recognised as his sister Juliet. He looked even more powerfully masculine and attractive than she remembered. His commanding presence was awesome, drawing the eye of everyone in the park. A group of people had moved to speak to him, but his eyes continued to follow her as she urged her horse on.

Unaware of what his daughter was thinking, and of the man who had held her attention for a moment, her father fell in beside her. Turning her head once more, she saw that Marcus was still looking at her—but he might not have recognised her, dressed in her finery and riding a splendid horse and in the company of a gentleman.

Marcus watched the man reach across to her and gently touch her cheek in an intimate gesture. That was the moment he realised that he was looking at a familiar figure, and his heart took a savage and painful leap at the sight of her.

In a moment of unconscious spontaneity he stepped forward, wanting reassurance that she was not an apparition, but the two riders disappeared as the crowd closed round them.

Juliet moved to stand beside her brother. 'Marcus—who was that? Do you know them?'

'I thought the lady looked familiar, that is all,' he answered, his gaze fastened to the place where she had disappeared, hoping she would come back into view. But she was gone.

He must have been mistaken. It could not have been Lowena. It was not possible. But, as much as he told himself that, part of him still wanted to believe it. Relief at seeing her again—safe and looking well—washed over him like a tidal wave. But if it *had* been Lowena, then who was the man— and what did she mean to him?

Could she…? Had she…? *No*, screamed a voice

inside his head. The thought of Lowena—that beautiful girl—and that man being lovers was not to be borne. These images and visions of the two of them together were without sequence or logic. What he was thinking made no sense.

The brief softening emotion he had felt a moment before had vanished. In its place was something steel-hard. A hot crimson rage and a sickening jealousy such as he had never known boiled inside him like fiery acid at the thought of another man touching her.

He'd spent the last few weeks searching for her—even seeking out Nessa in Saltash to throw some light on her whereabouts—only to find Nessa had also disappeared. He had been a damned fool.

Seething inwardly, he damned her conniving little heart.

Between her sighting of Marcus in the park and Lady Wychwood's social event later that day—the largest society event she had attended so far—Lowena was existing in a state of great anxiety. The excitement of the social whirl into which she had been thrust, and which she had initially enjoyed, was waning, and she was beginning to find it all rather tedious. She longed for the fresh country air of the West Country and the smell and the sound of the sea.

Casting a critical eye at her reflection in the long mirror, she accepted the fan and reticule her maid gave her and, picking up her skirts, went in search of her father.

The stunned admiration on his face when he saw her coming down the stairs bolstered Lowena's faltering confidence.

'You look absolutely breathtaking—and very elegant. This is a proud moment for me: escorting my beautiful daughter to a social event at the prestigious Lady Wychwood's house. And my wife, of course,' he was quick to add, when his smiling wife, resplendent in a gown of saffron silk, appeared at the top of the stairs.

The streets around Lady Wychwood's elegant house overlooking Green Park were filled with the rattle of carriages and the jingle of harness, accompanied by the voices of coachmen and lackeys.

Climbing the steps to the house, sandwiched between her father and Deborah, Lowena knew she looked her best. Her dress suited her to perfection—although she had acknowledged some doubts about the deep décolletage which, in her opinion, was cut far too low. But Deborah had assured her that it was simply perfect, for it displayed to advantage the full, rich curves of her breasts and shoulders.

With a warm, searching smile, her father offered her his arm. 'Are you ready?'

She nodded, and laid her gloved hand on his arm.

A liveried footman stepped aside as Sir Robert Wesley and his wife and daughter swept into the marble-floored hall. Lowena concentrated on keeping her mind perfectly blank. On entering the large salon, which was filled to capacity, a festive air prevailing, they paused, and Lowena's eyes swept the large number of assembled guests dressed in their finery. Her nervousness was superseded by a blissful sense of unreality. She was met by a wave of light and heat and the smell of perfume and powdered wigs.

It wasn't a ball, as such, it was an informal affair. But there was music and dancing in the ballroom if one wished for it. The buzz of conversation was punctuated by the fluttering of fans and the swishing of silk gowns. She had never seen so many fashionable people gathered together all glittering with jewels.

Exuding luxury and fashionable elegance, the walls were hung with ivory silk, delicately worked with a gold and green design, and the colours were reflected in the upholstery and in the heavy curtains hung at the French windows, which opened onto a terrace and the flower-filled gardens. The windows were open wide, to catch the coolness of the evening and to allow guests to wander outside, and for those guests who sought other entertainment two adjoining rooms had been set aside for gaming.

Lady Wychwood, a striking middle-aged widow, was flitting among her guests. Like a queen, she reigned supreme, bedecked in sparkling jewels and with her richly coloured silk skirts spread about her.

Helping themselves to glasses of champagne from a silver tray, the three of them stood and surveyed the glittering company.

'It's rather splendid, isn't it?' Deborah commented, smiling across the room at a lady she was acquainted with.

'As usual,' her husband replied, 'it's what you expect at Lady Wychwood's affairs.' He glanced at his daughter, feeling immensely proud of her and her composure. He knew how difficult it must be for her, this first proper outing into society. 'How are you bearing up, Lowena?' he asked softly, his eyes twinkling down at her.

Lowena smiled, beginning to relax. 'Relieved that you are with me—but I'd like to go out onto the terrace and take a look at the garden before it's too dark to see anything. Would you mind if I slipped away for a moment?'

'Not at all. There is someone I must speak to, and then I will join you.'

Lowena paused on the wide terrace before stepping down into the beautiful garden. The sun had almost set, leaving the sky a deep blue with several shades of pink on the horizon. As she strolled along the paths she was surrounded by clambering sweet-scented roses and honeysuckle, and the foliage of tall flowering shrubs. The air was warm and humid, and filled with the hum of insects.

Looking back at the house, she saw an elegant, slender young woman dressed in a fashionable rose-pink gown walking quickly towards her. It was Juliet, Marcus's sister. She was a pretty brunette, with friendly blue eyes.

'Lowena, how lovely to see you again after all this time,' she said, greeting her warmly, obviously genuinely pleased to see her. 'We've just arrived. When I looked onto the terrace I thought I recognised you. I couldn't believe my eyes. So Marcus was right. It *was* you he saw in the park.'

'Yes—yes, it was.'

'Well, I have to say that I am quite astonished to find you here, of all places. I see your circumstances are much changed. It's been a long time since I was down in Cornwall, but it's good to have Mama and Marcus to stay for a while. They arrived yesterday. I'm so glad Marcus is home at last—the children adore him. No doubt he will be eager to get back to Cornwall and that mine of his, but I'm hoping Mama extends her visit.'

'I'm sure she can be persuaded. She spoke of you often and I know how much she misses you. She's been looking forward to this visit. Is she with you tonight?'

'No. She wasn't feeling too well—a headache. She wanted an early night. Ah, here is my brother,' Juliet said, looking beyond Lowena to the house. 'I must tell you that he is a little out of sorts just now,' she confided softly, looking at Lowena with quiet concern. 'I think it must have something to do with seeing you earlier and then you disappearing before he had chance to speak to you. He has told me that you left Cornwall under mysterious circumstances. He was quite put out about it and has been searching for you ever since. Have a care… Marcus is not a man to be reasoned with when he's in one of his adverse moods.'

With her back to Marcus, Lowena smiled at Juliet. 'Oh, I think I can manage Captain Carberry.'

'Here you are, Juliet. We wondered where you had disappeared to.'

It was Marcus who had come into the garden, and he stood behind her. Lowena knew it. She could feel it. She didn't need to turn for verification. She would sense his presence whenever she was near him—always. There was nothing she could do to change that. Nor would she want to.

She stood for a moment before turning to look at him, breathing in the scent of the roses, seeing their petals shining as if they'd been polished. She exhaled slowly, then turned.

Taken completely off guard, Marcus gaped at her. 'Good Lord! Lowena…' He was suddenly lost for words. He had only ever seen Lowena in simple day-to-day clothes, and then in the dark grey dress of a servant, and this transformation into a fashionable young lady was astounding.

The familiar voice struck straight at Lowena's heart as she watched him come towards her, and she felt it fill and almost burst with the joy of seeing him. She fought to calm her rioting nerves and maintain her equilibrium—to ignore the seductive pull of his eyes and voice.

Resplendent in black and white, his lustrous black hair brushed neatly back and secured at his nape, he looked unbearably handsome. He was just as she remembered, and when she looked into the lean, bronzed, formidable face, the instant she met his silver-grey eyes she felt a shaking begin in her limbs.

His presence swept away everything around her, and once again she was back in Cornwall.

She could see the blue sky, feel the wind on her face and taste the salt of the sea on her lips. In an ecstasy of love she wanted to cast herself into his arms, and yet her heart had already made its choice between distancing herself from him and the happiness that could be hers for a moment in his arms.

His face was expressionless, remote, and his silver-grey eyes gleamed hard and cold. Her heart fell and her joy in seeing him again melted away. He looked away from her and concentrated his gaze on a group of people who had come out onto the terrace, as if he could not stand the sight of her.

He was fighting her, Lowena thought, trying to shut her out, and for the moment he was succeeding. At that moment she would have done or said anything to reach him. She could not believe that this cold, remote stranger was the same tender, passionate man who had made love to her.

She tried to put those thoughts out of her mind. She grieved for the life she had known before, but she had a new life now—the life that had been stolen from her by her grandmother in her wickedness—and it was a life with promise.

Marcus towered over her, and Lowena almost retreated from those fierce eyes. But she steeled herself, and stood her ground before his accusing glare.

'I'm sorry. You take me by surprise,' Lowena said with cool civility, prepared to be on the defensive, recognising that the stern set of his face and the thin line of his lips did not suggest much tolerance or forgiveness. She was determined to speak to him with a calm maturity and not to let anger and confused emotions get the better of her. 'I thought never to see you again.'

Marcus cocked a handsome brow as he gave her a lengthy inspection. 'Obviously.'

Lowena had spent many cold winters in Cornwall. She had seen the lake on the Carberry estate ice over. But nothing had chilled her as much as Marcus's voice at that moment. It froze her heart, too. The tension was palpable. His look was threatening, and a sense of force was distilled and harnessed in his stance. She could feel his simmering anger.

In spite of her subterfuge, and the time they had been apart, Marcus knew the conversation must take a polite course.

'Do you often ride in the park?' he asked, his voice cool.

'Yes. I love London—and riding out. There is so much to see and do, and the park is extremely pleasant.'

'Your accomplishments astound me,' Marcus said sardonically. 'I had no idea you could ride.'

'How could you? I didn't learn until I went to live in Devon. I was taught by a master.'

'I don't doubt it. You will remember my sister Juliet and her husband Lord Simon Mallory?' he said, standing aside and turning to his sister and then to her husband, who had come to join his wife.

'Yes, of course I do,' Lowena said, smiling at Juliet. She had not met her husband, though. She had not been working at Tregarrick in the days before Juliet had gone to London to marry Lord Mallory.

'I've just been telling Lowena how lovely it is to see her again,' Juliet said, her tone warm with obvious sincerity.

'It is the first big society event I have attended since I came to London. I must confess to feeling like a fish out of water,' Lowena admitted, lowering her voice to a conspiratorial whisper.

Eager to be introduced to this vivacious young woman, Simon reached out his hand, his handsome face breaking into a brilliant reassuring smile and his blue eyes twinkling with delight. 'Your servant, Miss Trevanion,' he said, bending over and pressing a gallant kiss on the back of her hand. 'I'm very pleased to meet you.'

'Thank you.' For a moment Lowena was tempted to inform him that her name was Wesley now, but she held back, not yet ready to divulge her new identity to a stranger. But she liked Juliet's husband at once. 'Please—you must call me Lowena. Everyone does.'

'And you must call me Simon.'

'You look well, Lowena,' Juliet said, turning to her stony-faced brother. 'Don't you agree, Marcus?'

'Never better,' he ground out.

Dressed in her gown of pale green, with the tightly fitted bodice that forced her breasts high and exposed a daring expanse of flesh, and her heavy, glorious hair twisted into burnished curls at the crown, Lowena stood in resentful silence while Marcus's gaze slid boldly over her from the top of her shining hair to the toes of her satin slippers.

She actually flinched at the coldness in his eyes as they raked over her, but she raised her chin and held her ground, clutching her fan in front of her. 'I am perfectly well,' she replied. 'As you can see, I have survived very well since leaving Tregarrick.'

'I'm sure you have.'

'And how do you like London?' Juliet asked, aware of the tension between these two, which could be cut with a knife.

'Very much—although I confess to being overawed at first. There is so much to do and see and experience—I love the parks, and the Vauxhall Gardens are particularly beautiful.'

'Indeed they are,' Juliet agreed, then was suddenly distracted when she saw a lady trying to get her attention on the terrace. Excusing herself, Juliet left to speak to her, Simon following in her wake.

'You may find the gardens at Vauxhall so during the day,' Marcus retorted, 'but at night they are altogether different.'

Lowena stiffened. 'Really? Please explain what you mean by that.' She was unable to look away from his ice-cold eyes.

'Only that at night they are not so genteel—in fact they really do become pleasure gardens in every respect after dark. Sexual intrigue stalks the remote avenues when ladies of the town frequent those dark walks.'

Confused by this information, she asked, 'Pardon me—but what are you talking about?'

'It must be an intoxicating experience to stroll along Vauxhall's Grand Walk on the arm of a gentleman—even if you *are* only his mistress and he is twice your age. Why, if you play your cards right, Lowena, you could become the greatest demi-rep in London.'

She stared at him, unable to believe he was

saying these awful things to her. 'What—what's a demi-rep?' she asked in all innocence. She really hadn't the faintest idea, but she had a vague idea that it wasn't complimentary.

He cocked a sleek dark brow. 'Do you *really* need me to spell it out?'

His meaning hit her like a slap in the face. She was stricken. Her cheeks filled with heat. 'No. I understand you perfectly.'

He smiled thinly. 'I thought you might.'

His deliberate insult sliced through her, and she now knew what he was thinking—though horrified, appalled and deeply hurt that he could even *think* that of her, she had no intention of enlightening him.

'How dare you say that to me? I may have lived all my life in the country, away from the sleaze and corruption of London, but I would have to be a simple and naïve fool not to know the implication of what you are saying. Your standards are so perfect you consider yourself an authority to judge me, I suppose?' she uttered with equal sarcasm, her cheeks aflame, suppressing the desire to hit him over the head with anything that was to hand. 'I wonder why, when you have such a propensity to insult me, you deign to speak to me at all.'

He arched his brow infuriatingly. 'And I wonder how, since you left Tregarrick in such haste, you managed to fall on your feet in no time at all.'

Lowena recoiled as though she'd been stung. 'It wasn't like that. You don't know anything about what happened to me after I left. Little did I realise when I went to work at Tregarrick that your brother was a predatory amorist, and my virtue some kind of challenge to him, regardless of my station. And now, because of what you have just accused me of being, you no doubt think it was all *my* fault.'

Marcus stepped closer to her, his eyes penetrating, cold and ruthless, his jaw tightening ominously. When she had left him at Tregarrick she had looked like a wounded child. Now he was confronted with a woman he didn't recognise—an enraged, beautiful virago.

'I have never said that.'

'I have no doubt you think it. You are a monster, Marcus Carberry, and I can't imagine why I let you make love to me.'

His lips twisted laconically. 'You are right. I must seem like a monster to you. Tell me something I don't already know. This man who keeps you—he treats you well?'

Raising her eyebrows, she said coolly, 'I confess that the gentleman you speak of and I have become…close. He treats me very well and I want for nothing. Indeed, I have come to love him dearly.'

Jealousy ripped through Marcus on hearing those endearing words for another man on her lips. Her apparent lack of contrition fuelled his anger even further.

'So you admit it, then?'

'I have nothing to admit—at least nothing that signifies.'

He bent his body so that his face was level with hers. 'So you value yourself so little that you are prepared to sell yourself to this man?' he said, knowing full well that his attitude must seem brutal to her, but so mired in suspicion that he couldn't help himself. 'I am surprised you have settled for an older man when you rejected my brother's attentions.'

Despite this outrageous attack on her character, which she would not have believed in him, Lowena let her soft lips break into a smile. 'One man is much like another—and the difference between the gentleman you saw me with earlier and your brother is that I did not *choose* your brother. He chose me—and my new status is certainly an improvement on that.' Slanting him an amused look from the corner of her eye, she said, 'Why, the way you are behaving you are beginning to sound like a jealous suitor—which, of course, we both know you are not. I really cannot understand why you are making such a fuss.'

'Do you expect me to act reasonably when you failed to inform us where you had gone? When you left Tregarrick we assumed you would be returning. After the consideration my mother has shown towards you over the years, do you not think she deserved better than a short note? I *demand* to know what you have to say for yourself,' he said, in an icy, authoritative tone that Lowena resented.

She had the grace to look contrite, but she continued to defend her actions. 'Yes, you are right—and I do apologise for not being more open—but you have no right to demand anything from me,' she retorted, sparks of anger darting from her narrowed eyes. 'There isn't a man born who will tell me what I will and will not do. Do not forget that *you* told me I had to leave Tregarrick—and you were right to do so. Living with the compliant, obedient deference of a domestic servant was not for me any more.'

'I know I told you to leave, but you had little money and no connections—I did not want you to leave until we had found you a suitable place with a good family. I also wanted to be certain that after—'

'What, Marcus? That after our night of pleasure I was not with child? Is that what you were afraid of?' Lowena's smile was one of irony. 'You need not concern yourself. There is no child. In your arrogance you thought you knew what was best for me. Why, anyone would think that because I took it upon myself to leave I was setting myself on a path to financial and moral ruination.'

It was clear she could not begin to understand just how concerned Marcus had been, how relentless his search to find her.

'Well, you need not concern yourself any longer,' she said, tossing her head and glaring at him, her eyes sparking ire, her chin set firm. 'Neither my finances nor my morals are any the worse for leaving Tregarrick. Now, please excuse me. This conversation is going nowhere. I think enough has been said between us.'

Her words brought a feral gleam to his eyes. 'Have a care, Lowena. Do not fight me.'

And, before she could walk away, with a startling jerk he pulled her into his arms, his mouth capturing hers in a desperate kiss born out of frustration and an unappeased hunger for her which had increased a thousand fold since they'd been apart.

But Lowena didn't care for his reasons. His sudden kiss set spark to tinder, unlocking all the hidden passions she had held in check since the night he had made love to her. It was just what she wanted, what she needed, and her reaction was to wrap her arms around his neck and kiss him back with a hunger of her own.

As he crushed her pliant body to his, spearing his fingers through her hair, his head filled with the fragrance of her, Marcus felt the passion flare in her, felt her heart race. He felt a burgeoning pleasure and an astonished joy that was almost beyond bearing. He deepened the kiss and she shivered. He felt it bone-deep. A moment later he finally forced himself to lift his head and he gazed down into her eyes, his anger unappeased despite her surrender.

'Tell me again how you have come to care for your lover, Lowena… You would do well to remember that men do not marry the women they choose as their mistresses. Do you respond so wantonly to *his* kiss as you have to mine? Tell me he means nothing to you—if you can.'

'I owe you no explanations.'

'You may be as haughty as you wish, but I think your flight from Tregarrick has not brought you the independence you so desire. *Why* are you with him?' he persisted.

Lowena listened to him with outrage burning inside her, wanting to fling her new-found status in his face. But for some unfathomable reason she desired more to keep her relationship with her father from him. Let him wallow in his jealousy and anger a while longer.

With as much dignity as she could muster, she replied evasively, 'I am with him for the usual reasons.'

'Money, influence and a very comfortable position, I expect,' Marcus summarised with scathing disgust.

Tilting her head to one side, Lowena looked at him. 'Why, Marcus, I cannot imagine why what I do should concern you so. Are you jealous, by any chance?'

Marcus's sardonic gaze swept over her lovely face and the full soft mouth that positively invited a man to kiss it. Tendrils of her hair drifted like whispered secrets against the curve of her cheek, precisely where his lips had been just moments before. His eyes dropped to the swell of her breasts, trembling invitingly above the neckline of her gown. Desire poured through him like molten rock. She had a body that was created for a man's hands—a body that could drive a man to lust.

Recollecting himself, he averted his gaze, felt his pulse hammering. He had known her as intimately as it was possible for a man to know a woman, and it had been her first taste of pleasure, yet he wanted more from her. Knowing that she was giving the pleasures he wanted to experience again for himself to another man sent ripples of unrest into the hollow place that was his soul. Yes, damn it, he was jealous. It was an emotion he had only felt once before, for one woman, and he despised himself for his sudden weakness.

'You are beautiful—but you are also amoral. I congratulate you on your success in snaring a wealthy man, but I thought you were different from that—that you were a woman with a heart, not some mercenary little opportunist.'

This pious condemnation from him of all people was too much for Lowena. She drew herself up, her eyes blazing. 'I think you have said quite enough. I will not stand here to listen to you accuse me of being mercenary, lacking in morals and an opportunist.'

'Why not?' he bit out, wanting to hurt her as much as she had hurt him. 'Evidently you are all those things.'

'And *you* are arrogant and overbearing. I owe you nothing. My life is my own, to make of it what I will, and neither you nor anyone else will tell me how to live it—especially you.'

Marcus glared at her. And then without another word he turned on his heel and strode swiftly away.

Lowena watched him stride along the terrace

and disappear into the house, and knew that in all probability he had just left her life for ever.

Raising her hand, she touched her lips. That kiss, vibrant and alive, soft, insistent and sensual, invaded her mind. Her reaction to it—her submission—terrified her. She'd wanted more—much more. She'd wanted it to go on and on, and to kiss him back with soul-destroying passion.

Disappointment overwhelmed her and she bitterly faced the awful truth that physically she was no more immune to Marcus Carberry now than she had been at Tregarrick. She felt the serenity she had acquired over the past weeks melt away, leaving her grieving for the man who was no longer a part of her life—grieving for the man she loved…for love him she did. Of that there was no doubt.

She could withstand his insults, his anger, but not his smile, his touch, his kiss—the kiss that twisted her insides into knots, that made her burn, that wreaked havoc on her heart, her body and her soul. She was still as susceptible as she ever had been. She wished she could resist that wanton streak he had uncovered in her but she was helpless to do so. Marcus had turned her into some kind of wild creature—someone she didn't recognise.

But, she asked herself, how could she possibly love a man who had hurt her and insulted her as he had done? It would seem there was no protection against love once it had you in its power. From the instant she had seen him on his return from America she had admitted that she loved him, and now she felt despair flooding over her like a great wave. She really shouldn't have deceived him…doing nothing to alleviate his suspicion that her father was her lover.

She had thought she was secure in this new world with her father, but just a moment spent with Marcus had shown her it was nothing but a fantasy—a bubble that had burst with just one look at his face.

Forcing back her dammed-up tears, she turned to see her father walking towards her. Immediately she pinned a smile to her face and went to meet him.

Frowning, Robert Wesley looked towards the French windows through which the gentleman who had been speaking to Lowena had disappeared. 'Do you know that gentleman?'

When Lowena spoke she tried to keep her voice from trembling, to dispel the passion Marcus had roused in her. 'Yes. It was Captain Carberry—Marcus Carberry.'

Robert's eyes widened. 'The man who found you in the woods when you were a babe?'

'Yes, the same.'

'I see.' He studied her closely. 'I would like to meet him, but you seem put out, Lowena. Did he say something to upset you?'

She averted her eyes. 'No—although he was surprised to see me.'

'What? Here at Lady Wychwood's musical evening, or to see you at all?'

'Both, I suppose. The last time he saw me I was a servant in his house.'

'Lowena, I know you wrote to Lady Alice, but did you tell her where you were living—that we have been united after all this time?'

She shook her head, looking sheepish. 'No, I'm afraid I didn't.'

'But why not? For what reason? Did you not think that you might owe it to her?'

Lowena had the grace to look contrite. 'You are right. I should have told her. But I—I didn't want Marcus to know. When I left I considered it in my own best interests not only to terminate my employment, but to terminate my relationship with him.'

Robert noted the catch in her voice. He glanced at her sharply. 'Relationship? Did he hurt you in some way? Did he upset you?'

'Our last encounter was…unpleasant.'

Robert's face tightened as a terrible suspicion

began to take root. 'What happened between the two of you, Lowena? Was his behaviour towards you inappropriate?'

Lowena felt heat stain her cheeks and she looked away. She couldn't possibly tell her father how, as a servant in Marcus Carberry's house, she had willingly, shamefully, let him into her bed—how she was unable to blot out of her mind the exquisite sweetness of the intimacy they had shared, how it had felt to be held in his arms and how the memory kept coming back to torment her and that there was nothing she could do about it. That sometimes she didn't even want to.

And so she looked for another answer to her father's question and said, 'He told me I had to leave. It may not seem important now, but at the time it was—to me. He wanted to find me a suitable position—probably as a governess or something of that nature—with a good family. I was angry and very upset. I told him not to concern himself—that my life was my own and I would make my own way. As I said, my leaving was—unpleasant. Too many things were said—by both of us. We did not part on the best of terms.'

Digesting what she had told him, Robert studied her unhappy face for a moment, feeling uneasy and sensing there was more to her relationship with Captain Carberry than she was prepared to admit. But he would not press her.

'You are a grown woman, Lowena, who knows her own mind and is her own mistress, so I won't interfere in what is not my affair. It is too late for me to begin playing the heavy-handed father now. However, I did not come down in yesterday's shower, and I sense there is something else—something you are not telling me. I felt when you first came to me that you were unhappy about something. I'm a good listener, if you want to talk about it.'

She shook her head. 'It's nothing—truly. Please don't worry about me.'

'When I saw him just now, the Captain looked decidedly put out about something.'

'I'm afraid he was—*very* put out. It's all so silly, really...'

'He *does* know you are my daughter? He must, since society has done nothing gossip about me turning up in London with you.'

She flushed and looked away. 'No. He—he only arrived in London yesterday. It would seem he hasn't had time to catch up on the gossip. I—I didn't tell him about you—he didn't give me the chance.'

'I see. So who does he *think* I am?'

When she failed to answer he took her arm and turned her to face him.

'Well?'

Lowena hesitated to answer. After all, it was hardly the sort of thing a daughter would say to her father. Regardless of this, a mischievous twinkle entered her eyes. 'He—well, he assumed that you and I—because he saw us together in the park—that we are...'

Comprehension dawned and, seeing the funny side of it, Robert threw back his head and laughed out loud. 'For a man who is getting on in years, whose youth is just a distant memory, that is the most flattering thing that has happened to me in a long time. I feel twenty years younger. If Marcus Carberry believes that, then he has been well and truly duped. Oh, my dear—wait until I tell Deborah.'

'I know. I can imagine just how furious he will be when he finds out.'

'He will not remain for long in ignorance. He only has to ask any one of these guests and they will enlighten him as to your identity. I should speak to him...'

'Yes—but not immediately,' Lowena said, mischief still lighting her eyes. 'Let him remain in ignorance just a while longer.'

Robert chuckled. 'That is cruel.'

'I know,' she said, linking her arm through his. 'But it's fun.'

'Not the kind of fun Deborah was referring to when you first appeared in London.'

'I know,' she said, laughing, 'but I'm learning.'

Robert's face settled in more serious lines. 'You do know that no matter what happens, Lowena, you can always count on my full support, don't you?' he said gently.

His quiet offering touched Lowena deeply. 'Of course I do,' she said, walking close beside him along the path towards the house. 'But it won't come to that. My time spent at Tregarrick in the employment of the Carberry family is well and truly in the past.'

'You seem angry, Marcus. What has happened?' Juliet asked when he came in from the garden.

'What has happened? I would have thought it quite obvious. Lowena left us to begin an affair with a man who is old enough to be her father,' he uttered dispassionately, keeping his words devoid of concern, determined not to let Juliet see how much Lowena's affair angered him. 'Ever since she walked out of Tregarrick I have been making desperate enquiries into her whereabouts—it was as if she'd disappeared into thin air. And now I know the reason why I couldn't find her. The existence of a lover is the only thing that makes sense.'

'You are jumping to conclusions, Marcus. Did Lowena actually *tell* you that the gentleman you saw her with is her lover?'

'She didn't have to.'

'There might be an innocent explanation for her being with him.'

Marcus fixed his ice-cold eyes on his sister. 'What sort of explanation could she possibly have? They were together—he even touched her face, for God's sake, for all to see.'

Furiously he looked away. The bewitching, artless young woman who had always held a place in his heart—the woman he had made love to so passionately—had turned out to be as cold and calculating as Isabel.

'There has to be another explanation. It think it's time we found out the truth.

They didn't have long to wait.

Marcus watched the French windows, knowing the exact moment that Lowena entered on the arm of the man he had seen her with in the park.

'Good Lord!' exclaimed the gentleman next to him softly. He had paused on his way to the refreshment room to speak to Marcus. 'What an exquisite creature—far too exquisite to be flesh and blood. Wesley's damn lucky, if you ask me.'

'Wesley?' queried Marcus.

'Sir Robert Wesley—from your part of the world. Well, Devon—just over the border.'

'Really?' Marcus murmured, his interest pricked. 'I am not familiar with the name.'

He watched Lowena come closer. His anger having dissipated somewhat, he had to admit that she was a breathtaking vision. Meeting her hot, amber gaze across the distance that separated them, he saw she looked as dangerous as a suppressed tropical storm.

'Some would say she has landed on her feet,' he said.

'I'll say. It would seem this young lady is the fruit of an affair Wesley had with her mother— dead now, I believe. Can't say if they were ever married. All a bit of a mystery, really.' He sighed, shaking his head mournfully and moving on.

Marcus stood rooted to the spot, the revelation grinding through his brain like a million hammers. Burning rage at his own stupidity and blindness poured through him. At last everything was beginning to fall into place. But why had she not said anything? And how long had she known about the family that had abandoned her?

'Well, well!' Juliet breathed, having made her own enquiries and utterly delighted by what she had been told concerning Sir Robert Wesley.

Coming to stand beside Marcus, she smiled into his stunned face. 'It would appear Lowena is Sir Robert Wesley's natural *daughter*. What a turn-out. Who would have thought it?'

'Who, indeed?' Marcus replied, beginning to feel like a complete and utter idiot as he remembered how he had been so ready to judge and condemn as he watched the object of his gaze now walking gracefully across the room, her hand resting on Sir Robert's arm, keeping her head high, her deep red hair resembling a beacon of light. 'She'll regret this.'

Juliet laughed softly. 'More like you'll regret your accusation. You were too hasty to judge her, and if her father is aware of it he will be none too pleased. You, dear brother, are going to be down on your knees for a very long time, begging for her forgiveness.'

'You know I never go down on my knees,' he retorted dryly. 'What do you know about Sir Robert?'

'He lives in Devon—an old family, by all accounts. He's wealthy—extremely so—and the owner of a silver mine. At least you have something in common. He has no other offspring. Whether Lowena is legitimate or not remains to be seen, but whatever the case she will be a very rich young woman.'

'Then she must watch out for fortune-hunters.'

'That is true. She's about to become one of the most sought-after young ladies in London. Are we likely to see *you* in the running, Marcus?' Juliet asked, eyeing her brother closely.

'I'm afraid not. She wouldn't consider me, even with a gun against her head.'

Juliet laughed softly. 'Be that as it may, Marcus, I think we should go and speak to them. After all you have played a large part in her life. I'm sure Sir Robert would like to meet you.'

As the evening progressed Lowena was acutely aware of Marcus's presence, feeling his razor-sharp gaze on her as he prowled among the guests. He seemed to radiate a barely leashed strength and power. There was something primitive about him, and she felt that his elegant attire and indolence were nothing but a front meant to lull the unwary into believing he was a civilised being while disguising the fact that he was a dangerous savage.

She found the memory of their altercation and their kiss still very much on her mind. It made her feel quite ill even at the same time as her pride forced her to lift her chin and rebelliously face him across the room, meeting his ruthless stare in mutual animosity as she took to the floor in the ballroom with an exuberant young man.

With his shoulder propped against a pillar, his brows drawn together in thoughtful concentration, Marcus watched Lowena dancing the intricate, lively steps of a country dance. Her movements were dainty and graceful, and she was looking at her partner with the most innocent expression on her face.

He continued to watch her, and when she again took to the floor and took her place in a progressive dance, where one's partner constantly changed, observed how her face positively glowed with whispered compliments. He experienced an acute feeling of jealousy and wanted to annihilate every one of her partners.

Ever since that night he had made love to her his tortured imaginings had caused him to exist in a state of righteous fury, and he didn't know how much longer he could stand it. The memory of what they had shared became more alive with each passing day. It touched him and lived inside him, was visual and tactile, had odour and taste and warmth. It had been perfect, and because he was powerless to banish the memory from his mind he longed to savour its potency once more.

Never had he seen her look so provocatively

lovely, so regal and bewitching—and he would not rest until she belonged to him.

He argued with himself—asked himself why he was behaving like a churl towards her. Was it because she had damaged his male pride by leaving him so abruptly at Tregarrick? Was it because she had taunted him by making him believe that the man who was her father was her lover?

Whatever the reason, it was time he made amends. At Tregarrick she had told him that she loved him. Did she still love him? Or had he broken her spirit and driven a stake through her heart? But then he smiled, remembering how, in the garden tonight, she had stood up to him as no other would dare to. No—her spirit was still intact. And God help him if he should ever destroy that.

Pushing himself away from the pillar, he drew himself up to his full height, telling himself that something must be done to heal the breach between them before it destroyed them both.

Chapter Nine

Breathless, her feet aching and her head spinning, Lowena declined the next admirer who tried to claim her in the dance. Excusing herself to her father and Deborah, she made her way to the ladies' retiring room. Secretly she had hoped that Marcus's anger towards her might have lessened, and that he would ask her to partner him in the dance.

But as she had twirled about the floor she had been aware of his tall figure, of him watching her. There had been a tension in his stance, and his expression had been dark and brooding.

Any hopes she'd had of ending the night without another confrontation with him were quashed when she emerged from the retiring room and he stepped in front of her.

'At last,' he said with impatience. 'I was beginning to think I would never get you alone. I want to talk to you.'

Taking her arm, he drew her into an alcove, away from curious eyes. Shaking her arm free, she glanced up at him.

She was uncertain of his mood after their angry and extremely bitter exchange earlier, which had opened up so many painful wounds between them, and her expression was wary. His face was etched with tension, his eyes as hard as granite. With his relentless ways and implacable will he must have now found out the truth, and had followed her to the retiring room to intercept her.

'Go away,' she retorted irately. 'I have no wish to speak to you.'

'On the contrary. There are things we have to discuss.'

'Then if I am to remain,' she said sharply, 'I would be grateful if you would observe the proprieties. I have no wish to be the subject of idle or malicious gossip.'

His smile was one of condescension. 'If you are afraid that there will be a repetition of my earlier conduct, I will set your mind at rest. I simply want to talk to you. Until you have answered all my questions you are quite safe.'

She glanced at him warily. 'And afterwards?'

His eyes gleamed wickedly. 'We shall see.'

Lowena glared at the handsome, forceful, dynamic man towering over her, looking so disgustingly self-assured. 'Anything we had to say has been said. After everything that has happened, how dare you feel you have the right to approach me? There will be more than a few raised eyebrows if you are seen loitering outside the ladies' rest room.'

'It is worth the risk to get you alone. You look as if you are enjoying yourself,' he commented, noticing her high colour and shining eyes.

'Very much—although I confess to feeling a little exhausted. What is it you want to talk to me about? Your attitude earlier and all those dreadful things you accused me of being were unforgivable.'

As Marcus looked down at her he reminded himself that no matter what she did or said he must be patient and understanding. But with her chin raised defiantly high and her eyes hurling scornful daggers at him it was all he could do to bridle his temper.

'What the hell did you think you were playing at, letting me believe Sir Robert Wesley was your lover? Damn it, Lowena, you should have *told* me he was your father.'

Lowena quivered, half with apprehension about his reaction to the news of her true identity and half with relief that he knew at last. Her face working with her emotions, which had for the moment got the better of her, she gazed up at him reluctantly. 'Yes, I should, and for what it's worth I am sorry.'

Marcus eyed her warily. 'You are?'

'Yes, but you had so clearly already made up your mind about the situation.'

His eyes shone softly down into hers. 'I could happily shake you.'

'I'm sure you could.'

'You made a complete idiot of me with that silly charade.'

'I think you made an idiot of yourself without any help from me. You shouldn't have been in such a hurry to think the worst of me.'

'You didn't enlighten me. In fact you were enjoying every moment of my discomfort. Faced with such evidence, you cannot blame me for thinking you had got caught up in some sleazy affair. And you played along with it—no doubt enjoying watching me make a fool of myself. I congratulate you. You are a superb actress, whose talents would be best suited on the stage.'

'I should have told you who he was—and I would have if you hadn't jumped to the wrong conclusion. You were so pig-headed about it that I couldn't resist letting you suffer in ignorance a while longer. I would have introduced you if you hadn't been in a temper.'

'With good reason.'

'Maybe.'

'How did you find out that Sir Robert Wesley is your father?'

'Nessa told me.'

'Nessa?'

'Yes. She knew all along. It was Nessa who left me in the woods that day—the day you found me. She told me everything I've wanted to know all my life.'

He stared at her in disbelief. 'And you knew this when you left?'

'Yes.'

'And yet you didn't think to tell me—or my mother? She deserved better from you, Lowena. It was badly done. She was sick with worry when you didn't return.'

'I'm sorry.'

Her apology took him off guard and he raised an eyebrow.

'I hate myself for hurting Lady Alice. When I told her I was going away with Nessa I had only just found out who my parents were and that my father—whom Nessa had been told was dead— was alive. The knowledge was so immense I hadn't had time to take it in. I couldn't bring myself to speak of it.'

'And Sir Robert? Did he know about you?'

'No, not until I turned up on his doorstep. At the time I was born he was in Mexico. My mother died shortly after my birth. Nessa, who was my mother's maid, told me my grandmother was a hard, unfeeling woman. When my father returned to England she didn't tell him he had a daughter. He loved my mother and would have married her.'

'And your grandmother? What happened when your mother died? Why didn't she keep you with her?'

'She didn't want me. She couldn't bear the scandal an illegitimate child would bring. If Nessa hadn't taken me she would have sent me to the orphanage.'

'Good Lord! I cannot believe Nessa has known the truth all these years. Why didn't she tell you before? Why keep it from you?'

Lowena gave him a brief account of Nessa's circumstances at the time, and the events of the day she'd left Lowena's grandmother's house, taking her to find her father and what she'd found at Castle Creek.

'When you found me and took me to live with Izzy Nessa found work at Tregarrick. It meant she could keep an eye on me. When she saw I was happy and well looked after, she decided to remain silent.'

'But Nessa was leaving her employment at Tregarrick. Was that why she decided to tell you?'

'It was one of the reasons.'

'And the other?'

'She had just found out that my father was alive.'

'And your grandmother? Is she still alive?'

Lowena shook her head. 'No. There was a fire. The whole of Beresford Hall was burned to the ground. She—she couldn't get out in time.'

'I see. How do you feel about that?'

'I don't know. What she did was cruel. She ignored my existence. I doubt even had she still been alive she would have welcomed me with open arms.' She looked up at him. 'Were you angry when I didn't return to Tregarrick?'

He looked at her sharply. 'Yes—if you must know I was furious. But most of my anger was out of concern for you—and the greatest part of it was directed at myself. After all, it was my fault that you fled.'

'Juliet told me that you looked for me?'

'Of course I did. I care about you, Lowena—more than you realise. I deeply regret asking you to leave Tregarrick—handing down rulings and opinions as if, in my arrogance, I knew what was best for you. I underestimated you—and you soon put me in my place. It didn't take me long to realise what I had done—what I had lost. I desperately wanted to know you were all right. I went to Saltash to see Nessa, thinking she must know where I could find you—only to be told when I got there that her aunt had died and Nessa had vanished.'

'She came to Castle Creek to find me. She's still there.'

Lowena glanced towards the refreshment room just in time to see her father and Deborah disappearing through the door.

'I think it's time I introduced you to my father and stepmother.'

'Did you tell him that I thought you were his mistress?'

'Of course.'

Marcus rolled his eyes. 'Good Lord, Lowena. Have you no mercy? Is my shame not bad enough? No doubt he is impatient to meet me at dawn in some secluded place and offer me a choice of weapons.'

'The idea did have a certain appeal, but he's more likely to offer you a glass of his finest brandy. He did see the funny side, and was rather flattered that someone as old as he is still thought handsome enough to have secured a young paramour. Although I don't think Deborah—his wife—was quite so amused.'

Marcus's eyes softened. 'I'm glad I was mistaken. And are you enjoying London? You appear to have fitted in well with your new life.'

She smiled. It was a cynical smile. 'New life? Yes. I suppose it is. But it is not what I sought.'

'No?'

She shook her head. 'Finding out who I am does not mark a happy ending to all that has gone before. It is simply a beginning—the ushering in of a new phase in my life. Naturally I am happy that I know who I am at last, where I come from and that I have an identity—and I have grown to love my father dearly. But this life...' She sighed. 'In truth there are times when I find it hard to laugh and smile with people I don't know and perhaps wouldn't like it if I did. I'm not very good at it, I'm afraid.'

'You appeared to be at ease when dancing with your admirers.'

A light flared in her eyes and she drew herself up haughtily, preparing herself for another assault by his temper. 'And why not? I was enjoying myself—and, as you will have seen, I have learned to dance without stepping on toes.'

Tired of sniping and bickering, Marcus let his temper be mollified and a smile of admiration broke across his features. 'What a little spitfire you are when you're angry...' He chuckled softly. 'Are you disappointed that I did not dance with you?'

Lowena looked at him incredulously, relieved to see that his black scowl had disappeared and his face had relaxed into pleasanter lines. 'Dance with me! I could cheerfully murder you.'

'I would come back to haunt you, Lowena,' he threatened, a slow, roguish grin dawning across his handsome features, his silver gaze locking on hers. 'I swear I will be a hundred times more formidable when my body has been reduced to dust. You will see me everywhere. My ghost will give you no rest.'

Having lost the battle to remain aloof, Lowena was unable to repress her answering smile, and could feel laughter bubble up in her chest. 'That's absolute rubbish. I don't believe in ghosts.'

'I'm not sure I quite believe that. Since you are clearly reluctant to let me haunt you, I shall just have to make sure that I remain alive long enough to harass you in the flesh,' he teased. 'Now, isn't it about time you introduced me to your father? Before I forget myself and repeat my actions of earlier and kiss you into submission.'

Lowena bit back a smile at his quip, happy to let her anger melt because she still loved him to distraction. 'Really, Marcus, you do confound me. Have you no mercy?'

The remnants of mirth gleaming in his eyes slowly dissolved as he laid his hand tenderly against her cheek. 'None,' he replied obligingly.

Lowena's father and Deborah were located in the refreshment room. Sir Robert was expecting them.

Marcus took his proffered hand and introduced himself, watching Sir Robert's face for a reaction. His eyes measured Marcus in a slow, exacting way that gave him every assurance that he was successfully assessing him. Then the older man smiled and nodded slightly. Seeming satisfied, he introduced him to Deborah.

Marcus bowed gallantly and told her that he was enchanted to meet her. Then he smiled into her eyes in a way that made her feel as if she'd just received an enormous compliment.

'I am happy to make your acquaintance, Captain Carberry,' Deborah said courteously, her piercing eyes assessing him with fascinated curiosity. 'You and Lowena have had—how shall I put it?—a slight misunderstanding, I believe?' Deborah looked from Lowena to Marcus with a mischievous twinkle lighting her eyes. 'It has been resolved, I trust?'

Marcus grinned, knowing precisely to what she was referring, and had the grace to look contrite.

'Absolutely, Lady Wesley. And I hope the misunderstanding did not cause offence, for it was unintentionally done.'

Robert chuckled. 'I am sure it was—but I have not been so amused in a long time.'

'I'm relieved to hear it.'

'I have a great deal to thank you for,' Robert said on a more serious note. 'Had you not found Lowena that day when she was a babe, I shudder to think what might have become of her. She has told me the circumstances of her birth, and of her grandmother's insistence that she leave her home. My only regret is that I was in Mexico at the time and did not know of Lowena's existence until she came to Devon to look for me. I wish the maid had come forward with the truth earlier. It would have saved a lot of heartache, and Lowena and I would not have been deprived of each other all these years. However, nothing can change what has been done, so it us up to us to make the most of what we have now.'

After making polite conversation for several more minutes, Marcus turned to Lowena.

'Come, Lowena, dance with me...' He glanced at Sir Robert. 'With your permission, Sir Robert?'

'Of course you have it,' he replied, happy that everything seemed to be resolved between his daughter and Captain Carberry.

There was no time for Lowena to react. Already Marcus was taking her hand and drawing her away from her father towards the room where couples twirled around the dance floor beneath glittering crystal chandeliers.

Lowena walked into his arms and felt his arm slide about her waist, bringing her close against the solid strength of his body. His left hand closed round her fingers and suddenly she was being whirled gently around in the arms of this man who danced with the easy grace of a man who had spent most of his adult life on a dance floor instead of a battlefield.

She should have felt overpowered, especially with almost every eye in the room focused on them, but instead, feeling Marcus's broad shoulders beneath her gloved hand and his arm encircling her waist like a band of steel, she felt safe and protected.

'You dance divinely,' she complimented him softly.

'I'm supposed to say that to *you*.'

'Really?' She frowned. 'It would seem I have much to learn.'

'You will find that society has rules to govern absolutely everything.'

'It seems to me that society requires a female to be utterly useless. Independence holds a certain appeal.'

He smiled down at her. 'There are many who would say that independence is vastly overrated and an odd notion for a woman to have.'

'Maybe, but I would still value it—although I suppose I would be condemned by society for having such ambition.'

Gazing at her downcast face, lowering his head to hers, Marcus murmured, 'Lift up your head and smile at me. Look as though you've never enjoyed a dance more.' His eyes twinkled wickedly. 'Feel free to flirt with me, if you like, but do not on any account look humble or meek.'

Lowena drew a shaking breath and a smile curved her lips. 'Smiling I can do—but flirting is definitely out. Look where it got me before.'

'How can I possibly forget?'

'I know the rules of society and I broke them all like a shameless wanton when I—when I...' Her voice trailed away. She was too embarrassed to go on.

'And who is to know that but you and I?' he murmured, his voice surprisingly gentle. 'I will not look too far afield for explanations, but what happened between us happened because we were attracted to each other. I wanted you, and I know it was what you wanted.'

The sudden glamour of his lazy smile was almost as effective as his admission. She flushed hotly. 'I—I think our emotions were running high that night—and before that on the night you kissed me. It wasn't all your fault. In hindsight you had merely offered to walk me to the cottage, and instead of letting you do just that like a stupid girl I told you that I loved you. What happened after that was mutual, not seduction—even though I felt seduced at the time.'

And afterwards she remembered how she'd felt unbearably sad, knowing nothing could possibly come of it.

'I refuse to regret or apologise for what happened,' he said. 'We wanted each other. It was as simple as that. I admit that the blame is entirely mine. You were innocent and totally inexperienced. I treated you very badly and I'm not proud of myself. By my actions I have wronged you. I fully admit that and hold myself accountable. Now, try to relax and enjoy the dance.'

'I am relaxed.'

'Your body tells me something different.'

'I think, Marcus, that my body is my own affair.' She was acutely aware of his hand against the small of her back, and she had a sudden impulse to shy away.

'I well remember what your body looks like, Lowena.' His eyelids were lowered over his eyes as he looked down at her upturned face, gently flushed a delicate pink by his remark. 'I remember everything about it—every curve, every hollow and every inviting, secret place.'

He grinned at the shock that registered in her eyes and spun her round more vigorously than the dance required.'

Lowena's attempt to chastise him for his forward remark failed when she saw the sparkling humour in his eyes. A smile curved her lips. 'You're enjoying this, aren't you?'

'Every minute,' he admitted shamelessly. 'After all, you did leave me high and dry when you left Tregarrick, and you made a fool of me by letting me believe your father was your lover. I must take my revenge where I can.'

His voice was deceptively soft, and Lowena suddenly felt a stirring of unease. She considered ending the dance prematurely, but the intensity of his gaze, devouring her with a ravenous hunger, was enough to keep her trapped in his arms.

Reading her mind, he said, 'Do you want to leave me, Lowena?'

As they twirled about the floor Lowena felt her heart begin to beat heavily. She knew she should not let him hold her so close, but she did not try to pull back. It was almost as if she were under some sort of spell. His lips were hovering just above her own. She looked into his eyes, and in the silver-grey depths she saw something relentless and challenging. She felt a quivering inside, but it was not fear.

'No.'

His gaze lingered on her face. 'You know, Lowena, you could have such power if you only knew how to wield it.'

She frowned, curious as to what he meant. 'What are you talking about?'

'If a woman goes about it the right way, she can twist a man around her finger. Some women know this instinctively. You, Lowena, do not.'

Marcus's eyes continued to hold hers. She tried to appear calm and in control, while melting inside. 'I think you are playing a game with me, and I'm not sure now to play.'

'You are right. I *am* playing a game with you and I do not intend to let you win. But,' he said slowly, his eyes lingering on her mouth, 'I can teach you how to play.'

'You forget that you have already tried that.'

'To my satisfaction.'

Knowing that he was referring to the night she had surrendered herself completely to him, she said, 'You have just admitted to playing a game with me and said that you do not intend to let me win. What, then, do you want from me?'

Marcus wasn't smiling now. His face had taken

on a serious expression. And in the moment that followed, with her heart beating wildly, Lowena felt again that wild surge of excitement and anticipation.

'I want you to be my wife. Marry me, Lowena.'

His voice had become low and soft in her ears, and Lowena had to delve deeply into her reserve of will to dispel the slow numbing of her senses. Their surroundings disappeared into a haze. She was completely stunned by what he had said, but somehow she carried on dancing.

Unable to work out where his proposal had come from, she was amazed that her voice sounded so calm and controlled. 'Goodness! You really are full of surprises. Why, Marcus? Why do you want to marry me now? You didn't want to marry me before I left your family's employ. Why now? Am I expected to be flattered by this?'

'Not at all. Since you left Tregarrick you have been forever in my thoughts—plaguing me, torturing me. Dear Lord, Lowena! You sorely test my restraint. Don't you *know* how much of a temptation you are to me?'

Her mind reeling with the shock of what he was saying, Lowena could only stare at him as a torrent of emotions overwhelmed her.

'I want you, Lowena,' he murmured. 'I want you to be my wife.'

Understanding dawned with his meaningful gaze. Despite the other dancers and the sound of the music, it was as if a deafening silence engulfed them. Lowena stared at him in confused shock as she understood the truth of what he was asking of her.

'I want to marry you,' he repeated, watching her closely.

She raised her eyes to his and what he saw in their innermost depths—a confusion of doubt, pain and a little fear—almost took his breath.

'I cannot believe that you want this. I have certainly not encouraged it.'

'Unconsciously you have encouraged it every time we have been together. Have you any objections to me as a husband?'

Lowena looked directly into his face just above her own, feeling herself respond to the dark intimacy in his voice. His expression was gentle, understanding—soft as she had not seen it for a long time. And there, plain for her to see, was the sincerity of his words.

'No, it is simply that your proposal has taken me by surprise. I may no longer be a servant—indeed, my elevation into the world of the gentry makes me altogether more desirable in the marriage mart, I realise that—but inside I am still the same person.'

What she said was true, and Marcus realised how his proposal must seem to her. But he also knew that after finding her again, even had she still been a servant, it made no difference. He would still want her to be his wife.

However, instinct and experience told Marcus that she might not be as eager to fall into his arms as he had thought. Still, it was nothing that a little tender persuasion couldn't solve, and he was prepared to use it to further his cause if logic and honesty weren't enough to persuade her.

'You are not just any woman, Lowena, and I cannot tell you the devastation I felt when you didn't return to Tregarrick. I have given marriage to you a great deal of thought—even before I came to London. Servant or princess—it makes no difference to the way I feel about you. So what do you say? What is your answer?'

The strains of the music died away and as they left the dance floor Marcus took her arm.

'Will you at least think about it?'

All Lowena's past experiences with this man rose up to overwhelm her. What he was asking of her was something she had always dreamed of— never, ever believing it would happen. Heaven help her, it was all she had ever wanted—and now it had.

But she could not forget that he had cast her

out, leading her to believe he had no place for her in his heart or in his home. And now her circumstances had changed he had changed his mind. Like a fool, she still wanted him, and he knew how she felt—had she not *told* him that she loved him? She damned herself for doing so. But despite his supreme confidence that he could have it all his way, she would not let him.

Pausing as he returned her to her father, she looked up at him. He was looking at her intently and his magnetic gaze stirred her painfully 'Your proposal has taken me unawares, Marcus. You must give me time. This is your game, not mine.'

'It is a game we can both play, Lowena. In a strange kind of way we are engaged in a power struggle, you and I. Do you not see the power you could have over me?'

'How? By becoming your wife?'

When he opened his mouth to speak, she looked away.

'I don't want to have power over you, Marcus. That is not my way. The games you play are played by your rules, not mine, so in my book that makes me the winner.'

'Dear Lord, Lowena, you are the most stubborn female I have ever come across. My behaviour was disgraceful when I asked you to leave Tregarrick, but I am prepared to atone for that.

I ask you to be my wife. I am offering you my name and all I possess.'

'Yes, and I thank you—with all my heart. But please give me time to think about it.'

His features softened and his eyes warmed. He was amazed how easily she could touch him—to the core of his being, to his very essence—without even trying. 'You must forgive my haste, but the past weeks without you have not taught me any degree of restraint. You can have no idea how much I have missed you.'

'And I you, Marcus.'

He wanted to take hope from her short reply. He wanted to infuse the words with both meaning and promise. But if he was to win her then he must be patient.

'Now, please excuse me,' she murmured. 'I will return to my father. Goodbye, Marcus.'

The following morning Lowena was alone in the garden, reliving the night just past and unable to believe that Marcus had asked her to be his wife. Why had she not accepted his proposal right away? Why had she hesitated? Was it because deep inside her heart she could not forgive him for sending her away from Tregarrick?

She had said nothing to her father and Deborah about what had transpired on the dance floor, and after bidding them goodnight she had headed directly to her room with a fixed smile on her face. Dismissing her maid, she had stared blindly out of her window. The energy she had forced into her parting from Marcus and into her easy conversation about the ball with her father and Deborah had vanished.

Now, covering her face with her hands, she faced the truth that physically she was no more immune to Marcus now than she had been when she had worked for his family. She could not withstand his smile, his touch, his kiss—the kiss that twisted her insides into knots; that made her burn; that wreaked havoc on her heart, her body and her soul.

Unlike many men of his background he was a private man—and, she suspected, careful in his friendships. And then there was Isabel—a woman he couldn't bring himself to speak of. What Lowena did know was that she had hurt him very badly, inflicting emotional injuries on him that no woman should.

Lowena felt a lump of constricting sorrow in her chest. When she thought deeply about it she realised how he must have suffered when Isabel had married Edward, and how difficult his decision to ask her, Lowena, to marry him, must have been. And what a blow to his pride when she had not accepted him outright.

She had gone through a great deal of deliberation and heart-searching since last night. She could hardly believe how deep her feelings were running, and the sudden joy coursing through her body melted the very core of her being. She loved Marcus, and that perfect certainty filled her heart and stilled any anxiety she might otherwise have had. The feeling was so strong there was no room for anything else.

She suspected that he was thinking of returning early to Cornwall. On that thought, and impatient to see him and tell him how she felt, she ordered the carriage.

On reaching the Mallory house, Lowena was relieved to find that Juliet, Simon and Lady Alice had taken the children to the park. She was pleased when she was told that Marcus was at home.

Reaching the study, Lowena knocked gently on the door. When there was no response, she opened it and quietly stepped inside. Marcus was standing by the window, unaware of her presence.

For a moment she drank in the sight of him, waiting for him to notice her. All the harsh things she had said to him at the ball had mellowed into a desire just to see him. He'd removed his jacket, and beneath the white shirt his muscles flexed as he stood up straight, lifting his hand and combing his fingers through his dark hair.

His stance was sombre. She took in the sheer male beauty of this man who wanted to make her his wife, feeling her blood run warm. He was everything a man ought to be. She was aware of the aura of calm authority and strength that always surrounded him, that was evident in his voice and lent purpose to his movements.

As if sensing her presence he turned, his shoulders stiffening and his face stony and preoccupied. His expression became guarded as he gave her a lengthy inspection, his eyes as brittle as glass.

Taking a deep breath, she walked towards him. Her stomach was in knots. What if he no longer wanted her? Her pulse was racing faster than ever.

'Well,' he said, his eyes locked on hers, cold and dispassionate. He was in complete control. 'You certainly know how to make an entrance. You take me wholly by surprise.' One dark brow lifted in questioning arrogance. 'To what do I owe the honour of this visit? No doubt you have considered my proposal of marriage and have come to reject my offer.'

Although hurt and appalled by his biting tone, Lowena knew she had come too far to stop now.

Drawing a long breath, she said, 'If you want me to go away I will, Marcus. You only have to say.'

She was relieved when she saw his granite features relax a little.'

'No—please stay.'

Swallowing past the awful lump of constriction in her throat, she moved uncertainly towards him, feeling momentarily at a loss to know what to say.

'Why are you here?'

His soft voice was more intimidating than a raised one. Pinning her eyes with his, he hooked his thumbs into the waistband of his trousers and remained several feet away from her.

'I want to tell you that I have considered your proposal of marriage most seriously...' she answered in an aching whisper.

'I see.' His eyes probed hers, wary, expectant—hopeful.

'Marcus—why are you making this difficult for me?' she asked.

She spoke with such quiet dignity that Marcus felt his heart begin to melt. Her glorious amber eyes, sparkling with suppressed tears, were looking at him with no trace of defiance and without guile.

'Am I?'

'Yes—this is silly. Although I don't suppose I

can blame you after my coolness towards you last night. I will do anything to atone if I have angered or upset you in any way.'

One dark brow lifted in questioning arrogance and his firm lips twisted with irony. 'Anything?'

'Yes,' she whispered, looking into his fathomless eyes. Her throat ached, and she was trying hard not to cry. 'Marcus—please don't be like this. You have no reason to be. I cannot bear it,' she whispered wretchedly. 'Please don't shut me out.'

Her soft plea wrung his heart. 'So what have you decided? Is it—favourable?'

Lowena was relieved to hear the harsh edge of his voice tempered at last. 'Yes. I—I've come to tell you that I would like to accept your proposal— if you'll still have me, that is.'

He saw the tears shimmering in her eyes, and one that traced unheeded down her cheek. His heart wrenched and, unable go on torturing her when he had no reason to, he said with a raw ache in his voice, 'And do you really want to be my wife, Lowena?'

She searched his face, feeling her heart turn over exactly the way it always did when he looked at her as he was looking at her now. She saw the glow in his eyes kindle slowly into flame, and deep within her she felt the answering stirrings of longing—a longing to feel the tormenting sweetness of his caress, the stormy passion of his kiss and the earth-shattering joy of his body possessing hers.

'Yes. More than anything else that is what I want.'

'Thank God for that,' he murmured huskily. 'As an experienced man of the world, I never would have believed that I could fall victim to a beautiful, innocent young woman who has blithely incurred all my displeasure by leaving me and then having doubts about becoming my wife when I finally find her again. You, my love, have the power to amuse, enchant, bewitch and infuriate me as no other woman has done before. These past weeks have been hellish. I only hope that you have felt my absence as keenly as I have felt yours during the time we have been apart.'

The tenderness in Marcus's eyes warmed Lowena's heart. 'Yes, I have,' she confessed. 'When I left you, and before I met my father, everything suddenly seemed so empty and meaningless.'

Marcus's lips curved in a soft, satisfied smile and tenderness washed through him at the sincere honesty of her reply.

'I'm sorry,' she went on. 'I was still upset and angry that you had told me to leave Tregarrick.'

'I understand that now.' Suddenly his smile was lazy, and his eyes settled on her moist lips with hungry ardour. 'I can think of many pleasurable ways of showing me you are sorry for turning me down.'

Hot colour burned Lowena's cheeks and she smiled. 'I would like to.'

'Then if you come here you can show me, and cry in my arms if you want to. And while you do I will tell you just how much you have come to mean to me. And when I've done that, and we are of one accord, I will kiss you.'

Tortured by her tears, and loving him so much, Lowena moved the few steps towards him. But, unable to wait, he reached out and snatched her into his arms, wrapping them about her as she wept happily against his chest, wetting his shirt with her tears. He clasped her tighter, kissing the top of her shining head, inhaling the sweet, familiar sent of her.

'Dear Lord, I've missed you,' he told her, his voice a ravaged whisper.

'I'm sorry,' she said brokenly, still sobbing. 'I've missed you too—so much. I couldn't fight my feelings, however much I tried. They are too strong for me.'

'Don't,' he begged, unable to bear her tears. Turning her face to his, he touched her mouth with his with an aching tenderness. 'Don't cry any more, sweetheart. You're tearing me apart.'

'I don't mean to. I don't seem to be able to help it,' she said, smiling through her tears as he proceeded to kiss the droplets from her cheeks.

Placing his finger beneath her chin, he tilted her face to his. 'Don't ever leave me again, Lowena. Even if I ask you to—which I won't. I asked you to leave because I wanted you out of the house—somewhere I didn't have to see you. I reasoned that if you were no longer there I'd stop feeling wretched... I'd stop wanting you. You'd stop invading my mind. I thought I could exist without you—how wrong I was. You'd been gone less than a week when I saw the truth of what I'd done.'

'Please don't—there is no need to torture yourself like this, Marcus,' Lowena whispered, deeply moved by his words.

'I couldn't endure a time like that again without you—not knowing where you were, what had happened to you. I'd cut myself off from caring for anyone for so long—maintaining the careful emotional distance I had developed over the years to protect myself. Then all of a sudden there you were, and I wanted you—quite desperately.'

'I wish you had told me then.'

'I was a fool not to. You have done what no other woman has been capable of doing. When I returned from America and saw you—all grown up and more beautiful than I remembered—I was offered hope and forced to test the susceptibility of my own heart. You have broken through my guise of stoic reticence. The simple truth is that I was strongly attracted to you. You were far too beautiful for any man to turn his back on.'

'And yet you sent me away. It was because of Isabel, wasn't it? I know she hurt you very badly.'

'Yes, she did. I admit it. You knew her. You must have known what she was like.'

'I was living with Izzy at the time, and didn't go to the house. I saw her from time to time in the carriage, or riding out, but I didn't know her—I never spoke to her. She was very beautiful, that I do know,' Lowena said, remembering the woman—tall and slender as a willow, with flaxen hair and cornflower-blue eyes.

'Yes, she was, and I was certain she returned my feelings. In fact, she swore her undying love.'

Lowena hated Isabel for hurting him, for turning him into a cynical man who was reluctant to marry and refused to believe in love. She realised that although Marcus wanted her, Lowena, he hadn't wanted to open himself up for more hurt. Yes, he wanted her in a physical sense—he'd shown her that and told her as much. But Isabel had damaged him. He'd put a wall around himself, but it wasn't insurmountable after all, for he had asked her to be his wife.

'I can't begin to imagine how you must have felt, but I can imagine the pain of it.'

'Looking back, I don't know if the pain I felt was caused by losing her or by Edward taking something that was mine. I didn't see myself as a victim. There was nothing to be gained by placing blame. And they were happy together, if just for a short time. But I didn't want to watch them settled and living at Tregarrick. It was better that I got on with my own life. I told myself that I would never again allow myself to become enamoured by a woman.'

'I don't wonder at your reluctance. But not every woman is like Isabel.'

'You are absolutely right. It was simply that she hurt my unguarded heart so badly,' he said, remembering Isabel and how, even with the width of the Atlantic Ocean between them, he had been unable to forget her. 'When I left America, for me the war was over. I told myself that what mattered now was getting on with my life. And yet those left-over thorns were still stuck in my flesh and posing problems.'

'And what happened to change that?'

He looked at the proud beauty before him. Placing his hand gently on the curve of her cheek, he felt the pain of a moment before dissolve as he looked into the depths of her eyes and saw her goodness and understanding.

'You did.'

'So you did want me?'

Taking her face between his hands, he looked deep into her glorious eyes. His expression held no laughter when he searched the hidden depths with his own, and when he spoke his voice was husky.

'Want you? How can you ask me that? My attraction to you is both powerful and undeniable. I have told you that I sent you away because I was afraid of what you were making me feel. The force of my feelings astounded me. At first I was quite bewildered by the emotion I felt in my heart. I couldn't really describe what I felt for you because I didn't have any words. All I knew was that I felt strange, wonderful—different from anything I had ever expected to feel or ever wanted to feel again. It was as if I had spent my whole life waiting for you to be there.'

'I have always been here—since the day you found me.'

'Yes, you have. I have wanted you ever since you were a sixteen-year-old girl—one minute filled with childlike innocence and the next with the beauty of a woman and the wisdom of someone twice your age. And now you have a new identity, a new place in the world, but you are still full of strange, shifting shadows, and I ask myself if I shall ever truly know who you are.'

'Know that I am only a woman who loves you. That is the truth.'

Drawn to the beauty of the bewitching amber eyes looking into his, he lowered his head at last and his mouth covered hers in an endless, drugging kiss as his arms tightened around her. Trembling with a joy that was almost impossible to contain, Lowena abandoned herself to his embrace, pressing herself close to him.

His kiss, full of longing and bittersweet, induced a whole range of uncontrollable feelings within Lowena, and her eyes fluttered closed when she felt the stirring of immense pleasure sigh through her body. All she was conscious of was Marcus's mouth on her own, kissing her with commanding strength and passion. He deprived her of thought, leaving only feelings, and they filled her with such a sense of languorous pleasure that she seemed to be floating. He was as warm as she remembered, and the masculine scent of him seemed to surround her...

Chapter Ten

When at last they drew apart, Marcus took her chin between his fingers and tilted her head until the light shone in the amber depths of her eyes.

'There is one thing more I have to ask you, my love,' he said, tracing her jaw and cheek with his forefinger, his gaze compelling. 'How soon can we be married?'

She smiled at him, a soft pink flush mantling her cheeks. With a raised brow he waited silently, expectantly, for her answer.

'I would say right now, if it could be arranged, but I don't think my father and Deborah will allow us to get off that lightly. Arrangements will have to be made, so I suppose we'll have to patient.'

His heart ecstatic in its joy, with a groan Marcus pulled her against his chest with stunning force, crushing her against him. 'My beautiful, darling girl, I shall insist that arrangements are

made right away—within the next two weeks—
I shall obtain a special licence, here, in London.'

Her lips broke into a smile of delight. 'What?
No banns?'

'No. My impatience to make you my wife is
great indeed. Besides, I have no intention of allowing anyone to come forward to ban a union
between us.'

'They wouldn't dare!' She laughed. 'But I have
to consider my father. I have spoken to him, and
he knows how I feel about you and that you want
to marry me. But he has only just become used
to having a daughter and suddenly you intend to
snatch me away.'

He grinned down at her. 'I am sure he will wish
us well. Besides, Devon is practically next door.
We can visit and he will be more than welcome
in our home.'

'Home! It will not be easy for me, returning to
Tregarrick as your wife. As an employee of your
family I was accepted as such, but there will be a
complete change in the household's attitude towards
me. I expect there will be a distinct reserve—even
resentment—now I am no longer one of them.'

'I will write to the housekeeper. They will
know by then who you are, and by the time we
get there you will be accepted as my wife.'

'But I am not trained to oversee a household.'

'My mother will help you. You'll soon get the hang of things.'

'And Edward? How do you think *he* will react to our marriage?'

He shrugged. 'That does not concern me. He will deal with it in his own way.'

It wasn't until later, when Lowena was alone in her room, that the full realisation of what she was about to do set in—she would be married to Marcus before the month was out. Just the thought of being his wife warmed her heart and set her pulses racing, but she was disappointed that he hadn't told her that he loved her, which would make their union perfect...

Everyone was delighted at the way things had turned out for Marcus and Lowena—in particular Lady Alice, who was relieved that Lowena had been found and that she was united with her father. The two families came together to discuss the happy event of their wedding, although Lowena insisted that she didn't want much fuss— that she wanted it to be a quiet family affair.

'No sooner do I find I have a daughter than she leaves me,' Sir Robert said as he embraced her. 'But if this is what you want and you are happy then that is the most important thing.'

'We are not far. We will see each other often.

Now I have found you I will not be away from you for long periods, I promise you.'

'Now, where will the wedding take place?' asked Lady Alice, already mentally listing the many arrangements.

'Here—in London,' Marcus stated, 'At St George's Church in Hanover Square—if that is agreeable to you, Sir Robert?'

'Why not wait until we are back in Cornwall?' Lady Alice asked.

'Because a long delay seems pointless, and because I want my sister and her family at our wedding. I would not wish to drag them all that way.'

'But—what about Edward?' Lady Alice said tentatively. 'I know the two of you are not...close, but would you not like to have your brother present?'

Marcus looked at his mother directly, his expression suddenly hard. 'Of course I would—and you know how I wish things could have been different between us—but Edward's behaviour to both you and me in the past has not endeared him to either of us. No, we will marry here in London. I am impatient to return to Cornwall, but I think St George's Church will be more convenient for the guests.'

'But there is still so much to do—not to mention Lowena's bridal gown,' Deborah said. 'It is virtually impossible to arrange a wedding on a scale that befits the daughter of Sir Robert in two weeks. And do not forget that we have bridesmaids to find.'

'I don't see why that should be a problem. Juliet has two young daughters. I am sure they'd be overjoyed to be Lowena's bridesmaids.'

'I agree with Deborah,' Lady Alice remarked. 'I think a little more time is needed.'

'My dear mother,' Marcus said, not in the slightest perturbed by the objections being raised. 'I am sure you and Deborah are two of the most competent and capable women in London. I have every confidence that you will be able to arrange food, flowers and bridesmaids in time.'

'But we can't possibly!' Deborah said.

Marcus grinned at them all, casually propping one booted foot on the opposite knee and gently stroking the palm of Lowena's hand with his thumb inside the folds of her skirt, knowing how susceptible she was to his caress when he heard her breath catch in her throat and saw a pink flush mantle her cheeks.

'Yes, you can. Two weeks at the most,' he insisted implacably, trying to maintain his straining patience and calm the escalating pulse-rate caused by the closeness of the magnificent young woman by his side.

* * *

For the next two weeks everything was rushed and planned, and ordered and contrived to make the wedding occasion a memorable one.

When the day of the wedding finally arrived, and they were surrounded by a family gathering and a few friends, Lowena and Marcus gazed lovingly into each other's eyes as they spoke their vows, unaware of Lady Alice and Juliet dabbing away their tears of happiness and Sir Robert looking proudly on.

It was the most poignant moment of Marcus's life. His expression was so intense, so profoundly proud, that Lowena's heart ached.

Afterwards Marcus took his wife in his arms and kissed her with a passion that left her breathless. He was unable to believe that this exquisite creature in her gown if ivory satin and silver lace belonged to him at last. With her large amber eyes and her hair cascading in abundant red and gold curls, framing her enchanting face, she was a vision of radiant, breathtaking beauty.

Standing in the shadows across the square stood a silent observer—Edward, Lord Carberry, only today having arrived in London. He was watching his brother's wedding. Guests in their finery milled around the bride and groom with smiling, happy faces, having just emerged from the church. Marcus had his arm about his bride.

On seeing such family happiness, Edward gave a reflective cynical smile.

Conscience! The irony of it! He hadn't realised until recently that he had one, and it wasn't the first time he had regretted the things he had done. Everything he touched, he destroyed. Since Isabel had died he hadn't given much thought to his behaviour, and he wasn't proud of what he had become.

Edward had heard that Lowena had discovered her identity—that Sir Robert Wesley of Devon was her father. The name was familiar to him. Sir Robert was immensely wealthy, by all accounts—owned a silver mine and was well respected.

He watched his brother hand his beautiful new wife into the carriage, in a drifting swirl of ivory satin and lace, and sit beside her. Marcus's pride and the love he felt for his bride was evident in his face. It was a scene Edward would have liked to be part of. Marcus's marriage, and seeing his happiness and the love he bore his bride, made his own wretchedness and loneliness seem more profound.

There was no one to see his face as he turned away, his stormy eyes filled with sorrow. For the first time in his life he stood apart from himself and examined his soul. Alcoholic drink had always been a thing he could take or leave alone. Now, as he turned towards the nearest hostelry, he needed one badly.

At last they were alone. They were staying with Juliet until they left for Cornwall, and their room was a cosy place to be.

Marcus drew his wife into his arms. 'Dear Lord, you're incredible, Lowena. Have you any idea how lovely you are—and how rare?' he murmured, touching the smooth cheek of this artless young woman with unconscious reverence, unable to believe that she was his wife.

His words, combined with the touch of his fingertips against her cheek and the deep, compelling timbre of his voice, had a seductive impact on Lowena. She could not believe the pulsing happiness that glowed inside her, or the exquisite sensations speeding through her veins.

For a long moment they gazed at each other, feeling more exposed to each other than ever before.

'I never knew I could feel this wonderful wanting…' Lowena breathed as they lay together, gently placing her lips at the corner of his mouth. 'I want you to love me, Marcus—like you did before.'

'I *do* love you,' he whispered. 'More than you will ever know. 'You have come to mean everything to me. I have loved you from the minute I lifted you into my arms that day I found you in the woods. Who would have thought then that I would end up marrying you?'

'I always hoped,' she murmured simply, her face aglow. 'I'm glad that you love me.'

Heat erupted inside her, spreading through her body as his lips found hers. He had kissed her before, but this time it was different. Within the sanctity of marriage this time there was no guilt, no nagging feeling that what they were doing was wrong. It was a kiss of infinite tenderness—a kiss that quickly escalated to something more.

They loved each other until dawn, and Lowena gloried in her power to arouse and bring pleasure to this wonderful man. She felt an overwhelming sense of wonder that their bodies could react to each other in an instant, that they could become one. That wonder soared within her as his lips murmured against her mouth, his body claiming hers. They moved together in a timeless rhythm and Lowena thought that everything was perfect and would last for ever.

When she lifted her eyes to his, Marcus saw sweet acceptance and all the love in the world concentrated in their fathomless amber depths. He also saw the promise of a perfect future together, of his unborn children and of quiet joy.

Never had Lowena believed she could be so happy as she settled into her marriage at the cottage at Tregarrick. Wanting to give the newly wedded couple privacy, Lady Alice had been more than happy to remain with Juliet in London indefinitely.

During the day Marcus immersed himself in his work, spending a large part of each day at the mine, and when he was not at the mine they would spend time together, riding through the surrounding countryside and generally just enjoying being together. At other times Marcus could be found fastened in his study, poring over his business investments and seeking other enterprises in which to invest his time and money.

Lowena saw nothing of Edward. Marcus told her that he'd made a brief visit to London and had returned to Tregarrick recently. Marcus had met him when riding home from the mine and had been surprised when Edward had reined in to speak to him. He had asked about the mine and quietly congratulated him on his marriage before riding on.

'Something has changed,' Marcus told his wife. He was puzzled by his brother's behaviour, but he welcomed any change for the better in their relationship. 'He seemed different, somehow.'

'Different? In what way?'

Her question went unanswered for a moment, as Marcus thought of his meeting with his brother, and then he told her.

They had met on the road when Marcus had been riding home from the mine. Edward had been riding in the opposite direction, and he'd halted his horse and waited for Marcus to reach him.

They'd sat their horses, looking at each other.

'Well, Marcus?' Edward had said.

'I thought you were still in London,' Marcus had replied, thinking his brother looked detached and very tired. There had been something in his eyes he hadn't seen before—something akin to torment. 'I'd hoped to see you, but I had to get back.'

Edward had nodded. 'You are married now.' He'd smiled thinly when Marcus's gaze had sharpened. 'I heard you had married Lowena, who has found her family at long last. What a turn-up, eh? I congratulate you both. You're a lucky man. I envy you. Rest assured that she will be safe from me in the future.'

Marcus had looked at him a long time, thinking, *I'm a fool. You took Isabel and wrecked my life—and then Lowena. And yet...*

'I'm glad to hear it, Edward. And you? Is there no one?'

Edward had sighed and shaken his head. 'Isabel is a hard act to follow—besides, can a man who has lived the life I have find what we had again?' His eyes had met his brother's. 'I've done a lot of thinking recently...about what I did to you—and her. I should not have let her ride that day. I blame myself for her death, Marcus. More than you or anybody else possibly could. I'll never stop blaming myself till the day I die. It's suddenly important to me that that you know that.'

Marcus had expected him to be the Edward he knew. He had not been prepared to see a change in him, and had been shocked by the outward show of feeling. He hadn't been the brother he knew—always so confident and sure, often cruel. He had not expected to see a grave, tormented man and the black depression that had seemed to cloak him.

'Why, Edward? Why—after all this time?'

He'd shrugged. 'I don't want to live the rest of my life knowing you think ill of me. I've grief enough to suit even you.'

'All my life I believed you hated me.'

He'd shaken his head. 'I thought I did—but that's not what I feel. I *do* feel hate—but not for you. For myself.'

Edward had looked at Marcus for a long, slow time, and then he'd looked ahead of him and ridden on.

'And you, Marcus? Lowena asked softly now. 'Will you be able to forgive him his harsh treatment of you and your mother over the years?'

Marcus sighed. 'The enmity between us goes back to childhood. It became more virulent with the passing of years but he was never my enemy. I became his.'

'Can you find it in yourself to forgive him for Isabel?'

He thought a moment before speaking. 'I was immeasurably hurt and angry at the time. In the beginning I think he took Isabel as an exercise in proving his superiority as the older brother, but then I genuinely felt he loved her. When I came back from America and saw you—how Edward was doing his damnedest to seduce you—I felt it was happening all over again.'

'But forgiveness,' Lowena persisted. 'Can you do that?'

'Yes, I would like to think so. Now, after all this time, I feel I *can* forgive him. Despite his attitude, I think he has suffered in his own way—

first losing the mother he adored, at a time in his life when he so needed her, and then Isabel. It left him with a well of bitterness and loneliness. I'd like to think we could become reconciled.'

'Reconciliation and redemption can defy anything that's gone before, Marcus—forgiveness, too, if you let it. You didn't turn the other way when he approached you today. One thing I learned when I was growing up is that it's easy to condemn, but harder being compassionate. It seems to me you have shown compassion for your half-brother, even if the reason is hard for you to understand just now.'

Marcus smiled softly. 'You have a beautiful hcad on your shoulders, Lowena Carberry, and a wise one—full of goodness. However, I've no intention of acting like the caring brother all of a sudden, but I will welcome his hand of friendship if he offers it.'

Lowena listened to the wind growing stronger as the day wore on. By early evening it was blowing with a force she found terrifying. When one of the servants came from the hall to tell them that a ship was in difficulty off the cursed cove, in danger of floundering on the rocks, and that Lord Carberry was there and needed all the help he could get, Lowena immediately reached for her cloak, hoping to be of help to any survivors should the worst happen.

'Send word to my husband at the mine, Mrs Seagrove. Tell him what has happened and where I am,' she said to the housekeeper. 'And find what you can in the way of blankets.'

Mrs Seagrove had done exactly that, and was about to send one of the grooms to the cove with the blankets when the door was thrust open.

'Lowena?' Marcus's voice was sharp and loud, and could be heard above the storm.

Mrs Seagrove came hurrying out of the kitchen. 'Oh, sir. The mistress isn't here. I sent one of the servants to the mine to fetch you. A ship was seen to be in difficulties in the rising gale. You must have seen for yourself if you came home by the coastal path.'

'I didn't come that way,' he said, feeling the first stirrings of alarm. 'I rode back through the woods.'

'I expect everyone from the village will have gone to help.'

'And Lowena?'

'She went to join Lord Carberry in the cove.' Marcus stared at her, his eyes wide with disbelief— and something else Mrs Seagrove didn't like. 'He wanted all the help he could get…'

'And she *went*?' Marcus said, frantic for his wife's safety.

'There is great concern for those on board. If the vessel hits the rocks there may be no survivors. It will be merciful if they can be rescued.'

Marcus turned away. Since when had Edward shown consideration for anybody—let alone shown them mercy? he thought furiously, thrusting the amicable conversation he'd had with his brother just days ago out of his mind. He wouldn't put it past Edward to have lured the ship onto the rocks himself, in order to steal its cargo. God help the poor devils on board.

Without more ado he left the house, his sights solidly fixed ahead. It was still daylight, but the light was fading. Rain and low cloud made visibility difficult. On reaching the coastal path he found the mist swirling around him, but it was a mist whipped up by the gale-force wind from the sea and not the ghostly stillness of fog.

Arriving at the clifftop above the cove the locals believed was cursed, due to the ships having floundered on the needle-like rocks in the past, he secured his horse and pushed his way through the furze bushes. He saw that all was pandemonium down below on the beach. It was worse than he had expected.

The gale had become a tempest. Storm-driven waves crashed upon the rocks, sending plumes of spray high into the air. The tide was riding high, thundering onto the shore, the waves capped with curls of foam.

Marcus saw Edward. He had his telescope and was looking at the vessel. Men and women had collected on the shore, watching helplessly, waiting for the inevitable. In desperation his eyes searched for Lowena—and then he saw her, standing close to Edward, her cloak billowing about her like a giant kite.

In its moment of peril the vessel was pitching violently. Unable to change course, it was being tossed up and down, blind and helpless, at the mercy of the elements with the wind driving it to a deathly trap.

Hurrying to Lowena's side, Marcus placed his arm about her waist. Turning her head to look at him, her expression registered the horror she was feeling. Neither of them spoke. They watched as the bulk of the vessel seemed to rear up and then collapse with a sound like thunder as it hit the jagged rocks. There was a terrible rending of timbers, followed by the total collapse of rigging and masts.

Lowena closed her eyes to shut out the scene of the stricken ship, her frozen lips sending up a silent prayer for the unfortunates on board. The crew—about fifteen or twenty men—could be seen on the deck, clinging on to anything that might save them.

'What can be done to help them?' she cried, raising her voice to be heard above the storm. The wind whipped the words away as soon as she had uttered them.

'Very little,' Edward replied, having come to stand beside his brother. His face was drawn and anxious, in an expression not often witnessed. 'It's too far out to be reached.'

As he said this one of the crew could be seen falling into the water. His arms flailed once before he was swept away. Nobody would be strong enough to swim against the surges of the water.

Seeing this, Marcus was galvaniscd into action. He turned to the men from the village and told them to fetch one of the boats that had been dragged up the beach for safety. When someone like Marcus assumed command, others obeyed, and soon the men were pulling a large rowing boat down to the water's edge. He ran towards it and slotted the oars into the rowlocks, turning as Lowena, beside herself with terror because she knew what he was about to do, tried to pull him back.

'No, Marcus! You cannot go out there. It's too dangerous. I beg of you not to go.'

'She's right!' Edward shouted. 'Don't be a fool, man. It would be suicidal.'

'I can't stand by and watch them drown,' Marcus told him. 'There's a chance some of them can be rescued. There's no time to waste and it will be dark soon. The rocks beneath the water are holding her, but when she is swept free she will be dashed against the cliff face and battered to pieces within minutes.'

'And you along with her!' Lowena cried. 'Please, Marcus. I couldn't bear it if anything happened to you.'

'I have to try, Lowena. I couldn't live with myself if I didn't do something. If I can save just one soul it will be worth it.' He looked at the men gathered round. 'I need just one man to come with me. Just one to man an oar. More and there will be no room for survivors.'

There was a shuffling among them as they moved back. Nobody was willing to risk their life.

Seeing their reluctance, Edward uttered a sound of disgust. In this moment of extreme danger, and perhaps death, his brother was prepared to risk his life to aid his fellow man. In the face of Marcus's courageous determination, Edward felt admiration surge through him.

'Damn it all. Get in,' Edward said to Marcus, climbing into the boat and taking up one of the oars.

Marcus stared at him. 'You don't have to do this.'

'Neither do you. I cannot think of any combination of circumstances that would make me risk my life, but I cannot allow you to do this alone. Get in. There are people to be saved and we're wasting time.'

Lowena watched with paralysed anguish as Marcus sat beside his brother and took hold of an oar. She stared after them, her pulse racing like a maddened thing, sensing impending doom as she watched them battle the savage sea. Sick with worry, all colour having drained out of her face, she was insensible to the fact that her feet were sinking into the wet sand.

She felt so small and insignificant, standing there with the vast expanse of water before her—so alone. How could Marcus possibly survive the savage sea?

Every time the boat sank into a trough her blood ran cold. In her terrible, heart-rending anguish she wanted to scream, to cry out her husband's name, but she remained silent. She stood straight and still, her eyes staring out of her stricken face, her mind frayed with worry.

And so she waited as the unbearable, unearthly storm seemed to go on and on. No one moved and all eyes remained fixed in concentration on the boat heading for the stricken vessel. The scene was like a fatalistic tableau.

Both Marcus and Edward were good, strong

oarsmen, moving the oars with precision with every stroke as they battled against the waves. For the first time in their lives they were in unison—together—striving for the same thing. Their very isolation seemed to tighten their bond. Marcus fleetingly thought it a strange situation to be in, but Edward's presence and support inspired confidence.

All around them was boiling water, swirling and crashing against the cliff. Through the spray and foam they tried to keep their eyes on the ship battling against the elements.

They were soon drenched by the spray soaking through their clothes. They were shocked by the coldness of the water but had no time to dwell on it. They had to keep moving. The activity helped to keep their circulation going, but the growing cold and the unrelenting wind were in danger of dulling their senses.

There was no respite. It was a miracle they weren't overturned. Both men called on every ounce of skill they possessed to hold course.

As they approached the vessel they heard a massive crack, and more of the ship broke up. With waves pounding against the hull, it was shifting all the time. The men clinging to the vessel for dear life watched them, hopeful of rescue, but there was a danger of the boat getting caught up in the debris and trailing ropes.

'How many men?' Marcus shouted when they were close enough to be heard.

'Just eight of us left—others weren't so lucky.'

It was no easy matter, getting the men into the boat. How they managed it Marcus would never know. But they helped each other. With each man there was a danger he would miss the boat and fall into the sea. Marcus made sure they were evenly placed to keep balance in the boat.

They had just hauled the last man over the side when a giant wave hit them with all its force, tossing them against the vessel. The ship lurched and a spar crashed down, hitting the boat—and Edward, who was directly beneath it.

Blindly, desperately, Marcus made a frantic lunge in the direction he had last seen his brother, but he had gone over the side. Peering into the foam he saw him being tossed about by the savage force.

'Edward! For God's sake take my hand!'

Helpless, Marcus could only watch as Edward, unconscious and in no condition to save himself, was swept away by the foaming breakers.

As they reached shore men ran into the surf to take hold of the boat and drag it up the sand. That was when Lowena's heart soared in her breast and life began to flow through her anew. Suddenly she was running towards the boat with the rest of them.

The survivors of the wrecked vessel were helped ashore and blankets were produced and wrapped around their frozen bodies. Marcus was the last person to climb out of the boat. Lowena flung herself upon him and his arms went round her, holding her as she clung to him, unable to speak for all the gladness and relief that filled her heart.

'Thank God you are safe,' she murmured against his neck. 'I confess that I feared the worst.'

'They're all saved that could be saved. They'll be taken to the village and taken care of.'

When Lowena found the strength to step back her eyes searched for Edward, the wind whipping her hair across her face.

'Edward?' She looked to her husband for an answer.

He shook his head, his eyes tortured with the memory of how he'd tried to save him and his loss.

'He is dead?' she said, her expression one of sick disbelief.

Marcus nodded, his gaze going to what was left of the wrecked ship, which was just visible in the growing darkness. 'He was hit by a falling spar and toppled over the side of the boat. Despite my efforts to save him he was washed away.'

'I am truly sorry. I'm sure you did all you could.'

He nodded, his eyes drawn again towards the stricken vessel. 'In the time it took us to reach the ship I felt closer to my brother than I ever have before, at any point in my life.'

Lowena took his hand, tears welling in her eyes. 'Come, you are soaked to the skin and freezing cold. We must get you back to the house and out of those wet clothes and get you warm.'

After making sure that the survivors were being taken care of, Marcus and Lowena left the cove.

Edward's body was washed ashore with others the following day.

Marcus was deeply distressed over the death of his brother, and Lowena's heart went out to him. As Edward's next of kin he was now Lord Carberry of Tregarrick, and he knew what that would mean to him, and the drastic changes that would take place and affect his life.

But Lowena knew there would also be changes to her own life. When they moved up to the house she would be faced with the confusing business of running a large household and all those who were dependent on it for their subsistence. It was a task she was totally ignorant of, but she was resolved to play her part. She would learn from Marcus and

Lady Alice, and she would rationalise the myriad roles that suddenly faced her.

Considering this most unusual turn of events, Marcus was overcome. Despite the hostilities that had kept them apart all their lives, it wounded him terribly that he should discover and then lose his half-brother so quickly and in such tragic circumstances.

If there was one thing he had learned over the years, it was that what people had done or not done didn't seem to have much effect on how one felt about them. Marcus's heart was warmed by the knowledge that he had seen some goodness in his brother at the end, and that in the span of the time Edward had climbed into the boat and disappeared into the sea he'd loved him.

The day finally came when Lowena made the journey back to Beresford Hall in Devon. She was accompanied by Marcus and her father—and Nessa.

The house in which she had been born was nothing but a burned-out shell. An eerie, haunting silence reigned among the ruins of the house in which her mother had been raised and—as Nessa had told her—had loved. It struck deep into her heart when she tried to imagine what it had been like on the terrible day when her mother had died and Nessa had taken her away.

Most of the building had been destroyed. Some walls still stood, with big, gaping holes in them, and the giant chimney stacks still rose into the sky. Ivy clung to the crumbling walls of the once noble house, and it made her think of something beautiful after it had been through the throes of death. The wind blowing off the sea went whispering and searching the holes and crevices in the walls.

On her father's suggestion they left the ruins and went to the village church—her mother's final resting place. There she saw for herself the monuments and alabaster effigies of her Beresford ancestors. Her mother was buried beneath a solid stone slab in the churchyard, with a simple inscription informing those who chanced to look of her name, her birth and the date of her death.

Weighted down by a terrible sadness, Lowena felt tears fill her eyes as she placed a bouquet of flowers at its centre, trying to imagine what might have been had her father not been in Mexico and had he married her mother.

Taking a rose from the bouquet, she turned away, holding it to her nose to smell its sweet perfume. There was a lightness to her heart and a little smile playing on her lips as she walked to where Marcus stood waiting.

* * *

Marcus watched her come towards him. On seeing her smile, he felt his concern turn to relief and he opened his arms. Not for the first time since he had found her that day in the woods he felt a surge of protectiveness—an unusual twist to his normal desire whenever he was with her.

The force of her attraction was like the pull of the moon on the tides. It was something that went beyond all earthly understanding. Her laugh was infectious, and her smile had the power to light up the darkest corners of his heart. She was also volatile, warm and elusive, and he was certain she would never bore him.

All those qualities, combined with her honesty and the love she carried in her heart for him, made her a prize above all else...

* * * * *

If you enjoyed this story, you won't want to miss these other great reads from Helen Dickson:

A TRAITOR'S TOUCH
CAUGHT IN SCANDAL'S STORM
LUCY LANE AND THE LIEUTENANT
LORD LANSBURY'S CHRISTMAS WEDDING
ROYALIST ON THE RUN

MILLS & BOON®

& HISTORICAL

AWAKEN THE ROMANCE OF THE PAST

---

sneak peek at next month's titles...

In stores from 27th July 2017:

Marrying His Cinderella Countess – Louise Allen
A Ring for the Pregnant Debutante – Laura Martin
The Governess Heiress – Elizabeth Beacon
The Warrior's Damsel in Distress – Meriel Fuller
The Knight's Scarred Maiden – Nicole Locke
A Marriage Deal with the Outlaw – Harper St. George

Just can't wait?
Buy our books online before they hit the shops!
www.millsandboon.co.uk

Also available as eBooks.